BRETT NELSON

A TIME FOR REDEMPTION

Book Two of the "War Songs" series

"Holy, Holy,Holy" song lyrics by Reginald Heber, 1861, public domain.

"He Hideth My Soul" song lyrics by Fanny Crosby, 1890, public domain.

"Amazing Grace" song lyrics by John Newton, written 1772, published 1779, public domain.

Author Website: https://brettnelson-author.com/

Author Email: admin@BrettNelson-Author.com OR authorBrettNelson@gmail.com

Amazon Author Profile: https://www.amazon.com/stores/Brett-Nelson/author/B08D2C1YSC

Social Media:

Facebook: https://www.facebook.com/AuthorBrettNelson

Twitter: @Brett Nelson Author

Instagram: @author_brettnelson

YouTube: https://www.youtube.com/@AuthorBrettNelson

Goodreads: https://www.goodreads.com/author/show/20833445.Brett_Nelson

ISBN: 9798857746479 (paperback)

ISBN-13: 9798878094061 (hardback)

Cover Design: Alexandra V/Kingwood Creations

Alex Coheeney, manuscript editing.

Acknowledgement

"Another tale is told, now it's time to play." That may not be an exact quote, but Mary Higgins Clark, one of my all-time favorite authors, often said some version of that in her own author acknowledgements.

As an author, I've learned that I can write a story but never without the help of several talented people along the way. I want to give a very special thank you to Alicia G. Murphy, MD, Surgical and Clinical Pathologist, and retired blood bank technician Geneva Teeters, MT (ASCP). As a past surgical pathology transcriptionist, I know just enough medical jargon to be dangerous. These two brilliant women helped me to not only conceive a perfect medical situation for the story, but they also helped me to get it onto the paper without sounding like a complete idiot. This author takes full responsibility for any medical inaccuracies that remain within these pages.

Kudos go to my sidekicks Melissa Brown and Melanie Dyer. You help me to place the building blocks into the story through the entire process of writing a novel. Your feedback on everything from character analysis, to plotlines, to cover design, and deciding on book titles is instrumental. Thanks for not getting too sick of my author talk.

No novel is complete without the beta readers and proofreaders who help me polish the manuscript before it goes to the professional editor. I'm blessed with the best beta readers and proofreaders in the world, and I'll fight anyone who says otherwise. Ashley Brooke

Knight-Henderson, Melanie Dyer, Paula Brown, Geneva Teeters, and Teresa Nelson. I promise, one of these days when I make my first million, I'll share the wealth but until then...BIG HUGS!

As always, a huge thank you to Alexandra at Kingwood Creations for your amazing book cover designs. At this point, I think you're stuck with me so it's good that we're a great team. "Vielen Dank."

Alex Coheeney, you have killer editing skills. You rock, my man!

Dad, Mom, Chad, and Jen. I love you to the moon and back.

Readers—Without you, there'd be no reason to do this. Thank you for choosing this book among the millions from which you have to choose.

Also By

War Songs: A Time for Redemption (Book #2)

Unprotected

War Songs (Book #1)

When Raindrops Fall

Lost Song

A Christmas to Live For

Cast of Characters

<u>Humans</u>:

Arnold Collins

Alice Collins, Arnold's wife

Hyacinth Alekson

Earl, Arnold's friend

Pauline, Earl's wife, Alice's friend

Camden Riley, Hyacinth's friend

Aunt Deborah, Arnold's aunt

Lucas Perkins, Hyacinth's friend

Paige Alekson, Hyacinth's niece

Sheri Bennett, Hyacinth's best friend

Janie Davis, Hyacinth's friend

Nancy, Janie's friend

Felicia, Janie's friend

Spiritual Realm:

<u>Angels</u>:

Cingo, Protector Warrior, Hyacinth

Lutis (pronounced Loo-tis), protector warrior

Nitasah (pronounced Nuh-tah-suh)

Istus, upper ranking angel

Hortamen, protector warrior

Ahava (pronounced Uh-hov-uh), protector warrior, Alice

<u>Fallen Angels</u>:

Iracun (pronounced Ear-uh-kuhn)

Fraush (pronounced Frow-sh)

Mondaci (pronounced Mon-dock-ee)

Sané (pronounced Saw-nay), traitor warrior, Alice

Chapter 1

Hyacinth stepped onto the back porch in the early-morning pre-dawn hours and stared across the backyard with a rueful gaze. The threadbare Marilyn Monroe shirt that she had owned since she was a teenager, along with the short sleeping shorts, offered no protection against the cool morning air.

Moonlight spilled across the surface of the swimming pool with a shimmer while a thin, velvety veil of silver fog danced over the landscape in a beautiful yet haunting way.

She crossed her arms across her chest and drew in several deep breaths as unshed tears threatened to spill from behind her clenched eyelids.

With a heavy heart, her mind replayed her beloved husband's funeral. Even though months had passed, she still couldn't believe Jenner was gone.

The day of the funeral had been a brisk fall day with a nonstop gentle rain. Maple Hill Cemetery had been resplendent with trees laden in fiery hues of red, orange, and yellow. Despite the cold drenching rain, it was the kind of day that Jenner loved most. To most the weather was dismal, but she saw it as a fitting tribute as they laid him to rest.

She opened her eyes and released a deep breath. A curl of vapor escaped her mouth then quickly folded into the filmy, moisture-laden morning air. "Jenner, I miss you so much it hurts," she whispered.

The dulcet cries of a lone bird that echoed in the distance disrupted the otherwise quiet morning, and the gorgeous yet mournful sound was a perfect match to what she felt in her soul.

She scooted to the edge of the pool and sat Indian style. The cold from the concrete seeped through the thin fabric of her shorts but the discomfort barely registered into her consciousness.

The bird chittered another chorus of muted songs while a cold breeze raked through her shoulder-length hair. A pungent, sweet, earthy potpourri of scents drifted into her nostrils.

Throughout her life, like every other person who had ever roamed the Earth, she had known plenty of pain. The pain of losing her husband so early in life, however, had far eclipsed any of her other pains.

He was her best friend, her lover, her confidant, the very breath in her lungs. How she could ever survive the rest of her life without his calming, sometimes annoying presence was something she couldn't conceive.

The plans for their life would go forever unfulfilled. He wanted to visit the arid deserts of the Egyptian pyramids and traipse through dusty ancient tombs. She wanted to discover the wonders of the 15th century Inca citadel of Machu Picchu. He wanted to journey to the summit of Guatemala's Pacaya Volcano, peer into the Earth's core, and roast marshmallows over boiling lava, something she thought was a horrible idea. She wanted to swim, kayak, snorkel, and hike her way across the Galapagos Islands. He wanted to camp for a week in the Congo and laugh at playful chimpanzees as they swung from tree to tree.

A whisper of a smile broke through her grief. The closest she ever wanted to get to the Congo was a fancy five-star resort with a nice view of the rainforest while dining on scrumptious international cuisines.

Jenner's and her tastes were so varied, but here, as the bird issued yet another chorus of twitters, it dawned on her that they would never do the things that had never interested her, like roasting marshmallows over the lava flow of a rumbling volcano or watching playful chimpanzees swinging from tree branches.

The thought pricked at her heart with such ferocity that she broke into inconsolable tears. Her anguished cries carried into the far reaches of the silent night and meshed with the bird's songs, as though it was nature's soothing way of letting her know that she didn't have to bear her grief alone.

"Jenner," she cried aloud. "Oh, Jenner. I love you. I'll always love you."

Cingo crouched behind her and listened to the human's shaky voice. He loved his charges and didn't like to see them hurting. How he would love to shield them from all the hurts and pains, but they were often the things that drew humans into a stronger relationship with their Creator.

"Hello, Cingo."

Cingo didn't bother to glance up at Iracun, one of many powerful Traitor Warriors who walked the face of the Earth.

"Death. Such a horrible thing, eh?" Iracun said in a taunting voice of amusement.

"For a true believer, to be absent from the body is to be present with the Lord," Cingo answered, though his evil counterpart knew the Word of God just as well as he did. "For believers, death is an eternal reward, not a curse."

Iracun looked at the weeping human with disgust, then quivered his lip in a mocking crying gesture. "Looks like someone forgot to tell her."

Cingo shook his head. "Being a believer doesn't exempt them from grieving, and you know that, Iracun. They grieve, but they also have a larger hope that blossoms from their grief."

Iracun chuckled. "We'll see, my friend."

Chapter 2

As Arnold shuffled across the driveway, loose pebbles crunched under his feet in the quiet of the pre-dawn hours.

With a mug of coffee in one hand and his cane in the other, he ambled across the yard and eased into the swing. He couldn't recall the last time Alice and he had taken the time to enjoy such a simple luxury as swinging together to watch a blazing sunrise or sunset. Though they had been married for decades, they spent as much time apart as possible.

He glanced up at the sky, at the millions of stars that shone through the inky darkness of space with amazing brilliance. It was one of the good things about living in the country—even the dimmest stars shone brighter.

He pulled the coffee cup to his mouth and slurped down a sip of the liquid as he contemplated life.

The truck accident with the bus had taken two lives, but he had escaped with nothing worse than a concussion, a few broken ribs, and a hairline fracture in his left leg. "I wish I had died."

He had fallen asleep at the wheel, or close to it, of that much he was certain. According to the police report, though, the official cause of the deadly accident hadn't been his sleepy negligence but a heavy wooden beam lying across the road that neither the driver of the bus nor Arnold had seen until it was too late. Where it came from and why it was there the police had yet to determine.

His throat constricted with overwhelming emotion that he refused to let surface. Those people on that bus died. Their whole lives were ahead of them. *I have nothing in life but an unhappy marriage to a woman who doesn't love me and couldn't care less if I'm here or not.* He jerked his head back up at the sky with a stony glare. "Why couldn't You let me die instead of them?" He didn't believe God existed, yet it made him feel better to place the blame on a non-existent entity.

Fraush and Mondaci circled around him. "Maybe you'll get your wish to die sooner rather than later. At least if I have anything to say about it." Mondaci glanced up at Fraush with a smirk, but Fraush ignored the comment.

Once again, Arnold found himself ruminating on how and when his life and marriage had eroded into something that he no longer recognized. Alice used to love him, but now she didn't want to be in the same room with him.

Not that their crummy marriage was all her fault. Whenever possible, he always wanted to stretch out his trips across the country for as long as he could rather than rushing back to a loveless home. There was nothing to rush home to, and there hadn't been for quite some time.

He recalled many times over the years—more times than he could count—that he had rented a cheap motel room for a few days rather than going home. More times than not, he also found a hooker to help occupy his time, and never had he felt guilty for his many improprieties.

Enjoying time with a hooker was something that hadn't happened in a while though because old age hadn't been kind to him. He was old, fat, and ugly. Hookers were no longer interested in him, or at least he assumed they wouldn't want him, which was a slap in the face since they would do nearly anything for a few measly bucks. It was hard to believe that at one time he had been a catch, at least enough of one to catch the interest of a floozy.

"The good old days are over in more ways than one." The reality made him sad. He chugged another mouthful of coffee and forced himself to gag down the lukewarm swallow. He spat a string of profanities for no reason other than he liked using filthy language.

He tossed the half-drunk coffee onto the mostly dead grass and placed the empty mug on the swing next to him.

Against his intention, his thoughts went to the people on the bus. The only thing the police told him was that they were a traveling gospel band. He didn't have much use for Christians or their oppressive religion, but they didn't deserve to die at his hands in a fiery bus crash.

The police officer's words of encouragement rang in his ears: Nobody knows why, but a wooden beam was laying across the road. The accident wasn't your fault, so don't beat yourself up about it.

The guilt that plagued him for ruining so many people's lives was relentless. His mind couldn't let go of the victims or their families. The police's explanation for the accident absolved him from the blame, but still, a thousand what if's haunted him.

He wondered what their names were and if any of them had young children.

A light came on in the house. Alice was finally out of bed.

With a grunt, he stood to his feet, threaded a finger through the mug's handle, snatched up the cane, and made his way to the house.

"Home sweet home," he said, though the words were laced with sarcasm.

Chapter 3

Arnold plowed through the door and placed the coffee mug on the table with a loud thwack.

Alice stood at the counter in front of the coffee maker in her ratty floor length nightgown and robe, stirring creamer and sugar into her coffee. She glanced at him with a smirk. "Careful there. Don't break the fine china."

He looked down at the mug without cracking a smile. It was a bright orange pottery mug that melted into bright yellow toward the bottom and had the faded and cracked silhouette of a woman's form. It was a garage sale find that was probably more vintage in years than he was.

Alice had mocked him for buying a coffee mug at a garage sale, because who knew how many people before him had used it. He didn't care what she thought, though, and he even told her so when she repeated her opinion on the matter. Finally, she stopped mentioning it.

"What're you doing today?" he asked when she waddled across the kitchen and collapsed into a chair across from him, the joints of which tottered and squeaked under her not-so-small frame.

The set of chairs had been cheap relics when they bought them used at a flea market years ago. Every time she sat in one of them, he expected to hear the familiar squeak followed by the thud of her body hitting the floor. The thought of her squashing a chair and hitting the tile in humiliation used to cause a chuckle, and he often visualized such a scene as a form of entertainment. Now such thoughts brought a surge of shame, and he didn't know where such shame came from since it was something he had never experienced.

Since neither of them were as fit and trim as they used to be in their younger years, maybe he needed to invest in a sturdier table and chairs for both of their future safety.

She drew the cup to her mouth, blew the hot liquid, and took a succession of cautious sips.

Her wiry, peppery gray hair was styled in a scraggly bun at the nape of her neck, and her blue eyes were anemic and empty.

"Same thing I always do, I reckon," she snapped.

"Ah, playing poker with the hags, huh?" He snapped back.

She shot him a mean and spiteful look. "We're playing bridge today." When he shook his head and looked away, a rare trickle of compassion coursed through her. "How are you feeling this morning?"

"Fine and dandy."

"You looked like you were limping when you walked in."

He shrugged, unaccustomed to her voicing concern about anything that related to him, not that he thought she cared this time. "We're not spring chickens anymore. Sometimes old people limp."

"That, plus you dang near succeeded in killing yourself a few months ago." She opened her ever present cigarette case, popped one in her mouth, lit it, and sucked in a lungful of tarry death.

He was nothing special, that he knew, but chain-smoking was one of the most unattractive and unfeminine traits that a woman could adopt. "Next time I'll try to do a more thorough job of knocking myself off. That insurance policy of mine will surely keep you in enough cigarettes and fresh playing cards to last from now until Armageddon."

A resentful look flashed across her face. "Why do you always say such ugly stuff to me?"

The statement made him chuckle. It had been years since either of them had anything nice to say to the other. If it weren't for low blowing each other with insults, they would probably never speak.

Amid a slurry of profanities, she pushed herself up out of the chair in a huff but fell back into it when she lapsed into a series of phlegmy coughs.

In the jostle, her coffee sloshed over the side of the mug and onto the table. A smoldering length of ash fell from her cigarette onto the tabletop as she jerked to and fro hacking up a lung.

For a split second he worried that the spilled coffee and the singe of the ash would mar the surface of the wood, but the table was already a bunged-up piece of junk so what was a couple more scars amid a lifetime of them?

When she finally settled down, she wilted into the chair as though the fit had taken its toll on her. After a couple of seconds, she slipped the cigarette to her mouth for another long drag.

"I didn't mean to be so ugly to you," Arnold said. "We've been nasty to each other for so long that it comes naturally to me sometimes. I'll try to do better."

A cackle of laughter sent a billowy fluff of smoke drifting from her mouth. If she had horns and the smell of sulfur, it would be easy to see her as the spawn of the devil himself. Again, out of nowhere, the thought brought him another unexpected wave of shame.

"Don't bother," she said. "We're two dogs who are too old to learn new tricks."

Her attitude irked him. "Don't you ever look at us and—" he paused, unsure if he wanted to continue. "Don't you ever want us to do better for ourselves?"

She clutched the corners of the table and pulled herself up to a stiff standing stance then pressed her fingertips to the table to steady herself. "Honey, we both know that ship sailed a long time ago, so how about we let sleeping dogs lie?"

With that, she turned to leave.

"Yeah, that'd be great advice," he called to her retreating form. "If we were both dogs."

Fraush stood over Arnold's shoulder with an evil sneer.

Arnold blew out a heavy breath of exasperation.

"Yes," Fraush sneered. "Let's let sleeping dogs lie."

Chapter 4

Arnold dragged the push mower out of the backyard shed and pushed it over the stubbly dead and brown grass. According to doctor's orders, he needed to stay off his leg for a few more weeks, but he had never been good at following orders.

Even though it didn't need mowing since the brutal summer had scorched every yard in the neighborhood, doing so not only gave him a sense of purpose but also allowed him to take out his aggressions on the yard instead of his wife.

He was halfway finished with the front yard when his neighbor and good friend, Earl, rushed across the street and stood in front of the ditch to watch him with curiosity.

He muttered a profanity as he released his hand from the bail, killing the mower's racket and once again thrusting the neighborhood into its typical quietness. In his current bad mood, the last thing he needed was a visit from Earl.

As soon as the mower stalled, Earl rushed in his direction with an amused look. "Why in tarnation are you mowing the lawn? There ain't a green blade of grass nowhere in driving distance."

"I needed something to do."

Earl leaned in and nudged his friend's ribs with his elbow. "The neighbors will think you're crazy for mowing dead grass."

"Have you ever known me to give a darn about what people think about me?"

"If you need something to do, just run across the street and let me know. We could go to Bart's and throw down a few beers and shoot some pool."

"You have enough beer to float the Titanic over at your house. Why go buy it at the local watering hole?"

Earl shrugged. "Tapped beer always tastes better. Not to mention, the views are better at Bart's, if you catch my drift."

Arnold released a spastic laugh. If there was anything his friend was good at, it was giving a good laugh when it was needed. "Sorry to tell you, buddy, but you and I are in the same boat. Those women who hang over at Bart's wouldn't give the likes of you and me a second glance even if we were the only two men there."

"I don't know. Cassie Mae was giving me the eye a few nights ago."

"I hate to break it to you, but Cassie Mae was giving you the eye because she's a gold-digging tramp who'll latch onto anyone if she thinks she can con them out of a few bucks. If I were you, I'd steer clear of Cassie Mae."

Earl spread his arms apart. "Hey, at my age, a guy will take whatever attention he can get."

Though he spoke a good game, his friend wouldn't get within a ten-foot-pole's length of the woman. Her reputation was well known among the men of the town, yet someone always managed to get snookered by her wiles at least a time or two a month. Such topics were their typical guy banter, but still he played along by giving Earl a stern look. "In that case, keep your wallet hidden and check all her pockets before you leave. That's the best advice I can give to a yarn-head who ought to know better."

"Oh, you're no fun, but fine, I'll stick with my dear Pauline."

"Good decision for someone who's as dumb as a box of rocks," Arnold teased.

Earl crossed his arms and lasered a stare onto Arnold. "Now why are you out here mowing the lawn? Aren't you supposed to be on bedrest?"

"The doctor never mentioned bedrest. He said I needed to take it easy for a few months. It's been a few months, and I say it's time to get back to regular life."

"Mowing the lawn isn't taking it easy. You should be on the couch, channel surfing for as long as you can get away with it."

"Would you want to stay in the house all day long with Alice?"

Earl nodded. "Point taken. Pauline is at your house all day playing cards with Alice and the rest of the neighborhood hags, which gives me plenty of alone time."

"Now you know why I'd rather be on the road. My castle ain't even my castle anymore because I have four chain-smoking broads there from sun-up to sun-down."

"Have you heard back from the insurance company on your rig yet?"

"The police report ruled it an accident because of the beam in the road, so they're for sure going to pay out, but I haven't gotten a check yet."

Earl muttered a few choice obscenities. "Those insurance companies are nothing but scumbag rodents. We poor folks scrape by to pay that premium every single month, Johnny-on-the-spot, by golly, or they cancel us. When it comes time for them to pay out, they make us wait weeks, even months, before we get a single payout from them. I swear, every one of those thieves who work in the insurance industry will burn in—"

Arnold patted his arm to calm him. "Hold on. Us old codgers have to be careful not to give ourselves a brain aneurysm."

"I'm just saying, you know as well as I do that right now a bunch of con artists in suits are probably sitting in a conference room in a high-rise building looking for the best ways to screw you out of the money they owe you."

"Apparently they couldn't weasel their way out of paying this time because they've already told me how much I'm getting."

Earl looked at him with staunch skepticism. "Is it enough to buy a new rig?"

"A brand spanking new top-of-the-line one." He leaned in closer as though telling a deep, dark secret. "I'm getting one of those fancy, new-fangled rigs with a built-in television."

Earl's frown curled into a smile, and he dropped another profanity. "No way. Are you serious?"

"Serious as sin," Arnold said with no small amount of pride.

"Well, I'll be dipped and French fried," Earl proclaimed with a happy kick of his leg. "You may never have to come home again."

"I talked to one of my trucker buddies a few days ago, and he told me to be sure and get one with wi-fi and blue-something-or-other capability."

Earl's smile drew back into a frown, and he dropped another profanity. "What's a wi-fi?"

"Heck if I know. The boy tried to explain it and I still don't have a clue what he was talking about. I finally had to act like I knew what he was talking about to make him shut up and stop yammering about it. I figure if I've lived this long without needing a wi-fi, I can keep going for the rest of my life without one."

"It's probably one of those devices that you see people walking around with these days that they can't keep their heads out of. I'll be dickered if I don't hate today's technology. I don't know about you, but I'll head back to the seventies any time anyone wants to send me."

"Oh yeah, bell bottoms and potheads," Arnold held up his fingers in the sign of peace. "Sounds groovy. Sign me up." Everyone liked to romanticize the old days, but every decade had its own problems. He had lived through enough of them to know it was true.

"I'll take seventies potheads over people who never look up from their cell phones. At least potheads still know how to have fun. What's fun about people who are more interested in their phone than in the people right in front of them?"

As much as he hated to admit it, Arnold agreed, not that he wanted to go back to the seventies, though.

"Have you picked out your new rig yet?" Earl asked.

Arnold shook his head. "My buddy gave me some websites to look at, but I have no idea what that means either. I told him I planned to go and look around the local lot, but apparently that's uncool and old fashioned now. Everyone these days buys everything on the computer, even cars."

Earl let another profanity drop. "The whole dadburn world's gone computer crazy."

Chapter 5

The stench of smoke burned his nostrils and lungs. He tried to hold his breath as he flailed his arms in the darkness to clear the air around him, but it didn't help. When he couldn't hold it any longer, he sucked in another burning gulp, which sent him into stinging, spastic coughs.

Fresh air. He needed fresh air.

He clenched the steering wheel and screamed as loud as he could, but the only answer he received were ominous crackles and pops intermingled with deafening explosions followed by the tinkling of thousands of shards of glass hitting metal.

He tried to remember where he was and why, but his mind was a jumble of fragmented images that made no sense.

Fumes of burning oil and rubber stung his eyes and coated his tongue with a thick and hideous taste.

He pressed his lips and breathed through his nose to swallow down the noxious taste, but it was forever imprinted on his tongue. Even when he got out of this awful place, he would always taste burning oil and rubber.

He took it for as long as he could then opened his mouth and plugged his nose to ease the stinging in his nasal passages. The toxic fumes tasted so horrid that he retched and gagged.

Fear exploded inside him as the truth touched his consciousness. He was dead and in Hell. Everything he'd heard was true. There was a God. There was a devil. There was a Heaven. There was a Hell. While on Earth, he refused to believe a simple truth and now he was sentenced to damnation in the flames of Hell where burning rubber and oil would plague him for an eternity.

"God, help me!" He screamed until his throat was raw and sore.

"God, I believe you. Please save me," he screamed, then lapsed into more burning and hacking coughs.

It was too late. God had already banished him to the Lake of Fire. "Please, God. Give me another chance," he tried to scream, but the words came out in a pathetic whimper. Tears streaked down his face. He didn't remember the last time he had cried. "I thought you were a God of second chances." He whispered the words with an angry and broken heart.

"I thought you were a God of second chances." He said the words aloud, but maybe he didn't. Reality and fiction whirled in his mind, and he couldn't discern one from the other.

Another loud pop followed by the shattering of glass.

Pinpricks of pain sliced through his face and arms.

He held his arm up to see if he was bleeding, but the film of choking smoke was too thick to see through.

A rush of cool air blasted across his face, or maybe it was his mind playing cruel tricks on him.

The curtain of smoke parted enough that he could look out the truck window at gray pavement with a bright yellow stripe of paint. Further out were darkened trees dancing with elusive shadows.

Trees and pavement. His heart grew light with relief. He couldn't be in Hell because in Hell there were no trees and pavement—at least he didn't think so.

His eyes bugged open at the smeary sight of orange flickers peeking through a grime-coated windshield. Fire.

"God help me! If I'm not in Hell, then it can't be too late." He couldn't speak the words aloud, but he prayed that God would somehow hear his pleas.

Another shatter of glass followed by a blood-curdling scream.

***

<u>Present Day</u>

The sound jolted him from a deep sleep and made his skin crawl. His heart throbbed in his chest.

He sat up as droplets of sweat dribbled down his cheeks. He gasped for breath while his hands flew over his face, then his arms, then his chest.

He was home in bed, not in Hell.

His gaze went to the window that was cracked open enough to allow a tiny stream of fresh air to rush into the room. The sheer curtains fluttered in the breeze.

His spine stiffened when he heard that awful sound again. A woman screaming.

Was Alice in trouble?

He brought his feet to the floor and stood. He held his breath and craned his neck forward to listen.

When his lungs burned for the mercy of a fresh breath, he exhaled and sucked in another.

Another screech.

He nearly passed out with relief and turned to the window with a self-conscious laugh. He shoved the window all the way up and shivered despite the tepid air that attacked him with a vengeance. Again, he stood still to listen and within seconds another screech interrupted the night.

A screech owl. Not a woman, an owl.

He looked out the window, lost in his thoughts. No matter how many times he remembered that night, he couldn't believe that he had killed another human being. The knowledge brought no small amount of condemnation and self-loathing.

He had been tired that night, too tired to be behind the wheel, without a doubt. If he hadn't been stubborn and refused to pull over, a young man in the prime of his life would still be alive. If God existed, and that was a big if, he hated Him for allowing him to live, an old man with nothing to offer, while a young man died.

He thanked his lucky stars that a beam had been in the road, which was attributed as the official cause of the accident. If not for that, he would probably have a homicide conviction looming over his head. "Maybe there's a God up there somewhere after all," he said, even though he didn't believe it.

He laid back down and pulled the covers to his stubbly chin. He was wide awake and suspected that sleep wouldn't come again any time soon, so he slid his arm back from under the covers and turned on the clock radio for some noise.

His heart was heavy, so he wasn't in the mood for anything loud. He tuned past rock music and his favorite oldies and stopped on a late-night talk program. When he realized the speaker was a preacher, he wanted to skip past it. On the other hand, given his frequent night-mares, maybe listening to what the man had to say wouldn't hurt.

The man's words piqued his interest when he spoke about having hope despite the world around them having gone awry.

When the pastor gave a scripture, he bolted up, flicked on the table-side lamp, and pulled from the drawer the Bible that Aunt Deborah had given him. He flipped through the crinkly onion skin pages. Since he rarely had the desire to open the book, much less read it, it took him several times to stumble upon the book of Romans. Once there, he turned to chapter twelve, verse twelve.

Fraush appeared from the dark corner of the room and stepped to the man's bedside. He glanced first at the man with seething hatred then at the book pages that he searched through with focused tenacity. "So, you're in the mood for fairy tales, huh?"

Rejoice in hope, be patient in tribulation, be constant in prayer. Those were the words that the pastor had read. Arnold spoke the scriptures to himself. His gaze stuck to each word, and the pastor's calming voice melted into the background as he read the words once more, then once again.

"Rejoice in hope," he whispered aloud. He wracked his brain, but he couldn't make himself understand what it meant. "Rejoice in hope?" He glanced up at the darkened popcorn ceiling. "Rejoice in hope? In the hope of what?"

He pulled the Bible closer to his face and read the verse once again then dropped it to his lap in frustration. "Why is everything this book says so darned hard to understand?" Just once, he'd like to read something and instantly understand what it meant.

He scrubbed his hands over his face. "Am I so stupid that I can't understand a simple sentence?"

Fraush smiled. "Yes, you're too stupid to understand a simple sentence so why bother trying?"

Arnold dog eared the page, tossed the Bible aside, and rolled over to his side. He was too stupid to understand anything, so why bother trying?

Lutis stepped from the shadows at the foot of the bed. He ignored the traitorous fallen angel and focused on his human charge. "Trust in the Lord with all your heart and do not lean on your own understanding."

Fraush's rumble of laughter floated through the room.

Arnold turned over in bed at the preacher's next words.

"Proverbs 3:5 tells us to 'trust in the Lord with all your heart and to not lean on your own understanding. The heart commonly refers to a person's center of thinking and reasoning. When we don't understand what to do, or where to turn, or what to believe, rather than trusting in our own fallible notions and false fancies, we should turn to the supreme infallibility of God's word."

"But how do you do that?" Arnold whispered. "I've yet to see God send an angel to me because I didn't know what to do." All this religious hokey pokey annoys me.

The pastor continued. "Jeremiah warns us that when we humans place our trust in ourselves, our hearts depart from the Lord. We should turn our trust to infallible God, whose Word will never lead us astray. No matter what happens in life, our first course of action should always be to find out what God's word says then take Him at His Word."

"I'd love to take Him at his Word if I could understand anything that this blasted Bible says." Arnold blew out a breath of patience, picked up the Bible, and flipped open its pages to the dog eared one.

"Rejoice in hope." He read the words aloud. Rejoice in the hope of what, he didn't know, so he skipped to the next phrase.

"Be patient in tribulation." He paused to think about what it meant. Tribulation was a big word but one he had heard. All those crazy Christians liked to talk about it. When Jesus calls them away in the rapture, everyone else is left to be maimed and killed in the

Tribulation. To him, it all sounded like a bunch of bull hockey that religious people said to scare everyone else into accepting their fairytale Jesus. "Be patient in tribulation. Is this guy saying that the Tribulation is already here?" He slammed the Bible to his lap again and released a curse of annoyance.

He took several breaths to calm his nerves as his gaze floated down to the next phrase. Be constant in prayer.

He picked up the Bible and focused on each of the four words. "Be constant ... in prayer. Be constant in prayer. Finally, something that even an idiot like me can understand."

Chapter 6

Arnold skipped breakfast and stayed in his room until after lunch time. He released a slurry of profanities when a cackle of muted laughter drifted through his closed bedroom door. He tore off his pajama bottoms and threw on the same jeans he had worn yesterday then rifled through his closet for a t-shirt.

At the cheap mirror that hung on the back of the door, he took a quick survey of his appearance. He raked his fingers through a disheveled mop of hair then gave his face a rigorous rub. His t-shirt was clean but yellowed at the armpits and his jeans were frayed at the hems.

Though he had never been a dashing looking man, in his youth he had been passably handsome. The man of his early years had given over to an old, wrinkled, and haggard one with dark bags under his eyes.

He slipped his sock-covered feet into his house shoes and made his way to the door. Even before he opened it, the stench of stale cigarette smoke smacked his olfactory senses. When he stepped into the hallway a fresh smog of smoke wallowed over him. "I've never smoked a day in my life yet every day I smell like a dang chimney," he muttered as he walked toward the front of the house.

As he neared the dining room that served as the women's inner sanctum of card-playing, the appalling fog of smoke grew thicker. Alice delivered the punchline to an offensive joke that resulted in another smattering of husky laughter among the chain-smoking women.

The joke itself wasn't offensive to him since he'd told much worse in all his years, but hearing the words flow so easily from his wife's mouth was shocking despite knowing her propensity for foul language.

He jerked his head to the side and looked in the room as he passed by. "Don't you broads get tired of playing cards every day? How about going outside for a breath of fresh air for a change?"

Alice looked up with a cigarette dangling from her lips and flipped him the bird. She followed him with her extended finger until he disappeared.

"Nice, Alice. Real womanly of you."

She answered him with a few choice obscenities which sent the women into yet another cackle of laughter.

Arnold threw open the refrigerator as his blood boiled with rage. How dare she flip him off, especially in front of all those women.

"Can't you get your old man back on the road so we can have the place to ourselves again?" One of the women whispered with the subtlety of a train hitting a brick wall at full speed ahead.

"Believe me, nobody wants him out of my hair more than me," Alice snapped.

A few choice words of his own hit his tongue with an acidic rush, but as much as he hated to, he bit them back. Alice never stepped away from a fight, especially not with him, and he didn't have a fight in him today.

As cool air from the refrigerator swept over his body, his gaze lingered over the remnants of leftovers that sat on the shelves: a half full plastic-wrapped bowl of noodles and ground beef, a store-bought pecan pie with two pieces left, and a few spoons of green peas and pearl onions. He could probably scrounge a half-decent meal with the leftovers if he wanted, but he didn't.

Instead, he yanked open the deli drawer with a clatter, pulled out a zippered baggie of smoked bologna, and tossed it to the table.

Next, he grabbed the green Tupperware bowl that held a head of iceberg lettuce and the smaller red one that always held a sweet onion.

He placed the bounty on the table and shuffled to the bread canister and pulled out a loaf of off-brand white bread.

At the cabinet next to the sink, he snatched a tall drinking glass and filled it with ice and sweet tea. He gurgled down half of the beverage in a series of thirsty gulps then refilled it.

With a sigh, he lowered himself into the chair and constructed his sandwich with two layers of bologna piled high with lettuce and the meager few pieces of red onion.

On the windowsill, he spotted a bowl of anemic-looking tomatoes and another red onion. He pushed himself up with a grunt and sliced one of the tomatoes and the onion. As he carried the piled-up plate to the table, with a smile of satisfaction he visualized Alice going for the onion and realizing that he had beat her to it. Just to throw fuel on the fire of her fury, he intended to eat every single bite of the onion, leaving her with nothing.

With his sandwich finally completed, he picked up the top slice of bread and muttered his disdain when he realized he had forgotten the mayonnaise and mustard, a special blend of which he liked slathered on his sandwiches, but he didn't have the wherewithal to get up again, so he would eat it dry.

He topped the sandwich and looked at it for several seconds before digging in. The meal of kings it wasn't, but a filling meal it was.

***

<u>1970</u>

They had been blissfully married for a week.

Arnold stomped onto the porch of their scrawny one bedroom, one bath rented house and looked from one side to the other before bending down and placing a doormat in front of the door. With a smile, he stepped back and looked at it with pride as he recalled their trip to the local discount store last night.

***

Money was tight for them, but he could tell Alice wanted the summery doormat with the vibrant green trailing vines, the scattered playful red cardinals, and the fancy scripted "WELCOME" splashed across the center. Even discounted four dollars from the original price, they didn't have the extra money to spare, but he placed it in their cart with a smirky grin.

Alice looked up at him with wide and innocent eyes. "Honey, we can't afford that. We need to save our money for groceries." She pulled it out of the cart and placed it back on the shelf.

Arnold grabbed it and placed it back in the cart. "We need it, so we'll manage."

She shook her head and placed it back on the shelf. "Nobody needs a doormat."

"If we splurge and buy a little something every payday, we'll eventually have everything we need," he said.

"We'll never have everything we need because once we have it all, it'll be old and time to replace it." She hefted the mat from the cart and placed it back on the shelf. "For now, let's stick with essentials like groceries."

Arnold gestured at the mat. "I want to get it for you now. It's not that expensive."

She took a final look at it, waved the mat away, and pushed the cart a few steps forward. "That's a summer one anyway, and now it's the fall. It's so out of season."

He chuckled at the dismissive tone of her voice. Despite her attempt to make him think otherwise, she wanted it, and if she wanted it, she would have it. "If we don't get it now, it may not be here next time."

She pointed at the opposite end of the store. "Let's get our groceries bought. I'm ready to get home and start cooking dinner."

He took one last forlorn look at the doormat but left it sitting where she had placed it. His cheeks flamed at his embarrassing lack of funds, at not being able to get his bride everything her heart desired. One day he would be able to get her everything she wanted and more. He resolved it in his heart. He would do it or die trying.

***

<u>1970 – The Next Day</u>

He scuffed his feet across the doormat and flung the door open. The scent of food greeted him, filling him with a burst of pure joy. His momma could cook like no one else's business, but there was nothing better than coming home to his own house to enjoy a meal cooked by his own wife.

Every morning when he woke up, he was tempted to pinch himself to make sure he wasn't dreaming, but if he was, he never wanted to awaken. He was married to the most beautiful woman in the world, and he still couldn't believe it.

"Honey, I'm home." He hung his light jacket on the hook behind the door. Honey, I'm home. He would never in a million years get tired of saying those words.

His eyes widened when she entered the room in blue bell-bottom jeans and a sunshine yellow blouse.

She rushed into the living room and jumped into his arms with a happy smile. "I missed you so much today." She squealed when he tightened his arms around her and spun them both in circles.

She bent her legs up close to her thighs and tossed her head back as the living room moved around them at a dizzying speed. When she'd had enough, she straightened her legs and pushed them to the floor.

He released her from his grasp and stared at her with delight.

Embarrassed by his scrutiny, she pushed her hands through her brunette hair that was styled in her best attempt to replicate a popular trend that was all the craze. Her meager styling skills were nothing to brag about, but she thought she did a great job.

Arnold turned in the doorway and gestured outside. "You notice anything different?"

She stepped onto the threshold and glanced around the yard then the surrounding neighbors' yards. "I don't think so," she said with hesitance.

He took a few more steps out onto the porch and gestured for her to follow.

Under her feet was a different sensation of texture, so she looked down and for the first time saw the doormat from the discount store last night. "Arnold," she giggled. "What did you do?"

"They say that no home is complete without a doormat."

"Who says that?"

"I don't know, but if they said it then it must be true."

She squealed and again jumped into his arms. "Thank you. I love it." When he dropped her back to her feet, she took a couple of steps back and suddenly felt silly for reacting in such a way to something as mundane as a doormat.

Arnold turned his face to the sky and breathed in deeply. "Dinner smells amazing."

She stepped inside, took another look at the beautiful doormat then closed the door behind them. "I had a lot going on today, so McDonald's cheeseburgers and fries it is." She flashed him her best teasing smile.

He placed his hand on her cheek and caressed it with his thumb. "I'll eat at McDonald's every day of the week as long as you're here with me."

She shook her head and made her way back to the kitchen but stopped short of entering. She whirled around to face him with a flourish. "You have time to freshen up before dinner if you want."

"I'll clean up before bed. I want to spend time with you."

She giggled, patted his fanny, and pushed him toward the bath-room. "You've been in the factory all day and, forgive me for saying so, but you look and smell like it. Now go clean up."

He leaned in and pressed a gentle kiss to her lips. The subtle scent of baby powder that fragranced her skin caught his attention. He loved the way she smelled. "I'll be back in two shakes of a lamb's tail." He made a mad dash for the bathroom. "By the way, what's for dinner?" He unbuttoned his shirt as he walked.

In a flirtatious manner, she placed her hand on the doorframe, kicked her foot back in a dramatic pose, and fluttered her eyelashes. "There's only one way to find out, sailor."

He blew her a kiss and flew into the bathroom to take the fastest shower of his life.

Ten minutes later, he left the bathroom with his dark brown hair glistening with moisture and combed back in a sleek style.

He drifted across the room toward the kitchen then went back to the bathroom for a few splashes of his favorite cologne, Old Spice.

He rarely wore cologne but kept a bottle on hand for special occasions, mostly weddings and funerals. Now that he was married, he found that more occasions, even something as simple as dinner with his bride, was special enough.

In the kitchen, the harvest gold-colored oven door was open with Alice bent over it with plushy potholders clutched in her fingers.

He bolted to her side and took the potholders away from her. "Let me do that so you don't get burned."

She swatted his behind with a sassy look of faux offense. "I'm an independent woman. I don't need a man."

He kissed the tip of her nose. "I hope you need this man for now and many years to come."

She pointed at the oven. "Fine. While you do that, I'll get the salad from the fridge."

He leaned into the scorching wave of heat and pulled out a fragrant golden chicken followed by another square pan of spicy-smelling cornbread dressing. He placed the dressing atop a cooling rack on the counter and gazed over the stove at simmering pans of corn, green beans, and a brown substance that he guessed was gravy.

Alice placed a wooden bowl of salad on the table and pointed at the cornbread dressing. "Move that pan, hon. I need the cooling rack for the hot rolls."

His face lit up. "We're having hot rolls, too? Did you win a lucky round of Bingo while I was at work?" He opened the drawer and pulled out two potholders, tossed them to the counter, and moved the dressing on top of them.

She uncovered a baking sheet lined with four dinner rolls and pushed them into the oven then turned and gave an embarrassed shrug. "They're only the brown and serve kind. I could never make homemade ones like momma does."

He forced his back into a rigid stance. "I thought you were an independent woman. Independent women can do anything they set their minds to."

"Okay, fine, you caught me. I don't want to make homemade rolls, so brown and serve it is."

He nodded to the corner of the kitchen and their dilapidated table that was stabilized from wobbling by a folded-up piece of paper strategically placed under two of the legs. *One of these days, I'm buying you a kitchen table that doesn't wobble.* "How about I set the table?"

She grabbed serving spoons from a drawer and thrust them at him.

He pulled cheap plastic plates from a stack in the cabinet and thin, cheap cutlery from the drawer, and plunked them all on the table and aligned them with care. Their dishes were nothing but mismatched hand-me-downs from each of their mothers' castaways. *One of these days, I'm buying you the best china and silverware that money can buy.*

Within minutes, they were seated at the sad, wobbly table with steaming plates of food.

"This looks amazing." He grabbed his fork and shoved it into a slice of baked chicken.

Alice reached across the table to stop him from taking a bite. "Do you mind if we pray first?"

Pray? They'd never prayed together, so the request took him by surprise. He cleared his throat and set the fork down. "Yes, let's pray."

She gave him a subtle nod, indicating that he should do the honors. A film of sweat popped up on his forehead, and his heart pitter pattered in his chest.

She took his hands in hers and gave him an expectant look. "Go ahead," she whispered.

"I ... I've never prayed before. I ... don't know what to say." He tucked his head in shame.

"There's no right or wrong way to do it. You just say whatever's in your heart. Whatever you want God to hear."

He nodded and his leg began a nervous dance under the table. He cleared his throat, then again for good measure as he tried to formulate, on the spot, his first-ever prayer. His hands trembled, and it made him feel better when she gave them an encouraging squeeze. "Dear Holy and Almighty Jesus Christ and the Holy Spirit who hovers over the ... the triumphant waters, and who died to save us from all our sins and the ... trespassers that ... that ... encompass us," he said in his most authoritative voice. He'd heard a preacher say that at a funeral once, or maybe it was one of the few times he went to church with his grandparents. At this point, every prayer he'd ever heard was a jumble of thoughts.

Alice peeked at him and chuckled to herself at his thrust-out chin and the formal cadence with which he spoke.

"We're all sinners saved by grace, so we'll see each other again one day when our feet touch the golden streets of glory ... and the mahogany Tree of Life where Adam and Eve ate the first ... um ... apple." Another tidbit that he remembered from the preacher's prayer at the funeral. He may not have gotten the words exactly right, but it was all he could remember on the spur of the moment.

"Thank you, Jesus Christ, for all the farmers who grow our food and for the rain that feeds the crops and for the truck drivers who bring it to our tables. Amen."

He raised his head and dropped Alice's hands then just as quickly picked them back up and lowered his head again. "Oh, and Father on the most-high mountains of … of … Jeremiah. Thank you for letting the Patriots kick butt this weekend. Those boys did us proud. Amen."

Crap, I think I was supposed to say the most-high mountains of Jerusalem, I think. Does Jerusalem have mountains? He didn't know. How embarrassing.

He dropped Alice's hands and gave her a sheepish smile. It was probably the worst prayer God had ever heard.

"That was a beautiful prayer, Arnold." She tried to keep from laughing as she patted his hands. "Thank you."

He picked up the fork and shoveled a pile of peas onto it, but all but three fell back to the plate by the time he got it to his mouth.

Alice tore off a bite of hot roll and dipped it into a pool of gravy. "So, um, who's Jeremiah and where are his mountains?"

"I think I meant to say Jerusalem."

"Ah." She forked a bite of the chicken. It tasted good but was dry, the gravy had turned into a gelatinous mess, and the rolls weren't as soft as she'd have liked. Maybe with practice, she would get better.

"Yeah, I think it's probably better if I don't say 'butt' in my prayer next time, huh?" Arnold said.

She belted out a laugh. "That might be something to keep in mind for future prayers."

After a long dinner, Arnold stood to his feet. "You go to the living room and have a seat while I clean up in here."

She shook her head and picked up their plates. "You worked hard all day, so I'll do the cleaning. After I'm done, if you want, we'll watch a little television together before bed."

He removed the plates from her hands and spun her around as though they were on a dance floor. When they stopped, chest to chest, he said, "Thank you for a wonderful dinner, but what's the occasion for the fancy baked chicken and dressing?"

She shrugged. "It wasn't fancy. I just wanted to do something extra special for you because it's our first Friday night dinner as a married couple. I know we didn't have the money to spend that much on a whole chicken, but I thought it would be nice." She jerked her head toward the living room. "Now scoot while I clean up this mess."

He grabbed her hands in his. "Let's do it together."

She tried to argue, but he placed his finger over her lips. "I want to help you."

When the dishes were done, Alice swiped a moist cloth over the countertops while Arnold swept the floors.

They turned off the kitchen lights with a few minutes to spare before their program came on.

"Do you think forty years from now we'll still be this happy?" Alice asked when they were cuddled on the couch.

"I think we'll be even happier than we are now."

***

<u>Present Day</u>

The memory of happier days brought a sigh to Arnold's soul.

He looked down at the half-eaten bologna sandwich. His stomach felt like it was full of barbed wire, and his appetite was wrecked. He pushed the plate to the center of the table and looked up at the ceiling.

"I don't know if You're there, God. I don't even know if You exist, but if You do, I could use some help down here."

Lutis gave the human a smile that he would never see. "Seek Him with all your heart, and you shall find Him."

Mondaci materialized behind Lutis with a series of guttural laughs. "Not if we have anything to do with it," Mondaci said.

Chapter 7

Hyacinth lay in bed with a heavy heart. It was already almost ten o'clock, but she didn't have the discipline to get up and start the day. Their home, usually so full of love and life, was oppressive with an emptiness to which she would never grow accustomed.

She missed the sounds of Jenner awakening early in the mornings to work on his blog, trying not to interrupt her sleep yet managing to fill the house with a barrage of noises that a normal person could never sleep through.

She missed the often-annoying sounds of his video games that filtered through the hallways.

She missed the sounds of his electric razor buzzing through his omnipresent five o'clock shadow on Sunday mornings before church.

She missed the late evening sounds of his basketball pounding the concrete driveway and his triumphant whoops and hollers when the ball sailed through the net with an easy swish.

She regretted all the times she had flown out the door to admonish him when the ball hit the side of the house precariously close to the upstairs window. Now that he was gone, the price of a few pieces of replacement siding or a new window didn't seem as big of a deal.

She rolled over and glanced at the doorway that would never again usher in her husband's appearance.

On his blogging mornings, she often would roll over in bed and smile at his futile attempts at silence. She would stay in bed so he wouldn't know he'd awakened her only to close her eyes when he clopped up the stairs like a Clydesdale to surprise her with a steaming mug of coffee.

The way he bent down to press a gentle kiss to her forehead as the succulent scent of coffee awakened her senses. His gentle whispers of, "Wake up, my love. It's a new and wonderful day."

Wake up, my love. Oh, to hear those words from her beloved just one more time.

A trail of tears worked their way down her cheek and absorbed into her silk pillowcase. "Lord, I miss him so much, and my heart is full of pain, but I will always honor and worship You."

Cingo and Nitasah stood next to the bed with proud smiles. "She has a strong faith," Cingo said.

"Yes," Nitasah nodded. "But we know the enemy always attacks when they endure great trials."

"Our fallen counterparts are cowards," Cingo said.

"If her heart remains on God and the truth of His word, she won't fall prey to the hands of the enemy."

You now have sorrow, but I will see you again, and your heart will rejoice. Your joy no man will ever take from you.

The words of Jesus to his disciples in John 16:22 coursed through her mind like an unexpected cool breeze on a stifling hot day. The pain of loss was still there, but the precious Holy Spirit had never failed to bring her hope in the midst of her worst times. This, her biggest loss ever, would be no exception—of that she was sure.

Much like Jesus' promise to his disciples, she would one day see her husband again, and that promise helped to soften the grief in her heart.

The peal of the doorbell drew her from her musings. She sat up and crossed her arms across her chest. "Who on Earth could that be?"

She slid out of bed, tiptoed across the room, stuck her head into the hallway, and listened.

When the doorbell buzzed once again, she yelped, and her hand flew to her chest. She rushed to the foot of the bed, snatched up her robe, and tied it around her waist as she traipsed down the steps.

A smile lit her face as she opened the door. "Camden." She stepped aside so he could enter then closed the door behind him.

He paused, looked around the foyer, and popped his fist into his palm. "What're you doing today?"

"Sheri and I are having lunch. Other than that, I'm playing it by ear."

"Ah." He shoved his hands in his pockets and rocked back and forth on his feet.

"Is—" She eyed him cautiously. "Is everything okay?"

He nodded, but his eyes flooded with tears.

"Come here." She wrapped him in her arms and gave him a tight squeeze.

Neither of them said anything for several seconds, until he stepped out of her embrace, sniffed, and wiped the back of his hand against his nose.

She yanked several tissues from the foyer table and placed them in his fisted hand then headed toward the living room. "Come on in and have a seat."

He wiped the tissues across his nose then shoved them into his pocket and followed her. "Sorry for stopping by like this. I just ... I miss him today."

"Well, honey, you're always welcome here. No need to apologize." She settled into an armchair and covered her legs with the robe's length.

He fell into the sofa with a shrug. "I thought maybe since you're here alone now, you might not like us guys dropping by like we used to."

She clicked her tongue in disbelief. "You know better than that. I need you all, now more than ever."

"That's what Lucas said."

She gave him a definitive nod. "For once, listen to Lucas. He knows what he's talking about."

He rewarded her with a tight smile then stood and made his way to the fireplace where he pulled from the mantle a picture of Hyacinth and Jenner smiling and drenched under a waterfall. He had seen the picture a hundred times but never really saw it until now. "When did you guys go to a waterfall?"

"Two years ago, when we went on vacation in Fiji. Their pool was fabulous."

He turned and looked at her. "This is a pool? With all the rocks and foliage, I thought it was a real waterfall."

"Yeah," she giggled. "I think that was kind of the point."

He clutched the picture to his chest, sniffled, and glanced around the room. "Is it hard to stay here with him being gone?"

"It's harder some days than others."

He sat back down in his chair and looked at the picture. Jenner's goofy smile and messy wet hair gave him a wave of much-needed encouragement. He handed the picture over to her. "If I've told that boy once, I've told him a hundred times, he doesn't have the physique for shirtless."

She took the picture and glanced over it then set it on the lamp table between them. "He thought the world of you and Lucas, you know. He loved you like the brothers he never had."

Camden chuckled. "Yeah, and according to him we were the brothers he never wanted."

She slapped her palms to her thighs and stood to her feet. "How about a glass of tea?"

He shook his head and stood.

"You're not leaving," she pleaded. "You just got here."

He nodded at the front door. "Nah, I thought I'd mow the lawn today instead of tomorrow. It's supposed to be ten degrees hotter tomorrow, which means today is hot and tomorrow is hotter than hades."

She perched her arm on her hip. "I keep telling you, you and Lucas don't need to mow my lawn. I can hire someone to do it."

Camden perched his arm on his hip in a similar fashion. "Yeah, right, and give Jenner a reason to come back and haunt us from the great beyond? Because I have no doubt, if there's a way for him to do it, he will."

She leaned in and pecked his cheek. "If you guys ever get tired of doing it, just let me know. I don't expect you to take care of things around here forever. You and Lucas are growing boys with things to do."

"We don't mind doing it, but we'll let you know if things change."

She nodded her approval though every week when they showed up guilt weaved its way into her thoughts. "Speaking of things changing, you and Lucas haven't been over to swim in the pool lately."

He shrugged. "I just thought you might—"

"You guys have a key to the house and to the backyard fence," she interrupted. "You were always welcome to use it anytime you wanted, and nothing has changed."

"Okay. Thanks."

A shadow of sadness lurked deep in his eyes, a sadness she understood all too well. She clutched him in a fierce side hug. "I'll tell you what. How about you and Lucas come over for lunch next Saturday? We'll have ourselves a full-fledged pool party. A light lunch and swimming then a big cookout that night."

"Yeah, I guess," he said. "Sure."

Hyacinth squeezed his arm. "We all miss him, and nothing is the same anymore, but Jenner would want us to keep living our lives together."

Tears welled in his eyes, and he tried to squelch the cry that rose within him. "I'd better get started on the yard. Lucas will be here in a few minutes to weed eat while I mow." He grasped the brass knob and pulled the door open, inviting in an already mounting insufferable wave of heat.

"You guys could skip it this week if you wanted. This heat has killed everything in the yard."

"There are spots that need mown," he shrugged. "It'll give me something to do."

"I'll bring you guys a nice glass of tea in about half an hour."

"Sure, sounds great."

"Things will get better. We'll adjust, and with time, things will be fine. You'll see."

"Just don't mention a new normal. I swear, if I hear that stupid phrase one more time." He blew out a deep breath and stepped onto the porch. "When you bring out that tea, put some of those baby orange slices on the rim of the glasses. Lucas likes them."

Yeah, because Lucas likes them, she almost teased, but instead she nodded. "I'll pile you both up with as many baby oranges as you can eat."

Chapter 8

"If your enemy is hungry, give him something to eat. If he is thirsty, give him something to drink. In doing this, you will heap burning coals on his head."

Arnold sat in the parking lot of the mom-and-pop garden center, watching as people went in and out of the store carrying everything from potted plants to bags of mulch. He listened to the final few minutes of the radio preacher. He wondered, yet again, why he was drawn to the local Christian talk station. A station he had never listened to in his entire life, yet now he found himself tuning in at least once per day. Why spend so much time listening to someone yammer on about things and entities—especially entities—in which he didn't believe.

He glared at the radio and flipped it the bird. "What does that have to do with healing broken relationships?"

"I know what you're thinking," the man on the radio said. His voice was a mixture of calming amusement. "Heaping burning coals on the head of the person with whom you've suffered a loss of relationship? That sounds like the perfect revenge, right?"

The man released a soft chuckle, and Arnold was tempted to turn off the radio.

"Revenge, while it sounds sweet, isn't where we want to go, though. Especially if it's a relationship you want to salvage. Maybe if you're listening today, you're in a rift with your best friend. Maybe someone at church did or said something that made you feel pain. Maybe you're a wife who has become estranged from your husband."

The last part of the statement piqued Arnold's attention. He was a husband, not a wife, but surely whatever the man had to say would work just the same. He turned up the radio so he wouldn't miss a word.

"Whatever your situation, with whomever you've experienced a loss of relationship, instead of taking on a passive-aggressive approach, try doing something nice for them instead. How about baking your friend a batch of her favorite cookies or taking him to a local game? I know it seems like small things, but most people don't require grand overtures when it comes to seeking amends. An earnest and humble conversation coupled with simple gestures often works wonders."

"Hm," Arnold said.

Mondaci sat in the passenger seat and glared at the radio.

"Alice will never respond to such silly gestures," he growled. "Don't bother."

Arnold shook his head. "Who're you kidding. Fresh-baked cookies? Even if I could make them, she'd laugh me out of the house."

"If you need to make amends with your wife, take her on a walk at the local park then present her with a beautiful arrangement of her favorite fresh cut flowers. Or take her to a nearby local concert then give her a gift certificate to a day spa for a facial or massage. Small gestures could be just the push in the right direction that you need," the voice on the radio continued. "And believe it or not, sometimes even a simple earnest apology could be enough to smooth things over."

Arnold released a sarcastic guffaw as he turned off the radio. Maybe all those things would work with most women, but Alice is about as feminine as I am. As the thought rushed through his mind, he smiled.

"I guess I could buy the old hag a carton of cigarettes and a new deck of playing cards. That's something she'd appreciate."

He slammed his hand down onto the steering wheel. "Forget it, Arnold. You are past romantic overtures and so is she."

Mondaci smiled. "That's right."

Arnold pulled the truck into drive but kept his foot on the brake. Since it was early afternoon, he didn't want to go home and deal with Alice. "Maybe it's time to get back to work. If I'm careful, I can manage it."

He was never home during the day, so he had no ideas of how to fill his time. He could run by Earl's house and slam down a few beers because, without a doubt, his old hag Pauline was at his house playing cards with Alice.

That option didn't appeal to him, though. Drinking beer while WWF buffoons wrestled on the television sounded like a horrible way to spend an afternoon.

Then it hit him like a load of bricks atop the head.

***

As soon as his wheels hit the gravel and dirt parking lot, a cloak of dust clogged the air. He pulled to a stop and dragged himself out into the heat of the day.

He choked down a series of coughs as he made his way through the gritty plume. He hobbled along with his cane in hand, a pathetic little medical device he could probably do fine without, but in deference to getting back on his feet quickly, he forced himself to follow the doctor's orders.

His gaze went to the signage on the building he hadn't frequented in years. Bottom's Up Gentlemen's Club neon lighting sizzled on the wall, washing the cream-colored bricks in hues of hot pink and cobalt blue. Behind the words, the lighted silhouette of an irregularly voluptuous woman brought an unintentional smile. It was vulgar yet hilarious.

"Gentleman's club, my rear," he muttered as he walked into the cool building. Many sleazy men had walked through these doors, none of which would ever fall under the category of gentlemen.

In the lobby, a shabby, thick, dust-laden brocaded curtain separated the entertainment area from the general public's probing eyes. He dropped the required twenty-dollar entry fee onto the pock-marked wooden counter.

The prune-faced man picked up the twenty and shoved it into the drawer of a vintage-looking cash register that opened with squeaky clanks. He nodded to the curtain with a grunt, which Arnold accepted as his invitation to enter.

Though it had been over ten years since he'd been here, the place looked the same, down to the air that held a rusty fragrance intermingled with sweat and malty beer hops.

Ghoulish rock music blared from speakers that hung by chains from the ceiling.

On the way to the bar, his gaze went to the stage where three topless women swung on brass poles. He hoisted himself up onto a barstool. Walking in with a cane in front of all these virile young men was embarrassing so with a discreet motion he hid it between his legs.

"What'll ya have," asked the busty middle-aged bartender who was several years past the age of catching any man's ogling eyes. Truth be told, that was probably why she was banished to the day shift, far away from the busy nights and weekends.

He gave her a playful smile. "Sex on the Beach."

She tossed a soppy bar cloth to the wooden counter with a scowl and rubbed it across the surface, leaving thick rivulets of moisture. "Honey, you don't look like a cocktail drinker, and you're about as apt to get a sex on the beach as I am. Now, what'll ya have?"

"Whatever's on tap."

"I'm not in the business of readin' minds." She jerked her thumb over her shoulder at a dry-erase board that contained a beer menu written with a crude and scrawlish hand.

Though the penmanship was atrocious, it was easy to catch the gist. "How about a BarrelHouse? I haven't had one of those in ages. I remember one time—"

She whipped around, clearly dismissing him, and grabbed a tall beer glass that hung from a rack above the bar.

He fell silent as she thrust the glass under the spout, pulled down the tap handle, and dispensed a frothy, golden-orange liquid.

She plopped it in front of him without a smile. A decent bartender would have asked if he wanted anything else, but niceties weren't in this woman's repertoire, so he didn't expect it. "You got any nuts back there?"

Without looking down, she reached behind the bar and dropped a parchment-lined basket of peanuts and pretzels in front of him. A peanut flew out of the basket and spun on the counter for a few seconds before slowing to a stop.

He snatched a handful of the salty snacks into his fist and shoved them all into his mouth. "Any good entertainment on the main stage tonight?"

She grabbed her towel, wrung it over a sink behind the bar, and wiped it across the surface again. "Tonight's boys' night," she answered in a tone that was neither rude nor friendly.

"Boys' night? Isn't every night boys' night in a gentleman's club?"

"Thursday nights are always boys' night," she repeated. "Muscled hunks in G-strings is the nightly flavor every Thursday."

"What?" He sputtered. "Are you telling me that men dance naked? On the stage? Here?"

"Yep." She cackled at his outrage.

"This is a Gentlemen's Club, for heaven's sake. You're saying that men dance here." He glanced over his shoulder toward the dance floor then back at her with disgust. "Naked?"

She crossed her arms over her ample breast. "The new owners call it inclusivity, or inclusion, or some such malarky, but, hey, whatever floats your boat, I guess."

"Men actually come here to watch—" He gestured toward the stage, "—other men dance naked? Who wants to watch that?"

She dispensed another beer and sat it in front of him.

Thinking it was his, he reached for it, but she sneered at him, grabbed it up, and slurped half of it down in a series of gulps.

She slammed the glass onto the counter and let out a deep rolling belch then leaned in and whispered. "You'd be surprised how many twinkle toes there are in this town, and every one of them is here on Thursday nights."

Arnold was floored and repulsed by the thought. "Who wants to watch naked men writhe on a pole?"

"Who wants to watch naked women writhe on a pole? If it's okay for a woman to demean herself for you perverts' entertainment, I reckon it's okay for a man to do the same."

"If men want to watch men on a pole, I say start your own club and leave ours be," Arnold spat in a petulant tone. "What's this world coming to?"

***

Arnold left the establishment with a disgruntled huff after only two beers. He didn't want to be in a place where so-called men pranced on a stage while other men lusted after them, even if it was only for a few hours on Thursday nights.

He hoisted himself onto the truck seat, tossed the cane to the side, and pulled out of the parking lot with a screech of his tires. "I'd rather watch Alice strip naked and dance than dadburn men." To get both unwanted images out of his mind, he flipped on the Christian radio and listened as gun advocates talked about what the world would look like if citizens were ever stripped of their rights to own guns.

While he drove with no intended destination, his mind went back to the previous pastor who'd spoken about making amends with the people you love.

He whipped into the garden center and ran in and out in less than ten minutes. With care, he placed a rose bush for planting on the passenger side floor.

Alice would mock him from here to Kingdom Come if he took her roses from a florist, but maybe this would be enough to make a statement. He didn't know whether he still loved her, or vice versa, but it was worth a shot.

Chapter 9

It was nearly ten o'clock that night before the card playing ended and the women finally left to go home and annoy their own husbands. How the biddies played cards from morning until night every single day, Arnold couldn't figure out. He would be bored with it by noon.

He waited until Alice turned off the lights in the front of the house and retired to her room. Once the women left, she usually settled into her bed to watch television until she fell asleep.

When he knocked on her door and peeked in, she had released her bun, combed it out, and changed into her ankle length Laura Ingalls Wilder-esque nightgown.

She looked at him without smiling. "Yeah?"

He dismissed her brusque tone and stepped into the room clutching the rose bush to his chest. He tried to think of something charming to say but nothing came to mind since charm wasn't his thing. Instead, he thrust the plant in her direction. "I bought this for you."

Her head tilted back, and she looked at it as though it were a pipe bomb infused with the Ebola virus. "What is it?"

He glanced down at it and choked back an 'ask a stupid question, get a stupid answer' response. "It's a rose bush."

She picked up the remote and flicked on the television with a snort. "What's it for?"

"I thought we might plant it. It might be nice to have some fresh roses."

"By 'we,' I hope you mean 'you,' cause with these knees, I ain't planting no roses." She switched her focus back to the television as the creepy music from an episode of her favorite show, The Twilight Zone, filled the room.

"I thought it would be something fun we could do tomorrow ... together?"

"I'm playing cards tomorrow."

"You play cards every day. Can't you put that off for an hour?" He had to work hard at keeping the irritation out of his voice.

"I don't care about roses. Plant them yourself."

Her easy dismissal caused a pang of hurt in his heart. "You used to love roses."

She cut her eyes over at him with an exaggerated sigh. "I used to be young and pretty, too. What's your point? Things change. Get over it."

Mondaci and Fraush grinned at each other as they witnessed the scene. "Nothing will save this wretched relationship," Fraush gloated. "These people hate each other."

"For our sakes, we better assure it stays that way." Mondaci moved to Arnold's side and glowered into eyes that would never see him. "I hate you, human."

Arnold squeezed the thin plastic container that the roses were in, and soil cascaded to the floor. What he wanted to say to her were words that no man should ever utter to his wife, but he held them back. He turned to leave but paused just outside the door. "I know I've not been the most decent husband over the years, but do things have to stay like this? Don't you ever miss what we used to have?"

Her response was to click up the volume by several decibels.

His inclination was to rush over and empty the contents of the flowerpot onto her bed, but what would that do but make things worse than they already were.

He lumbered down the hallway and threw open the front door. He rested his cane against the doorway and hobbled onto the front porch. A discomfort shot through his leg as he stomped unaided down the steps and onto the grass of the front yard.

The songs of crickets filled the night, and the sky held a half-moon surrounded by stars flung into space above them.

The swampy, humid air of the night had replaced the brutal heat of the day. On the road, a car zipped past going too fast, and the thumpity-thump-thump of music trailed behind it before dissolving into the night.

He held the rose bush over his shoulder and used his anger to launch it through the air. Across the yard, it landed and somersaulted for another foot before coming to a stop.

The rustle of something in the bushes made him take a few steps toward the porch. He scanned the darkness in search of a threat then unleashed a string of obscenities when a cat darted no more than a foot in front of him and disappeared around the side of the neighbor's house.

"People and cats!" He yelled after it. "The world would be better off without them both." He lowered himself to the bottom step as his heart raced in his chest. The sound of his shout set the neighborhood dogs to barking.

"Shut up, Buster!" A man's screech filtered through the chorus of barks, which brought Arnold a much-needed chuckle.

***

<u>1970</u>

Pineapple in a sweet and savory glaze simmered on the stove while spicy chicken chunks slow baked in the oven. The two fragrances wrapped the house in a scent that felt like a warm hug.

With care, she arranged the secondhand plates and cheap silverware on the table atop a delicate pink tablecloth with red roses and green climbing vines that she had found at a thrift shop. She folded the coordinating cloth napkins—another thrift store find—and placed them atop the plates.

She gave the table a critical eye. It looked good but was sparse and needed something more.

With a snap of her fingers, she rushed to the bedroom where she snatched up a bundle of faux flowers that she had won at the county fair several months ago.

Having no vase, she bent the wire stems to varying lengths and arranged them in a gold-rimmed glass. She set it in the center of the table and stood back for another look. The avocado green and orange petals didn't go with the pink tablecloth and napkins, but it would do.

She stirred the pineapple glaze and turned the heat to the lowest setting.

A glance at the clock told her that Arnold would be home in the next ten minutes. She took another stab at arranging a few more flowers until they were just right.

Assured that there was nothing else she could do to improve the table aesthetic, she rushed to the bedroom to change from her cooking clothes to her favorite outfit: a sunshine yellow peasant blouse and white polyester pants.

In the bathroom, she ran a brush through her hair and slid in a pastel yellow hairband. With a giggle, she spritzed Charlie perfume into the air and walked into the scented cloud with a dramatic sway of her hips. She normally sprayed it directly onto her skin, but the fancy women in the movies always walked into the cloud, and she'd always wanted to try it. The simple act made her feel like her favorite actress, Lauren Bacall.

She held up her hand to an invisible suitor while attempting her best curtsey. "Why, thank you, dah-ling. I do look mah-ve-lous, don't I?" She said in a raspy voice. It sounded nothing like Lauren Bacall, but she pretended that it did.

The mirror above the dresser caught her reflection as she walked out of the room. "Oh, I almost forgot." She pulled the red earrings from her ears and replaced them with yellow metal dangles with painted daisies.

Many women of today would say that having dinner ready and changing into her best outfit for her husband were not only outdated practices but also a setback to the women's liberation movement. She didn't care, though. She loved her husband and didn't want to look like a frumpy shrew when he got home from a long day of work.

She ran her hands down her waist as she studied her side profile in the mirror. "You really could stand to lose a few pounds, dah-ling," she said, again with a Bacall rasp.

She sucked in a breath when the front door creaked open then creaked shut. She almost burst into the living room to greet him, but she paused, wanting to hear the words.

"I'm home, baby."

A flush burned over her cheeks. In the last few weeks, he had taken to calling her baby, and oh, how she loved those words. She adored the term of endearment, of being someone's 'baby.' Another setback for the women's liberation movement, she presumed, but again, she didn't care as much as most about such progressive movements.

She dashed out of the bedroom with what she feared was a goofy smile. "Hey, sweetie. How was your day?" She stood on her tippy toes to press a kiss to his cheek. As always, he smelled of sweat and chemicals, but it was a smell that suited him well.

"Now, is that a proper way for a wife to greet her husband after a hard day of work?" Arnold held out his arms to her. "Get over here and let's do it right."

When she paused and gave him a questioning glance, he rushed forward, lifted her off the ground, and spun her in circles.

Her bright laughter filled the room with the light of a thousand suns, and it did his heart good. He placed her back on the ground and leaned down to drop a kiss on her lips that were as soft as the silk pillowcase on which she slept. "I love you, baby."

"I love you." She popped his rear with her hand. "Now, go get cleaned up. Dinner's almost ready."

"I'm starved. What're we having?"

"Pineapple chicken on a bed of rice." She nodded toward the bedroom. "Now, scoot while I finish up in the kitchen."

***

1970

He crept down the hallway and glanced around the kitchen door. Alice was at the stove humming a song he didn't recognize while stirring a steaming pan.

As quietly as he could, he placed a crinkly parcel behind his back and sneaked behind her. He swept his lips across her neck in sensuous arcs.

She slung her arm back and scratched the back of his head with her polished nails. "Dinner's ready if you are."

He wrapped one arm around her waist and brought around the crinkly item.

She looked down at three red roses in a bed of baby's breath and fern leaves. Her hand flew to her neck.

When he wriggled the flowers back and forth with a chuckle, she clicked off the stove burners and accepted the roses. "Oh, Arnold, they're beautiful." She pressed her face into the cellophane and breathed in nature's perfume. Her heart jumped in her chest, and she had to work to keep from crying at the sweetness of the gesture. "Thank you so much. They're lovely, but you shouldn't have. We can't afford such extravagances."

He lifted her chin and looked into her eyes. "One of these days I'll have the money to give you a dozen red roses. Or a whole rose bush. Heck, one of these days I'll give you an entire yard of roses."

***

<u>Present Day</u>

A train blasted through town nearly a quarter of a mile away, the whistle of which drew him from his memories of the sweetness of days past.

His eyes went to the rose bush that lay on its side halfway across the yard. With a grunt, he went over to pick up the bundle from the ground.

He made a detour to the shed for a shovel and picked a spot in the backyard next to the clotheslines that had fallen into disuse thanks to the modern luxury of washers and dryers.

One of these days, I'll have the money to give you a dozen red roses. Or a whole rose bush. Heck, one of these days I'll give you an entire yard of roses. His promise to his bride all those years ago swirled in his mind.

He used his foot to thrust the shovel into the earth and pull out several heaps of dirt. His eyes roamed up to the house, and he released an exhale of deep sadness. "You may not love me anymore," he whispered into the night. "After all these years, I finally give you the rose bush that I promised."

Mondaci stepped out of the shadows with Fraush close at his heels. "We need to put a stop to this. Now."

Chapter 10

Arnold exited the elevator and made his way down the hallway. He should have called first, but it was too late for that now.

The luxurious carpet beneath his feet dulled the sound of the rap of his knuckles on the thick wooden door. Compared to his twenty-year-old, threadbare carpet at home, this was like walking on a bed of fluffy cotton.

He took a step back at the sound of chains disengaging from the door.

"Arnold, what a pleasant surprise," Aunt Deborah exclaimed with a bright grin that lit her face. She held out her arms to him. "How are you, dear?"

"I'm fine." He walked into her embrace. At first, the huggy-feely stuff made him uncomfortable around her, but over the months he had grown accustomed to it. Now he didn't give it a second thought.

After their prolonged hug, she gestured him into the condo. "Come in, come in."

He preceded her into the living room, and as with every visit, he marveled at the rich and opulent décor. He had no idea what the White House looked like inside, but he imagined her lifestyle must be like living in the White House.

"Oh, my," she proclaimed from behind him. "Look how well you're getting along after the accident."

He held up the cane and swirled it in the air. "Carrying this thing around makes me feel like a ninety-year-old man."

She patted him on the back as they sat. "I use my cane when I go outside of the house, too, because at our age we can't be too careful, can we? As long as you're safe and healthy, who cares what other people think."

"I suppose," he said. "It's hard to realize I ain't thirty anymore."

The statement made her smile and nod in affirmation. "It's amazing how quickly our lives pass by. It seems like once you get past your thirties, life passes faster and faster." She nestled back into the cair and spread a lap-sized quilt across her legs. "I must say, though, I wouldn't go back in time for anything."

He glanced around the elaborately furnished room that smelled of vanilla and sandalwood, with its original oil paintings, sparkling chandeliers, and rugs in rich jewel tones. Compared to the dumps she lived in during the earlier parts of her life, he didn't blame her. "With these swanky digs of yours, I wouldn't want to go back in time either."

She waved his words away with a flick of her wrist that glittered with a tasteful diamond tennis bracelet. "Dear, when I say that, it has nothing to do with finances. These things are meaningless trappings that will one day wilt away."

Spoken like a true rich person. Why some people like her always downplayed their good fortune, he would never understand. "Sure, I get it," he said with thinly veiled annoyance. "Surely you're not saying you'd give up this lifestyle for the squalor you lived in when you were younger, are you?"

"I won't say money doesn't make life easier in a lot of ways, because we all know it does. Could I give all this up tomorrow if I had to?" She tapped her chest with a contented smile. "In a heartbeat, I could, because I have Jesus in my heart, and that's all I need."

He had grown to love Aunt Deborah with all his heart despite their having nothing in common except a family bloodline, but in all the time they'd spent together lately, he still didn't know what to think about all her fanciful notions of religion.

When the room fell silent, she patted her thighs. "I'd love a glass of iced tea. Will you have one with me if I fix it?"

He stood and patted her arm. "Why don't you sit and let me get it this time?" When she hesitated, he held up his hands and wriggled his fingers with a sly smile. "I'll even wash my hands before I touch the ice."

"You're rotten to the core, you know it?" She giggled. "It's been a long time since I've had a man around to wait on me, so be my guest."

"Any special requests?"

"All I have is sweet tea, and there's a bowl in the refrigerator with citrus rounds." She shook her finger at him as though issuing a reprimand. "And don't skimp on the citrus. It makes all the difference in creating a wonderful glass of tea."

When he passed into the kitchen, a sudden feeling of discomfort hit him. It was the first time he'd been in the kitchen alone. He went to the cabinet and pulled down two of her fragile, fancy-looking beverage glasses that he always hated to drink from, being that he was such a klutz. Not to mention, the glasses were so diminutive in size that he could gulp the entire drink in about three healthy swigs. "Hey, I thought we might mix things up today. Which cabinet holds your Hooters glasses?" He called out, unsure if she would get it, but she rewarded him with a healthy laugh.

"Wouldn't you know it? I left those behind at the trailer park."

He washed and dried his hands then tossed ice into the glasses, all the way to the rim just like she liked. He grimaced when a piece of ice fell to the ground, bounced off his shoe, and slid under the refrigerator.

He contemplated whether to pull it out to retrieve it but decided against it. It would melt then dry, so he didn't see an issue.

He pulled a clear glass bowl of orange, lemon, and lime rounds from the refrigerator and arranged them on the edge of the glass, just like she always did. To his eyes, the presentation wasn't nearly as nice as hers, but he had a feeling she wouldn't judge his attempt.

"Here you go." He handed a glass down to her, placed a saucer and two teaspoons on the table between them, then retook his seat.

"How lovely. Thank you." She squeezed each of the citrus rounds and placed the rinds on the empty dish.

Arnold followed her lead and did the same, though with much less grace and tact. He could do without everything but the oranges, but he always did it her way for a little something different.

He nestled back into the chair and wished the television or the radio was on, just for the sake of noise. As much as he had grown to love Aunt Deborah, sometimes being in her presence unnerved him.

The antique clock on her wall counted down the seconds with a series of ticks that sounded louder than usual. If they were in a horror movie, it would be an ominous warning to viewers of terrible things yet to come.

"What are you thinking, dear?" Aunt Deborah's soft-spoken words shattered the silence between them.

"Nothing that rolls around in this head of mine bears saying aloud." He brought the glass to his lips and slurped down half the contents. The sweet and tangy elixir danced across his tastebuds then down his parched throat in a cold and refreshing rush.

"How's Alice?"

How did she always seem to know what was on his mind? Maybe God whispered into the ears of good people like her the secrets of bad people like him? "I suppose she's fine."

"I enjoyed seeing her the few times I came to your house to visit after the accident."

"I hate that she never spent any real time with you. It was the least she could do since you went out of your way to visit." His anger caused his heart to pound in his chest. He didn't know why her behavior toward Aunt Deborah had surprised him. Alice was as cold and unloving as a person could be. Why had he expected her to behave in a way that was any different than usual?

"Don't give it another thought because I haven't," she assured him.

He stared down at the glass where ice cubes touched the sides with dainty clinks. "How did you and Uncle Ted have such a happy marriage for all those years?"

Fraush and Mondaci materialized in the corner of the room. Fraush stepped behind Deborah while Mondaci stopped in front of Arnold.

Deborah tapped a French-tipped acrylic nail against her glass as she summoned her response. "Things weren't always happy for us, you know."

His gaze slid to the side until their eyes locked with one another. "They weren't?" Was it true, or was the admission nothing more than a little white lie she uttered to make him feel better about his train wreck of a life?

"Of course not. No relationship is ever perfect."

Her words made him feel better, like he wasn't a complete and utter failure.

"Now, don't get me wrong, we had a wonderful life and marriage, but things weren't always fine and dandy."

Fine and dandy. The phrase made him smile. His grandmother had always used it to describe everything from the suitability of a meal, to the feel of fabric between her fingers, to her many excursions with friends and family. Fine and dandy. They were words that would never describe anything about his life.

"I've not been a good husband." The admission caused a rare blush of embarrassment to tinge his cheeks with warmth. "I've spent so much time on the road the past couple of decades that Alice and I ... we've drifted."

It didn't take intelligence to realize his confession wasn't an easy one, so she settled into her seat and waited for him to continue. "People who drift apart can always drift back to each other," she finally said when he didn't continue.

Fraush stepped to the side of her chair and bent until they were face to face. He snarled a series of grunts in her direction.

Arnold shook his head. "Maybe for regular people but not for us."

"Why would you and Alice be different than other couples?"

"I don't know." He wasn't smart enough with words to know how to have conversations like this, and he wished he had said nothing at all.

"Sure, you do. Tell me why, with work, you and Alice can't have a wonderful marriage again."

"Because Alice doesn't care about having a good marriage." He hurled the words at her with a ferocity he hadn't intended. "All she cares about is playing cards with her hags all day and half the night."

"That's right. Feed on the burn of her rejection. Who needs her, anyway?" Mondaci's words, unheard by the humans, slithered into the room with a depressing heaviness.

"Whatever," Arnold muttered. "Who needs her, anyway."

Mondaci's hooting laughter resounded through the heavenlies in waves of thunder.

Lutis, Protector Warrior, moved into place beside Mondaci without speaking a word. With love in his eyes, he glanced down at Arnold.

Mondaci glared at Lutis then at the human.

"Maybe you need to try a different approach," Aunt Deborah said, unaware of the spiritual beings that bristled around them.

"What do you mean?" Arnold snapped.

Mondaci and Fraush bore their eyes into the woman. Though they didn't know what words she was about to speak, their hatred for her boiled inside them.

"When was the last time you took her out for a nice dinner, or you came home to surprise her with a lovely gift?"

Arnold sneered at the idea even though it was her good-hearted attempt to help. "We haven't been out to dinner in ages. I asked her if she'd like to do it a few weeks ago." He flung his arms in a dramatic gesture of anger. "She laughed and humiliated me in front of her card-playing witches."

Mondaci and Fraush glanced at each other with foul smiles.

"I know that must have hurt." Aunt Deborah nodded as though she understood. "Maybe you could try again. If it's been a while since you guys have done anything like that, you may need to extend an invitation more than once."

He shook his head. "Let's face it. I murdered a young kid, and my wife hates me. My lot in life is to be a miserable and guilty murderer whose wife can't stand him."

"Please don't say that, dear. You didn't murder anyone. It was an unfortunate accident and thinking otherwise helps no one. As for Alice, I think you need to keep trying until she softens."

"Softens? Alice?" Arnold barked a loud, sarcastic laugh. "That'll be the day when I'm nice to that old—" A slurry of profanities swirled through his mind, but out of respect for Aunt Deborah, he abstained from finishing the sentence.

"Try to think about it this way," Aunt Deborah continued. "If you and she haven't been close in a while, perhaps it embarrassed her when you asked in front of her friends. Maybe you could try again when it's just the two of you."

He gripped the sofa arm to keep from lashing out at her. "I gave her a rose bush as a gift the other night. I thought it would be nice if we could plant it in the yard, together, like we used to do years ago, but she wasn't interested. I'm done with trying to be nice to someone who doesn't care."

The hurt that dripped from his every word tore a hole in her heart. *Lord, help me to speak Your words, words that will bring peace and healing, she prayed. He's searching for something, and he doesn't even know what it is. You promise that anyone who seeks You with their heart will find You. Help me point him to You, so he can seek You with all his heart.*

"I don't have all the answers," Deborah soothed. "I do know this, though. The Apostle Paul says that our struggles are not against other humans but against the powers of worldly darkness and the spiritual forces of evil in the heavenly realms."

Here we go, Arnold fumed. *Cue the nutty religious talk. Why do people like her always think that religion is the answer for everything?* "Perfect, but how does that relate to me and Alice?"

"More than you probably think. This scripture tells me that though you and Alice aren't as close as you used to be, you and she aren't the real problem, so don't treat each other as though you are." She leaned forward and clutched his hands in hers. "On the surface, our struggles may seem like they're with other people, but all around us is a spiritual realm where good and evil reside. Our struggles are against the spiritual forces of evil in the heavenly places. They're roaring lions who seek people to devour with their lies."

Fraush stood in front of her and knelt to her level. He gazed into her unseeing eyes and unleashed a powerful growl. "That's right, lady. We're here, and no matter what you say, he's ours."

Chapter 11

As the brushy terrain of town blurred past, Arnold contemplated his time with Aunt Deborah. As usual, although their time together was short, she had given him plenty to consider.

His hands trembled on the steering wheel as her words replayed in his mind. Even though Alice had turned away his rosebush gift with clear disdain, Aunt Deborah had suggested he forgive her actions and maybe even try it again.

"The last thing I want is to give her yet another opportunity to rub my gifts in my face," he muttered as he drove past his home. He wasn't ready to see her much less be in the same house.

He pulled into the mom-and-pop gas station and dashed in and out for a twelve pack of beer. Ed, the chatty proprietor, had tried to commandeer him with his usual incessant blather, but he had fibbed and said he was in a hurry. In a hurry for what, he didn't know, but he would leave that to the good man's imagination.

He cracked open a can of beer and took a satisfying slug as he passed the local park but shook his head. Strange that he would feel guilty for drinking a few brews in front of kids since he had done it in the past without thinking twice.

At the last second, he pulled into Hickam's Goat Farm. George and Sharon Hickam owned at least a hundred goats of various varieties, especially tiny Pygmy and Fainting goats, both of which the local kids loved to visit.

When he pulled in, the Hickams' gift shop loomed into view. He had only been inside a time or two because they sold nothing he needed. Today, however, was different.

He jumped from the truck to the ground, and a cloud of dust rose around his ankles. He finished off his beer, crushed the can in his fist, and tossed it into the bed of the truck. At some point he would gather them and take them to the recycle center for the measly few cents they were worth.

He made his way to the gift shop and into a flowery and clean scent. Sharon was behind the register counting receipts while George stacked square, white items. When George turned to the door, he grinned. "Well, as I live and breathe. Arnold Collins."

"Hey, George." He held out his hand, and they shared an effusive handshake. "Did I catch you at closing time?"

"We're always open for our good friends."

Arnold smiled even though he'd never considered the couple as good friends. They were more acquaintances that they rarely saw other than in passing, but such was life in a small town where everyone knew everyone.

Sharon rushed from behind the counter, held out her hands, and gave him a gushy hug. "How's your sweet Alice? I can't even recall the last time I saw her."

"Alice is about as feisty as a nest of angry yellow jackets."

"Oh." She swatted his hand with a giggle. "I know we say it every time we see each other, and we never do it, but we need to go out for dinner one night. Do you guys ever go to The Haybale? They have great food, and on Friday and Saturday nights there's square dancing, believe it or not. We don't dance, but it's a hoot to watch."

Yeah, that'll be the day Alice gives up a card game for square dancing at The Haybale. "Give Alice a call. If you can talk her into it, we'll do it." He was comfortable suggesting it because Alice would never go for it.

George slapped his back. "What in the tarnation is an old scutter like you doing in our neck of the woods?"

"I thought I'd come by and watch your goats for a while, if you don't mind." He left off the part about the beers because he couldn't remember if they were teetotalers.

"Swing by anytime, friend. I usually make sure I'm out there when visitors are here to watch the goats, but I can trust you to not accidentally let them out." George shook his head. "People seem to think it's a petting zoo and that they can let themselves into the pasture whenever they want. A few weeks ago, we had to chase down over a hundred goats when some yahoo opened the gate and didn't shut it behind them. It's a miracle we found them all."

"I just came to look."

George walked him to the door. "Sharon will call Alice, so tell her to expect the call in the next day or two."

"Will do." At the door, Arnold turned back into the store. "Hey, Sharon. You got anything nice that Alice might like?"

"Oh, honey, there's nothing here that any woman wouldn't like, and it's all made of goat's milk, which is high in vitamin A and loads of other good things. I have hand soap, hand and body lotion, milk bath, lip balm, and deodorant. I even have homemade edibles made on the premises, like fudge, cheese, caramels ... well, listen to me going on. You get the picture."

"Could you throw a couple of things in a bag for her? Maybe hand soap and a hand lotion?" He didn't know if she used that kind of stuff, but at one time she would have loved it.

"Sure thing. What scents does she like?"

He had no idea, so he bunted the question back at her. "What do you think she'd like?"

She snapped her fingers and picked up a bar and a bottle. "My favorite is our newest scent, honey vanilla. It's to die for, even if I say so myself."

He plopped his debit card on the counter and left minutes later with his gift bag and promises that he and Alice would have dinner with them soon, all along knowing it would never happen.

He placed the gift in the cab of the truck, whipped out a couple of cans of beer, and made his way to the fence. He balanced one of them on the fence post and opened the other.

The farm was well over a hundred acres, so there was plenty of room for goats, horses, and cows to roam the land.

Massive trees speckled the pasture, providing the inhabitants with plenty of shade, as well as covered feeding troughs. In the distance, so far that they were nearly specks on the horizon, were thick groves of trees.

About a quarter of the way down the property stood the largest barn he had ever seen, red with white trim.

A chorus of goat bleats and cattle lows mingled on the breezes of the twilight evening. When three tiny Pygmy goats meandered in his direction, followed by two larger goats, he wished he had brought something to feed them.

He pushed open the gate and stepped in, locked it securely behind him, and laughed when the herd rushed in his direction.

He emptied his beer can, crumpled it, sat it on the nearest fence post, then bent to pet each of the goats. They crowded each other at his feet for attention.

"I wish I had brought you guys some treats." He patted two of the smaller goats' heads.

An odd sound mixed with the excited bleats. He turned and looked behind him. One of the larger goats had its hooves on the fence, and it stretched to reach the can of beer he had yet to drink. "Hey, get away from there. That's for me, not you."

When it increased its efforts, Arnold snatched away the can and placed it on the ground just outside the gate.

The goat dropped back to its feet, curled its lips, and gave Arnold an angry bleat.

Arnold made a fist and shook it at the goat. "Don't give me no attitude. I get enough of that at home from the old ball and chain."

The goat jutted its head, gave another angry bleat, then turned and walked away.

The other four goats who weren't mad at him congregated around his feet, and one of them nuzzled his hand. "I think your friend needs an attitude adjustment."

When the sun made its final dip below the horizon and cast the land in deeper shadows, he gave the goats some final loving then made his way to the gate.

Assured that it was locked and secured, he grabbed the untouched beer and took a long, satisfying drink. Along the fence line, a trio of horses ran with graceful beauty toward the back of the property. They were far enough away that he couldn't hear anything, so he closed his eyes and imagined the muted cadence of their hooves striking the earth beneath them.

Chapter 12

She gripped Arnold's hand a little tighter as they wove their way through the crowded Twenty-Second Annual Fall Festival. She had been many times, but this was her first as a married woman.

The air around them reeked of livestock, and she looked forward to moving on to the more aromatic areas of the festival. "Oh, honey, look." She released his hand and rushed to a pen that held the smallest goats she had ever seen.

She looked over the waist-high fence at the tiny animals that ran to and fro inside the pen. "Aren't they adorable?" She screeched as Arnold made his way to her side. "What kind are they?"

"I don't know. I've never seen goats this small." He had to admit they were the cutest things he had ever seen.

As though on cue, a woman approached them from behind. "They're a breed called Pygmy. They derive from a breed in West Africa and are among the rare few in the United States."

"Are they for sale?" Alice asked with hopeful eyes.

"Sorry, they're not."

Thank God, Arnold thought.

"There are so few in the United States, and the rare few are usually in zoos."

"Where did you get them?"

"My husband is a farmer, and we found them on vacation in Africa a couple of years ago. He arranged to import a few here to the United States as they became available. As far as I know, we're one of few private citizens in the entire country to own them, though I figure that'll change soon."

Alice's gaze moved from the speaking woman down to the scampering animals. "I love them so much. I wish we could have one someday."

Arnold placed his arm across her shoulders. An animal, even a cute baby goat, was not on his wish list, but he would give her anything she wanted. "Maybe one of these days we will."

The woman placed her hand on Alice's and jerked her head toward the pen. "In the meantime, they love it when people scratch their heads."

Alice's eyes grew wide. "Really?"

The woman reached down to pat the nearest one and within seconds all ten of them darted in her direction. She looked back up at Alice with a hearty laugh. "I could use a hand here, if you want to help."

It was all the encouragement she needed. With a light touch, Alice ran her fingers over one of the creature's soft and downy coat then broke into laughter when it nudged her hand with its snout and licked it.

When she looked up at him, her eyes snapped with pure happiness. Arnold had never seen her happier, and if it were possible, he had just fallen even more deeply in love. He had loved other women over the years, but until he met Alice, he had never known the depths of love that could grow in a man's heart. It was the most amazing feeling in the world.

Several of the goats rushed in her direction, hungry for her shows of affection.

A burst of joy hit him when she tossed her head back and laughed. She brushed her hands over as many of their backs as she could. When she looked up at him, her face was radiant.

"Their coats are so soft. Pet them," Alice said.

He was content just watching her, but at her beckoning he leaned down and scratched the nape of one of their necks.

When the goat moved on to the next person that walked up and thrust their hand into the pen, his hand gravitated to the same one that Alice petted. Their fingers met and a new surge of love burst inside him. He threaded his fingers through hers and they petted the animal together.

When she looked up at him, he pressed a gentle kiss to her lips. The world around them disappeared until the pop of a balloon followed by the wail of a child drew them back into the real world.

***

<u>Present Day</u>

A loud slamming noise drew him from the daydreams of yesteryear. Arnold glanced over his shoulder at Sharon who had ducked into her car and closed the door behind her.

Above him, a sliver of moon and a blanket of stars twinkled on the backdrop of a royal blue sky.

Sharon's lights bounced down the driveway for several seconds before turning left onto the main road and disappearing into the night.

Another slam drew his attention. This time, it was George closing the gift shop. As he made his way toward their house, he raised his hand in the air. "Good night, Arnold."

It embarrassed him to realize how long he must have been here. "I'll get out of your guys' hair now."

"No problem. Stay as long as you want."

With those parting words, Arnold was once again alone with his thoughts. His mind went back to the festival he had all but forgotten about over the years. Even now it surprised him how easily he could recall every detail of the night. The tinkly sound of the carousel music mixed with family chatter and laughter. The night lit with the soft lights of the carnival rides, including the Ferris wheel that they had ridden three times because once wasn't enough for Alice.

The air had been thick with the smokey fragrance of meat, buttery popcorn, and the intoxicating sweetness of caramel apples, cotton candy, and funnel cakes.

The night air had been a perfect balance of coolness that required only the lightest of layers.

On their way to the car, the smooth sounds of a local jazz band had provided the perfect soundtrack to the end of the perfect night.

They strolled hand in hand, and Arnold, in one swift movement, raised Alice's hand in the air and twirled her in circles. Her dress floated around her, and her elated laughter caused a warmth to spread through his heart.

To everyone around them, they probably looked like lunatics, but he was a lunatic in love and didn't care who knew it.

When the twirl stopped, they were chest to chest. She gazed into his eyes, and he into hers. Their hearts pitter pattered the rhythm of a song that only theirs could sing.

Crickets chirped, and the songs of nightbirds provided a tapestry of night music.

Across the parking lot a woman cradled closer to her man as the sound of his Ducati Super Sport motorcycle shredded the quiet of the night. It was a sound Arnold could recognize without seeing it, but in that moment, he had barely heard it.

As clear as day, even though he hadn't smelled it in years, he remembered Alice's floral scent that wafted around them, and how he could barely contain himself. That is what real happiness is. "I'll love you forever and ever, Alice Collins," he had whispered, and before she could respond he pulled her close for another kiss.

That kiss.

That beautiful, wonderful kiss.

"Those were the days," he muttered with bitterness as his heart yearned for the simplicity of when Alice and he had nothing but each other, and they were fine with that because each other was all they needed.

Now, they had more money than ever, yet they never looked at each other nor shared a pleasant word.

He went to the tree a few steps back and lowered to the ground. He leaned against the massive trunk and gazed into the heavens. His eyes locked onto Mars whose light shone down with its distinctive pinkish hue. "Why did I let things go so wrong in our life?" he whispered into the night. He didn't expect an answer, but he almost wished something, someone, would answer back and tell him how to get back what he had lost.

To his left, Fraush cast a worried look at Mondaci.

To his right, Lutis kept his own quiet watch.

"God, are You there?" Arnold's throat constricted with a rare emotion. "I don't know if You exist, and if You do, whether You even see or hear me."

"God, are You there?" Fraush mocked. He snarled and kicked his foot at the human. "You're pathetic, you know that?"

"I know I've messed up," Arnold pleaded. "My wife doesn't love me anymore, and it's all my fault."

"Of course, it's your fault," Mondaci taunted. "You may as well not even try to fix it because that relationship is too far gone. She doesn't love you anymore, so move on."

Arnold shook his head and spat a slew of obscenities. "What are you doing, Arnold? Are you an idiot? There's no use in fantasizing about things that will never happen. She doesn't love you anymore, so deal with it."

Fraush gave Mondaci a poke of encouragement in the ribs, followed by a malicious laugh.

Despite the despair in his heart, and that it was probably a fruitless act, he raised his eyes to Heaven once again. "I'm a horrible person who doesn't believe in You, but if You're there, I could use Your help." He swallowed down the urge to cry. Darned if he would shed a tear for a God who may or may not be up there listening to him. "If You're up there, and if You know I'm here, please help my wife to love me again."

Fraush kicked at the human. "God doesn't know you exist because you're nothing."

"You belong to your father, the devil." Lutis' mighty voice shook the heavens. His stare bore into the heavenly traitors who stared back at him without flinching. "You carry out your father's desires. He is a murderer and a liar in whom lies no truth. He is the father of lies."

Mondaci took a few steps toward Lutis and thrust a finger in his face. "Say what you will, Lutis. That human is ours."

"God! Are you there?" Arnold screamed at the top of his lungs, and as though sensing his anguish, or perhaps fearful of the outburst, the nature around him fell silent. For the first time in years, he broke down and wept. "Are You there?" he whispered.

As Lutis lowered to his knees, his love for this human grew stronger than ever, and he spoke aloud promises from God's word. The human couldn't hear his words with his ears, but perhaps they would somehow penetrate his heart. "Let anyone who is thirsty come to Me and drink. Whoever believes in Me, rivers of living water will flow from within them."

Chapter 13

Hyacinth watched out the kitchen window as she tossed a chickpea quinoa salad with a zesty lemon dressing.

Lucas and Camden, Jenner's best friends in the world, sailed remote-controlled boats across the surface of the pool while her best friend Sheri arranged plates and cups in the festive bright colors of summer on the table.

She whispered a prayer of gratitude at the bustle of playful activity that had returned to her home.

With the bowl of salad in one hand and a basket of warm and salty bread in the other, she breezed back outside. "You boys ready for lunch?" Their boisterous laughter lifted her spirits as she placed the salad on the table along with loads of other food. She bent down and kissed her niece, Paige, on top of her head. "How's our rent-a-kid doing?"

Paige swung her legs under the table as she munched on chicken nuggets. She held up a half-eaten one at Hyacinth. "You want a bite?"

"No, baby. You eat it." Hyacinth almost swooned at her cuteness. "Gosh, she seems so much older than this time last year."

"You eat it," Paige insisted.

She glanced up at Sheri with a grimace. "It's times like this when I miss having Jenner around." She leaned down and took a bite of the chicken nugget.

Paige thrust her arms in the air and laughed when Hyacinth made a big deal of how good it tasted.

Hyacinth turned at another round of laughter. Lucas and Camden sat at the edge of the pool Indian style, each holding a remote control. "What are they doing?"

"They started out racing the boats from one end of the pool to the other, but apparently that got boring so now they're crashing into each other to see who can sink the other's boat first."

"So, they're being typical boys." Hyacinth shook her head.

"Aren't those two always up to something crazy?"

Hyacinth watched with fondness as the two friends interacted. After Jenner's and Ellie's deaths, while everyone contended with varying levels of injury from the bus accident, their group had fallen away to deal with grief in their own ways. She had checked in with them on occasion, but that was about it. It was time, she finally decided, to bring them all back together.

She navigated around Paige's array of pool toys and placed a hand on each of the boys' heads. "Are you two having lunch with us?"

"I have to sink his boat first," Lucas said without looking up.

Hyacinth crossed her arms over her chest as she watched the two respectably nice boats clanking against each other. "Which of you plans to go down there to retrieve the sunken ship?"

"I thought we'd leave it down there," Camden said.

"You think so?" Hyacinth asked.

"It'll be our version of an homage to the Titanic." Camden placed one hand over his heart, stretched out his other arm dramatically, and cranked out a sadly off-tune version of "My Heart Will Go On."

"Sorry to disappoint you boys, but there'll be no sunken ships on my watch. Any shipwrecks must be raised before we close the pool for the season. Now, turn off those boats so we can eat."

"Fine," Camden said with a disgruntled tone then looked up and winked at her. "We'll be there in a few minutes."

"Make it a quick few minutes. We're hungry," she called over her shoulder as she made her way back to the table. "I swear, they're like babysitting two toddlers."

Sheri looked up from arranging flowers at the center of the table. "They may be toddlers," she leaned in and whispered, "but that Lucas is a cutie patootie."

"You're married." Hyacinth raised her eyebrows in a sordid manner even though she couldn't argue the point. He was cute in an attractive yet nerdy sort of way.

"What? I'm married, so I can't look?"

"Look all you want, hon." Hyacinth picked up the pitcher of sweet tea and poured it into glasses.

"You think you'll ever—" Sheri said with a subdued tone.

Hyacinth shook her head. "It's too early to even think about dating again."

"Sure, it's too soon now," Sheri nodded. "You're young, so someday you'll want to date again, though, right?"

Hyacinth exhaled a contemplative breath. "I can't imagine ever wanting to date again."

"Well, if you do, you do. If you don't, you don't." Sheri turned at the sound of footfalls rushing toward them.

As they thundered toward the table, Lucas grabbed Camden around the neck and rubbed his knuckles across his head. "It's noogie time."

Camden screamed and threw a series of punches.

"No roughhousing at the table, boys."

Paige raised her arms with a grin. "Noogie, noogie, noogie!"

Lucas tossed Camden to the side, gave Paige a sinister grin, and skulked toward her with a limping gait. "Who wants the next noogie?" He asked in a scary-sounding voice.

"Me, me, me," Paige squealed.

He pulled her from her seat, held her under his arm like a football, and rubbed his fist over her head, resulting in screeches and giggles of joy.

"Don't jostle her around too much," Hyacinth warned. "She's been eating."

When everyone was settled around the table and finally quiet, Hyacinth said a quick prayer.

After the food was eaten and plates pushed to the center of the table, she looked around at her friends with a grateful heart. "I asked you guys here today because we've all been through a lot of grief the last few months. We've all lost a lot, but from here on out, I want us to stay close to each other. Jenner and Ellie would want that."

Smiles melted and expressions became somber.

"Sometimes I feel ..." Lucas looked around the table with sad eyes. "Sometimes I feel angry. As a Christian, I know I shouldn't, but I do."

The urge to cry welled up from deep within her, but she forced down the feelings. "I find myself with anger a lot, too."

Relief flooded his face. "You do?"

"More than I'd like to admit. I think it's unhealthy to go through such grief then give in to guilt for being angry. What happened was horrible, senseless even. I think anger is a healthy emotion as long as we don't allow ourselves to get weighed down and bitter by it."

"Do you ever ... think about ... him," Lucas whispered. He didn't need to specify which him because everyone knew.

"I do," Camden answered with a tinge of anger in his voice. "Sometimes when I think about him, I dream about having five minutes in a dark alley with a baseball bat and that truck driver." He glanced around the table, grateful that no judgmental eyes stared back at him. "Then sometimes I wonder, who's behind the villain I often like to conjure in my mind? Who is he? What's his name? How old is he? Is he a believer?"

Silence fell around the table, and he realized they all probably had asked themselves the same questions.

Hyacinth took a few moments to contemplate her response. "The truck driver's name is Arnold Collins."

Sheri grasped her hand in a gesture of support.

Lucas and Camden's heads snapped up at the information.

"You know him?" Camden asked.

She shook her head. "I only know his name."

Lucas' eyes widened. "Are we going to take out a hit on him? If so, I may have a contact."

Everyone around the table relaxed into a ripple of soft laughter, and Hyacinth was glad for Lucas and his often-inappropriate banter. "Call me crazy, but I think we should keep hitmen as a last resort."

"What else do you know about him?" Camden asked.

"I requested a copy of the police report after the accident, but I kept it sealed in the envelope for weeks before I could read it. He's in his late sixties and married. He lives somewhere in Iowa."

Camden leaned back in his chair. "Iowa," he whispered to no one as the information sank in.

"So often I struggle with being angry at him, but lately, more and more, I find myself wondering if he knows Jesus. If not, is there anyone in his circle who can minister to him in that way? Since there's no way to know, I've made that a focus of many of my prayers the past few weeks. In the process, I've found that my anger toward him has dwindled a lot."

"I don't want to pray for him," Lucas teased. "I'd rather hire a hitman."

"Pray about it then let's talk about it later." Hyacinth leaned in and whispered. "I suggest we make sure he knows Jesus before we sic a hitman on him."

Chapter 14

The sound of impact was sickening.

Fire danced all around him in the darkness.

Screams penetrated through the sundry of pops and crackles.

He couldn't catch his breath and sweat dripped from his face.

A searing pain shot through his body.

As though by miracle, the smoke in the truck cabin parted.

He squinted through the cracked windshield glass in search of anything, anyone, to help him. His eyes searched the shadows when a face materialized through the other vehicle's windshield.

It was the face of a man who pounded on the glass with palpable fear stricken on his face. He screamed silent words that Arnold couldn't hear no matter how hard he tried.

"Help me," Arnold screamed.

The man's face was no longer in the other vehicle but was now in the rig with him. He stared into Arnold's eyes. "I'm going to die. I have a wife. I'm young. Why did you kill me?"

"I didn't mean to kill you," Arnold cried. "Please, help me."

The man shook his head. "I'm young. Why did you kill me?"

I'm young. The words pounded through Arnold's head like a roaring jackhammer vibrating the life out of him.

"I'm young. Why did you kill me?"

Arnold jumped as a flame exploded in the other vehicle. The heat shattered the windshield as wild flames licked the outer walls. Even from this far away, the singe of the heat bristled across his skin.

He glanced around the interior of his truck, but the man was no longer in the cab with him. He was back in the other vehicle.

His face danced inside the orange, yellow, and red flames. "I'm young." He reached an arm toward Arnold. "Why did you kill me?"

Arnold reached for him. "I'm sorry. I didn't mean to."

***

Present Day

"I'm sorry. I didn't mean to." He reached out to the young man, but his face dissolved into the flames before the horrid scene went dark and transitioned into the murky remains of his bedroom. "I didn't mean to kill you."

He bolted up in bed, grateful for the coolness that swept over his sweat-drenched skin. He slapped his hands over his face and wept. "I'm sorry. I didn't mean to kill you. I'm sorry."

As tears squeezed between his fingers and rolled down his arms, the ghost of the man in the bus floated through his mind and tormented him.

Mondaci stepped through the shadows and approached the bed where the human wept. "Coward," he shouted. "I may as well kill you now and get it over with, you sniveling fool."

Arnold stood to his feet and whipped off his shirt, underwear, and pajama pants because he couldn't tolerate the wet fabric that clung to his skin.

He slipped across the hall, removed a towel from the linen closet, and carried it back to his room.

As he wiped the moisture from his body another wave of emotion overcame him.

The apparition of the man from his dreams, of the man he had killed, flickered in and out of his consciousness like a gauzy mist that refused to evaporate under the intense scrutiny of the sun's rays. "God, forgive me," he cried. "I didn't mean to kill him."

"How can you pray for forgiveness to a God who doesn't even exist," Mondaci taunted. He knew God existed, but planting doubts in weak-minded humans was one of the best tools at deceiving them. After all, it worked with Eve in the Garden of Eden when Satan asked, "Did God really say you must not eat of this tree?" Lying and planting doubt was a brilliant tactic that he and his evil cohorts had used against humans since the beginning of time.

Arnold snatched clean clothes from the dresser drawer, angry and embarrassed that a dream had unhinged him in such a way that it drew him to tears. "Murdering an innocent person sure turns a guy into a weepy pansy," he muttered as he stepped into the fresh clothing.

After a few minutes perched on the edge of the bed it became clear he wouldn't go back to sleep anytime soon. He tiptoed down the hallway and turned on the television in the living room.

He cringed when the sound of a local car sales commercial with an annoyingly chipper actor blasted through the house. He nearly broke the remote pressing the down volume button while muttering several profanities. The last thing he needed was Alice coming out here, then he released a contemptuous laugh. Alice would have to care about him for her to get out of bed in the middle of the night to check on him.

She'd never done it in recent years, not even when he was so sick that he could barely stand, so why worry that she would do it now?

He released another string of profanities and wished she was here to listen and find out exactly what he thought of her.

As soon as the thought hit his mind a flood of guilt replaced the anger. The guilt was such a foreign emotion that he resented feeling it. "Why should I feel guilty about our relationship if she doesn't?"

He flipped through the channels and stopped on an episode of *Bonanza*, but his mind wouldn't focus on the classic show.

His spirit was heavy and wounded and sick, so he leaned his head against the chair back and closed his eyes. Against the image of the innocent man who burned in the flames. Against Alice and his loveless marriage. Even behind closed eyes the burning man and Alice still hovered in the darkness and haunted him with their images.

His lips quivered with emotion. "I'd rather die than feel like this."

Mondaci smiled. "Now we're talking. When things are this hopeless, you might as well do everyone a favor and give up."

"Everyone would be better off if I ended my life."

Mondaci sneered when Mortol, the demon specializing in suicide, stepped into place next to him. "Who called for you?"

Mortol waved his hand in front of Arnold's face, as though testing if the man could see him. "The only way to bring justice to the innocent man you killed that night is to kill yourself." A slithery laugh rolled off his tongue. "Do it. Do it now."

As soon as he uttered the words, Arnold couldn't believe he had said them. His life had been a disaster for as long as he could remember, but he had never, not once, considered taking his life. He shook his head, jumped out of the chair, and raced for the kitchen.

He turned on the light above the oven so he could see then pulled a bottle of scotch from the cabinet. With trembling hands, he poured a snifter glass half full and chugged every scorching drop.

A movement caught his eye outside the kitchen window. Dark shadows with evil motives swayed in the yard. He shook his head. "It's not demons dancing. It's the shadows of trees." His logic told him it was so, but fear lodged itself inside him.

"Look at those demons out there," Timora spoke words to feed into his fears. "If you're not careful, they'll come in and getcha."

When Arnold turned back to the window, the dancing shadows were still there. "Dancing demons." He scrunched his eyes until the man materialized, the man he had killed now burned in black flames. He danced with the demons.

Arnold gripped the sink with his fingers and willed logical thoughts into his mind. There's no such thing as dancing demons.

"I hate you," he said to the man in black flames. "You've ruined my life. I hate you! Go away!"

Odi, the demon of hate, stood next to him, smiling. "Hate, hate, hate, hate," he chanted.

"Fear, fear, fear, fear." Timora stepped to his other side and chanted along.

"Death, death, death, death." Caedis stepped behind them and joined in the chants.

Arnold gripped the whiskey bottle, sloshed another serving into the glass, and chugged it. It burned like fire all the way down, but he deserved it.

Mondaci stepped into the group with the other three. "Murderer, murderer, murderer, murderer."

Arnold grabbed his head with his hands and shook it. Something was wrong with him, and he didn't know what. "Stop it. Leave me alone."

A hoard of demons surrounded him, shouting out their morbid incantations.

"Stop it. Leave me alone." Arnold, bug eyed, yanked open one of the kitchen drawers and pulled out a long carving knife. He poured two more drinks and gulped them down then raced to the kitchen door and slung it open. "Leave me alone," he screamed at the demons who danced in the night.

The man in the black flames charged at him. "I'm young. Why did you kill me?"

Arnold shoved the knife in his direction. "I'm sorry. I didn't mean to kill you. Leave me alone."

"Avenge my death, you murderer," the man yelled. "Avenge my death."

Arnold held up the knife and swung it at the apparition.

"Avenge my death."

The moon glinted off the edge of the razor-sharp knife.

"Avenge your death," Arnold whispered as he looked at the blade.

"Avenge his death," Mortol whispered in his ear.

Arnold held the knife edge to his wrist. It bit into his skin until a trickle of blood ran down his arm.

"Avenge his death," Mortol roared. "Avenge his death. Do it."

He dug the knife deeper into his skin.

A chorus of demonic voices chanted at him in a chaotic frenzy. "Death. Avenge. Hate. Fear. Death. Avenge. Hate. Fear."

Lutis stood above the fray and spread his hands. "Behold, I have given you authority to tread on serpents and scorpions, over all the powers of the enemy, and nothing shall hurt you."

"The thief comes only to steal, kill, and destroy, but Jesus came so that you may have abundant life," Istus moved in next to Lutis and shouted.

"Submit yourselves to God. Resist the devil, and he will flee from you," said Hortamen.

Nitasah joined the heavenly beings. "Beloved, never avenge yourselves, but leave it to the wrath of God. 'Vengeance is mine and I will repay,' says the Lord."

"Your adversary, the devil, prowls around like a roaring lion, seeking someone to devour," Cingo said.

A ferocious growl reverberated through the heavens. Zapheous stepped into the fray. "He is ours." He pointed at his evil beings. "Get him and make him ours forever."

They swarmed him like a flock of vultures. "Death. Avenge. Hate. Fear. Death. Avenge. Hate. Fear."

"No weapon formed against you shall prosper. This is the heritage of the servants of the Lord," Seema proclaimed.

Arnold dropped to his knees and raised the knife to the sky as confusion and chaos clouded his mind. "Help me. I don't know what to do."

A commanding voice stilled the malevolent cacophony. "I am the Alpha and the Omega. I am He who is and who was and who is to come. I am the Almighty God. He who calls on the name of the Lord shall be saved."

The knife dropped to the concrete with a clatter, and every eye in the spiritual realm turned to look at the human.

Arnold's hands dropped to the ground. "God, if You're there, help me."

Chapter 15

Bleary-eyed, Arnold hated himself for resorting to prayer last night, especially to a God that didn't exist.

He clopped out of the bedroom and into the kitchen for a cup of hot coffee. To get through the day, he would need more than his typical two-cup morning fix.

He poured cream and sugar into his cup then walked past the dining room where Alice sat staring at the wall.

You waiting on your hags to get here? That's what he wanted to say. "You playing cards today?" He asked instead.

"Same as every other day," she answered without bothering to look up at him.

He walked halfway down the hallway then turned and went back. "How long will you play tonight?"

"Until we're done," she snapped.

Her scathing tone made him want to unleash a chain of obscenities, but in the interest of changing the dynamic of their relationship, he stifled the urge. "Do you want to quit early tonight? I'd like to take you out for dinner."

She released a cackle. "I'll have company."

She wasn't willing to try, and it was all he could do to push down his anger and humiliation. "You can't end the game early for one night so we can go out and enjoy a nice dinner?"

She narrowed her eyes and pursed her lips. "We ain't ended game night before ten in years. I don't reckon we'll start now."

"We haven't been to the Teranga Grille in years," he said with a hopeful tone. "We used to go there every year to celebrate our anniversary. I'll call all nice and proper and get us a reservation."

With a grunt, she stood from the table, picked up her coffee cup, and disappeared into the kitchen.

Heat radiated from his cheeks. He blew out a breath of exasperation and made his way back to his bedroom. "How dare you walk out on me like that." He imagined the pillow that leaned against the headboard was her face and punched it. As soon as he did it, guilt riddled him. Though their relationship had been virtually nonexistent for years, he would never hit a woman, and especially not Alice.

He sat on the edge of the bed and fixed an accusatory stare on the ceiling. "I don't know if You're up there anywhere, but if You are, I could use some help down here." He paused for a sign of a higher being having heard his pleas.

A bird landing on the windowsill.

An unexplained whisper blowing through the house.

A gauzy apparition appearing before him.

A horseshoe to the head would even work. That one he would deserve for expecting a nonexistent God to notice him.

He muttered a filthy word then looked back up at the ceiling with an apologetic grimace. "Sorry, God." Though he was certain no one was up there to listen, if a higher being did exist, he assumed He might not answer a prayer that included a dirty word, so he retracted it for good measure.

Mondaci stepped beside him and frowned. "You fool. Why waste your time praying to someone who doesn't exist?"

"I want my wife to love me again," Arnold murmured, more to himself than to God.

Mondaci leaned down and stared into the human's eyes. What he wouldn't give for the human to have even a short glimpse of him. The thought made him smile. "She doesn't love you anymore, and she never will."

"How do you make someone start loving you again?" Frustrated at the stupid words, Arnold plowed to his feet and paced the room.

"You can't make her love you, so why keep trying?" Mondaci said. "You two are done so deal with it."

He rushed out of the room and pounded down the hallway.

Mondaci flew after him with a devious smirk. He didn't know what was about to happen, but he was certain it wouldn't be pretty. He tapped his fingertips in anticipation of an ugly domestic scene.

Arnold jolted to a stop at the dining room where Alice once again sat. She stared at the same wall, but this time she held a smoldering cigarette between her fingers. A curl of smoke escaped her mouth while two bursts barreled from her nostrils with a repulsive scent.

"Well, isn't that a beautiful and womanly sight?" Mondaci released shrieking laughter.

The sight of her chain smoking coupled with frizzy, unkempt hair and unsmiling prune face always filled him with disgust. Maybe I'm better off without her. Maybe I should pack a bag, get an apartment, and find a whore to fulfill my needs.

The words blasted through his mind, and he was tempted to do just that, but he softened when she lowered the cigarette to the overflowing ashtray and tapped off a long pile of ash with a deep sigh.

Though she was old and weary, just like him, he somehow had the ability to see her not as old and weary but as the beautiful bride he had married all those years ago.

"Alice," Arnold said.

Mondaci jostled from one foot to the other as he focused on the humans. Maybe the human would pull out a knife and hack her into a bloody mess. Or maybe she would be the one to snap and lose her grip on reality and do the murdering.

Alice wrapped her lips around the cigarette and sucked in a deep breath without looking up at him.

"I've been the worst husband ever over the past decade. I stayed gone on the rig for days at a time, weeks even. On the occasions I was here, I wasn't really here. We didn't make it through all those lean years of having nothing to end up like this. We're not rich, but we have more money than ever. Let's make a change—a positive one."

"There ain't no need in trying to change anything." She stubbed the cigarette into the ashtray then pulled out and lit another.

"Do you not want to be married to me anymore?" Arnold held his breath, almost afraid to hear the answer.

Alice hefted herself up, placed her palms on the table, stared him down, and unleashed a trail of profanities. "Honey, I think we both know we'd have been better off if you had died in that truck accident."

Chapter 16

We'd have been better off if you had died in that truck accident.

The words thundered through his mind as he stumbled across the driveway and jumped into the truck.

We'd have been better off if you had died in that truck accident.

He slammed the door behind him and stared at the house.

Mondaci sat in the seat next to him with a grim grin. It hadn't ended with bloodshed, but the words Alice had said to Arnold were sure to slice through a weak human heart like a hot knife through warm butter.

They had said some horrible things to each other over the years, but Arnold never dreamed she would say such a despicable thing. As much as he loathed her, not one time had he wished her dead.

When she said it, it took several seconds for the words to weave through his jumbled disbelief. He had taken several steps back until he collided with the hallway wall then fled from the room.

As he slung open the door and staggered outside, he thought he heard her cackle of laughter, but maybe it had been his imagination. He hoped it was his imagination and that she wasn't that cruel and unloving.

A rapping sound on the window brought him out of his reverie and made him jump. He glared outside at one of the card-playing hags who waved at him with one hand as she passed by clutching a covered dish with the other.

Arnold flipped her the bird.

The woman held up her wrinkled and blue-veined hand and returned the gesture, adding a torrent of profanities. She gave him the look of death for several seconds then whirled around and laughed all the way to the front door where she let herself in without knocking.

Pauline walked past the truck a minute later, but she scuttered past without looking at him.

He wondered if she had seen the altercation with the other hag and was slipping past quietly or whether she hadn't noticed him. She was his friend's wife and lived across the street from them, so he waited until her back was to him before flipping her the bird. "The whole world and everyone in it can jump off a cliff for all I care."

Mondaci patted Arnold's back even though the man couldn't feel it. "Thanks to Adam and Eve's stupidity, we've been doing our best for centuries to point as many souls as possible to hell, with a lot of success, I might add."

Arnold started the truck, jerked it into reverse, and zoomed down the driveway. In the street, he threw it into drive and squealed away, but three seconds into laying rubber on the asphalt, the truck spluttered to a stop.

He beat the steering wheel with his palms and stamped his feet to the floorboard while pelting every distasteful curse word that popped into his mind.

He turned the key, but the engine wouldn't catch. He beat the steering wheel again. "Come on you worthless piece of—"

The engine rolled over and purred to life, but he gave it another round of obscenities, just because he was in the mood, and because the rusted rattletrap deserved it.

A few miles down the road, he swerved into the local watering hole. If Alice wanted him dead, maybe drinking and driving would be a good way to oblige her. With any luck, the local police could deliver to her the good news of his timely demise by day's end.

At the bar, he tossed down six bottleneck beers while Shania Twain blared from speakers that hung on chains above a pathetic attempt of a dance floor covered with peeling linoleum. Peeling linoleum and blathering drunks weren't a good combination, but what did he care if some cowboy broke an ankle?

Half an hour later, he strutted back to the truck with a heavy buzz but not enough that he couldn't drive home safely. The police would think differently about it, rightfully so, but what they didn't know wouldn't hurt them. "Alice might not get her wish today after all," he said as the truck engine whirred to life.

He laced his fingers together and leaned the back of his head into them while the vibrations from the truck lulled his wrath into a slow-burning anger. He didn't know where to go, but home wasn't an option. Maybe he would disappear, and Alice would never know what happened to him. "Not that she'd care. Her and the card-playing hags would throw the party of a lifetime." Disappearing into the night and never returning didn't sound like such a bad idea, but now that he thought about it, he wouldn't want to give his old woman that much satisfaction.

Two men teetered out the front doors of the bar and drew his attention with their obnoxious braying laughter. One of the men snatched the keys from the other, though neither appeared in the condition to be behind the wheel. When one leaned in and pressed a long and passionate kiss to the other's lips, Arnold grunted and turned away as his rage rekindled.

He wanted to put his fist through something and the window next to him was tempting, but he shook his head at the irrational thought. A bungled fist and a broken window wouldn't help matters.

When he straightened up and wrapped his fingers around the steering wheel, the glove box caught his attention. He leaned over, popped it open, and pulled out a hunting knife.

Mortol appeared on the seat, which brought a scowl from Mondaci. They glowered at each other for several seconds before bringing their focus back to the human.

Arnold pulled the knife from the sheath and gripped the leather handle in his fist. When he rotated the blade, the sun glinted off the razor-sharp edge.

He lowered it to his pants legs and dragged the blade across the denim that covered his thigh. With the minimal amount of pressure he applied, it bit into the fabric and created a trench but didn't cut all the way through.

He held up the knife and twirled it in the sun again then pushed the flat side of the blade against the underside of his wrist.

The metal was cool to the touch. All it would take was a slight raise to bring the blade to the perfect angle to cut through skin, arteries, and cartilage until he finally reached the bone. His fury would allow him to make the cut with ease, or maybe it wouldn't, but either way it wouldn't matter because his lifeblood would leak to the floor until nothing remained but a pitiful corpse that no one wanted or loved.

"Do it now," Mortol taunted. "End it all."

Arnold pressed the knife edge into his wrist. Blood pooled under the blade then slid in paths to the underside of his arm. "One good push and it can all be over in a couple of minutes."

"When the righteous cry for help, the Lord hears and delivers them out of all their troubles."

Mortol and Mondaci snapped their heads around to see who stood outside the window. Though it was raised, they heard his voice as though he were in the car with them.

"The Lord is near to the brokenhearted and saves the crushed in spirit."

"Beat it, Lutis. You aren't needed here," Fraush growled.

"Many are the afflictions of the righteous, but the Lord delivers him out of them all. He keeps all his bones. Not one of them is broken."

Arnold closed his eyes to gather the courage to do what he wanted.

"It can't hurt worse than the pain you already have, so do it and get it done," Mortol sneered.

An image floated before Arnold's mind. It was a woman's face in front of a bright light that prevented him from seeing her features.

Her voice was succinct, and her words flowed into his spirit like sweet honey. "You are God's. Don't give up hope. Seek Him, and you will find Him."

Chapter 17

Hyacinth's metal knitting needles clinked as soft instrumental praise and worship music drifted in the background. The scarf pattern was one that she had used so many times that she could almost do it with her eyes closed.

She hummed along to the song that played. It was an old one that had been popular years ago when she and Jenner had first begun to date.

She remembered the day like it happened yesterday.

***

<u>Several Years Ago</u>

Jenner rushed into her apartment out of breath, excited beyond anything she'd ever seen. He wore blue jeans and an emerald-green sweater, and his hair was crunchy and spikey in a popular style among men his age.

He waved strips of paper in the air. "You won't believe what I got us."

She swept aside her college textbook, glad to push Endothermic and Exothermic Reactions out of her mind. She sucked in a deep breath and transfigured her expression into one of shock. "Did we win the lottery? Because if so, I'm not spending another day in college."

He leaned in and gave her a quick peck on the lips. "Sorry, babe, but I wouldn't recommend giving up on the college degree just yet."

She slumped her shoulders and fell back into the chair in a dramatic swoop.

He fanned her with the strips of paper. "Trust me, this is so much better than winning the lottery."

"Lay it on me then."

"What are you doing on June 18th? It's on a Thursday night."

It was over a month away, so as far as she knew, her plans were wide open. "I have big plans of gorging on Ben & Jerry's and watching *Dirty Dancing*."

He bopped her on the head with the papers then fanned them in front of his face. "You can move *Dirty Dancing* to Friday night where it belongs because you and I have a date."

She moved in closer to examine the ticket stubs then looked up at him with a growing smile. "We're going to a Mercy Me concert?" He slapped the tickets on his palm with a proud smile. "Rumor has it that Amy Grant will be there to sing a few songs, but I don't know how true that is."

She squealed and wrapped her arms around him. "Mercy Me is my favorite group. Move over, *Dirty Dancing*."

***

Present Day

With a sigh, she brushed her sleeve across her eyes as she reveled in the precious memory that was so long ago yet seemed like it had just happened. She clutched her hand to her heart and squeezed her eyes shut. If she had known back then how short their life together would be, she would have done so many things differently.

She would have spent more time with him, made sure they traveled to more places, and didn't put off so many things until they had more time or money. What good is time and money if you don't spend every possible second with the people you love before they're gone? Time and money meant nothing without memories to go along with them.

"Oh, Jenner," she whispered. "There's so much we never got to do because I never dreamed that we didn't have fifty more years ahead of us. I miss you so much it hurts."

She knew where he was, though, which made her grief bearable. He was in the presence of the God to whom he had dedicated much of his adult life worshipping through music.

Serving in the praise and worship band had been everything to him, and though they had never made it to the ranks of Mercy Me, he took his responsibility with complete seriousness, and she loved that about him.

As her mind wandered, she reflected on that horrible moment on the bus. What had he seen? What had he felt?

The doctors assured her that he went quickly, but did they say such things simply to make people feel better about their loss? Did he feel a strong presence of the Holy Spirit as he drifted from this world into his heavenly reward?

"Uncle Jenn?"

Hyacinth opened her eyes and bolted up. She glanced over her shoulder at her niece, Paige, who walked into the room rubbing her eyes that were still heavy with sleep. "Hi, baby. Did you finally wake up?"

"I see Uncle Jenn."

Hyacinth held out her arms, and the girl ran into them. She wrapped her tight and cuddled her close. "I want to see Uncle Jenn too."

Within seconds the girl she couldn't love more if she was her own was fast asleep.

She leaned back in the seat and again closed her eyes. She prayed for peace for herself, for Paige, and for everyone who had loved Jenner. His absence was a tragic loss for everyone who ever knew him.

Protector Warrior Nitasah stepped into the room and looked at his charges with love. "You've lost so much, yet your faith has never wavered," he said to the human. "Your Holy Father in Heaven sees His faithful servant and is pleased."

The human never opened her eyes, but her lips moved in silent prayers as she sought refuge in the love of her heavenly Father.

"Pray, my child," Nitasah said. "Pray like never before, because his life depends on it."

***

Present Day

The second the stirring hit her heart Hyacinth's eyes popped open. A fervency aroused from deep inside her and the urge to pray strengthened.

She placed Paige on the sofa, pressed a kiss to her forehead, and ran her fingers through the silky blonde hair that needed a good brushing.

She walked across the room unsure of what she needed to do.

Nitasah followed at her heels. "Pray, my child. Pray for him now."

Tears flooded her eyes and her throat constricted with high emotions and urgency. She needed to pray, that much she knew, but about what or whom, she didn't know.

She clutched her arms to her chest and bowed her head. "Heavenly Father, someone out there needs You. I don't know who or why, but You know. Whoever this person is, I pray that You would give them a spirit of wisdom and discernment. May they draw closer to you in their time of need."

Motecca fell into step behind Nitasah. "Why are you worried about some person you don't even know? You're acting from a sense of pious flesh."

Though she believed in the power of prayer, a sudden sense of unease filled her, but she pushed it aside.

"I ask that You strip away any distractions or lies from the enemy in this person's life. Help them to turn their eyes away from worthless things that bring sinful pleasure and destruction. Instead, may they seek repentance that leads to the saving knowledge of truth. May they turn their eyes toward You so they can escape the traps of the devil who revels in taking them captive to do his evil will."

"Leave it to you weak Jesus lovers to pray for someone instead of reaching out a helping hand," Motecca said in a slithery, mocking tone.

Is this someone I know? Instead of praying for them am I supposed to physically help them in some way? Confusion flooded her mind.

"Don't listen to the enemy of your soul." Nitasah glared at Motecca as he said the words, then he directed his attention back to his human. "The enemy comes to distract you from your God-given purpose."

"I wonder if it's Sister Paulina," she wondered aloud. "She wasn't herself at church on Sunday. I had an urge to go and pray for her, but I didn't. Forgive my complacence, Lord. Praying for people out of the blue like that isn't in my comfort zone."

Motecca smiled. How little it took for humans to get off track, and most of the time the distractions were of their own doing and had nothing to do with the influence of the dark world.

"The Father forgives you for not acting on that discernment," Nitasah encouraged. "Someone else needs your prayers now, child. Pray."

"Father, I pray for Sister Paulina right now. Soothe her spirit and may she remove distractions that keep her from focusing solely on You." Even as she prayed the words, they were flat and empty. Something in her heart said that Sister Paulina wasn't the one who needed her intercession. "God, for whom would You have me pray?"

"You don't need to know who," Nitasah rebuked. "Just pray."

She shook her head. How arrogant to think that she needed to know every detail of those for whom she was led to pray. "Lord, I don't know if this person is within my sphere of influence. If so, please lead me to them if it be Your will. If not me, then I ask that You send someone to help them in their time of need, someone who can minister to their situation and open the door so that someone can proclaim Your gospel message in their life."

Impatient, Motecca whipped past Nitasah and stood directly in front of Hyacinth, who had paused in front of the marble-lined fireplace. "What a worthless action, praying for someone without praying for something specific. God can't answer your prayers if you don't even know what you're asking Him for!" With every fiber of his being, he hated this human for truly understanding the power of prayer.

"The devil was a murderer from the beginning," Nitasah unsheathed his sword with a metallic zing that pierced the heavens. He thrust the razor-sharp pointed end at the scraggly Traitor Warrior. "He has always hated truth because there is no truth in him. When he speaks, he speaks lies, for he is a liar and the father of lies."

Motecca wrapped his fingers around Nitasah's throat and squeezed. "Shut up, Nitasah, and let her do what she will."

Without an ounce of fear, Nitasah pressed the tip of the blade into the Traitor Warrior's flesh, and the repulsive smell of sulfur spilled from the wound. "Step away, Motecca."

With seething hatred, Motecca gave a final squeeze before unfurling his fingers and taking a guarded step back. He roared his displeasure at Nitasah before turning back to the human who had moved from the fireplace and now knelt between the sofa and the bookcase.

Her hands were raised, and her alto voice sang in soft worship. "Holy, holy, holy, though darkness hide Thee, though the eye of sinful man Thy glory may not see. Only Thou art holy, there is none beside Thee..."

Nitasah moved to stand between the woman and the Warrior Traitor. "Use your war songs to worship your Creator and in doing so you'll defeat your enemy."

After several minutes of singing, she fell silent and wept.

"Death," Nitasah said.

Motecca glanced at Nitasah then at the human, wondering what it meant.

Hyacinth raised her head with a perplexed expression. She yanked a tissue from the lamp table and pressed it against her eyes then stood to her feet.

She paced the length of the room several times with her hands tucked under her chin.

Motecca stepped up to the sleeping child on the couch and gazed at her.

Nitasah took a few steps forward as the demon looked at the child with interest. "Touch even a hair of the child and the Father will banish you to the Pits forever. She's off limits."

Before Motecca could respond, loud weeping made them turn.

"Lord, I don't know who needs You, but someone somewhere plans to harm themselves, to bring an end to their life. I lift them up to You right now. In this moment, let Your peace wash over them. Bring clarity and truth and the life-saving gospel into their life. You've sent the Holy Spirit to be our comforter, and that's the greatest force that can work in a person's life. If it can't be me, then I ask that You ordain someone in the flesh to minister to their need."

Mortol appeared in the room. He gave Nitasah an unnerving grin before approaching the woman. "Where does your Bible say that your flimsy prayers can stop another's death, even when it's self-inflicted?"

Hyacinth gripped her hands into fists. If she could see the creature in front of her, they would be nearly eye to eye. "Greater is He that is in me than he that is in the world." Her whispered words rumbled through the heavens with authority.

Mortol took a step back and glared at her. He was impotent against the truth of scripture and such knowledge made him seethe. "Is He really greater in you than he who is in the world? Just because an old-fashioned book says it, does it make it true?"

"Greater is He that is in me than he who is in the world," Hyacinth repeated, this time even louder.

"Death," Nitasah whispered in her direction.

Hyacinth opened her eyes, and her heart softened toward a person whose identity she didn't know. "Whoever you are, whatever you're going through, you are God's. Don't give up hope. Seek Him, and you will find Him."

Chapter 18

You are God's. Don't give up hope. Seek Him and you will find Him. The words floated through his mind, causing further confusion. How could he be God's when he didn't believe that God existed? Where would such a fanciful notion come from? he wondered, then attributed it to the equivalent of a six-pack of beer he drank at the bar.

He could hold his liquor as well as any, but maybe it was messing with his mind more than his buzz indicated. What other explanation could there be for such poppycock thoughts?

He dropped the knife on the seat next to him and ran his trembling hands through his hair. Everything that had just happened seemed lightyears away.

We'd have been better off if you had died in that truck accident.

The image of a faceless woman hovering in front of a bright light.

You are God's. Don't give up hope. Seek Him, and you will find Him.

"Arnold, you are losing your ever-loving mind." He shook his head, started the truck, threw it into reverse, and screeched out of the bar's parking lot. "Maybe the bar had rust in their pipes, and it poisoned the beer, and I'm hallucinating. Or maybe you're getting old, and it's time for the looney bin. That'll get me out of Alice's hair."

He didn't know what was going on, but he knew one thing. It was time to get back to work. He and Alice did better when they had half the country between them. The better part of their days was over, so there was no need in staying home where he wasn't wanted.

With his thoughts tumbling in every direction, he hit the interstate and drove for an hour to the nearest truck lot.

Rows of sparkling diesel rigs in every color imaginable lined the lot, and their majestic beauty made him smile.

He heaved himself out of the truck with a grunt and ambled around the parking lot until a cowboy dressed in black slacks, a red and black cowboy shirt, and a Stetson hat made his way toward Arnold. "Arnold Collins? As I live and breathe." The man gave him a hearty pat on the back. "Please tell me you're finally in the market for a new rig?"

"Bill, good to see you, man. I haven't been here in what, eight years? How in the world do you still work here after all this time? I know old skinflint Wadsworth doesn't pay that well."

Bill leaned in and nudged him in the ribs with a good-natured smile. "The old skinflint kicked the bucket last year, and I bought the place when Mrs. Wadsworth put it up for sale and moved to Palm Beach to live it up with the rest of the rich biddies of the world."

"Well, good for you, buddy." Arnold patted him on the back. "If anyone deserves success, it's you."

"Between this place and home, I'm mortgaged all the way up to my eyebrows, but at least I'm the man instead of answering to the man, so it's all good." The expression on his face underwent a subtle change, but his friendly smile remained. "What can I do you for? Are you finally ready to trade-in that old rattletrap semi of yours? I've been begging you to trade up for years now. I'll give you a good trade-in on your old rig."

"That would be swell, but I was in a darned wreck a few months back so it's a heap of metal in a junk yard right now." *I killed a young man who had more to live for than I have.* He tried his best to push the thought aside, but the nagging weight of guilt remained.

The man whistled then muttered an obscenity. "Oh, man, I hate to hear that, but you seem to be fine, thank the Good Lord."

"I had a concussion and a fractured leg. I still hobble around like a decrepit old man, but I'm getting around much better." *I fared way better than the other guy.* Again, he tried to push the thought aside. Guilt wouldn't bring the guy back.

The man gave him an affable nod. "Even without the trade-in, I can cut you a great deal since you've been such a good client over the years. I assume you got an insurance payout of some sort?"

"Forty-five thousand and some change," Arnold nodded. "It's about half what I need to replace it, but what're you gonna do? Insurance companies are the biggest scammers on the face of the planet. You pay heavy premiums all your life, then when it comes time for them to pay out, they do their best to nickel and dime you."

"They screw you like a hooker, but it ain't nearly as much fun." Bill released a chuckle and shook his head. "I have a clean 2019 Volvo VNL over here. 415,000 miles. It's $74,960, but I can bring it down to $70 thousand." He pointed across the lot. "Over there is a 2018 Freightliner Cascadia 126. She has a little more mileage on her, about 481k, but she still has a few good years left in her. $61,000, but, for a friend, I'll give her up for 57k."

"Call me crazy at this stage of my life, but I want a newer, honey of a ride."

The man's eyes lit up.

With dollar signs or shock? Arnold wondered. *Probably the dollar signs.*

"You want to ride with the big boys, eh?" The man sped up and stopped in front of a silver sleeper cab. "This is a 2022 Freightliner Cascadia. Only has a little over 200k miles. 400 horsepower and a 72" raised roof sleeper. It has a Detroit DD15 engine with battery powered HVAC system, heated and ventilated seats, heated hood mounted mirrors, satellite radio capability, and it's Bluetooth and Wi-Fi enabled. There's even a flatscreen tv in the sleeper. To put a cherry on top, the cab and sleeper cabin are both equipped with Bose sound, one of the best sound systems ever, in my humble opinion." He looked at Arnold with raised eyebrows. "If you want a sweet ride, you can't do much better than this beauty."

Most of it he understood, but the Wi-Fi and Bluetooth was lost on him. "How much?" He was afraid to hear the answer.

"$121,000, but I'll give her to you for $118k."

Arnold brushed his fingers over the silver body as his mind spun with the massive number. He had never in his life spent more than $70k on a semi. He would never live long enough to pay off such an expensive rig—not if he was lucky, anyway—and luck had never been on his side.

Bill kicked the wheel with the pointed end of his cowboy boot. "She's a fancy broad and will give you the cushiest ride of your life. We have some great cheaper options if this is more than you need," he added at Arnold's hesitance.

He allowed the information to toss around in his head for several seconds. "Can I take her for a spin before I decide?"

Bill jerked his head toward the building. "Let me run in and grab the keys."

Chapter 19

It was nearly eleven at night before the card game ended and the girls finally went home.

Alice emptied the contents of the heaped-up glass ashtrays into the trashcan then tossed them into hot soapy water for their daily cleaning.

She placed them atop the soppy dishtowel to airdry overnight and glanced over the kitchen and dining area. The house was old and dated, but it was as spic-and-span as a house could be.

She pulled a cigarette from her cracked and aged pleather cigarette case, put it in her mouth and lit it. The warm smoke trailed down her throat and infiltrated her lungs.

On the way to her bedroom, she detoured to the back porch and sat in a lawn chair that squeaked under her weight.

The melodic chirps and trills of frogs and crickets provided a peaceful backdrop, and birds in the distance sang their nocturnal goodnights.

As she took another drag of the cigarette, her thoughts wondered to the scene with Arnold earlier in the day. She shouldn't have told him that she'd be better off if he had died, but she was tired of him inviting her out to dinner or nights of dancing.

They hadn't given each other the time of day in so many years that his sudden invitations left her in an awkward position. In her heart, she was glad he hadn't died in the accident, but she wasn't interested in his wine and dine invitations. For better or worse, they had a way of life, and he needed to leave it be.

She leaned up and squinted in the dark at two red points of light at the far end of the yard. "What the—" She muttered a profanity, stood to her feet, and scuttled to the edge of the concrete porch.

When the two red orbs moved, seemingly in her direction, she backed up until her back was to the door. She stifled a laugh when a rabbit, not a malicious demon, bounded across the yard and stopped again a few feet from the porch.

It was the first time she had seen a rabbit on their property, especially at night, probably because she never stepped a foot outside unless she had a good reason. She and the rabbit stared each other down for a full minute before it hopped away and disappeared around the other side of the house.

Though it was uncomfortably warm out, she lowered herself back into her seat. She dropped the cigarette butt and snuffed the orange glow with the bottom of her shoe.

A feeling niggled at the edges of her consciousness once again as the incident with Arnold this morning loomed in her mind. Guilt wasn't an emotion she ever indulged, and she didn't like it intruding on her now.

＊＊＊

<u>1971</u>

Alice giggled like a schoolgirl as Arnold held his hands tight against her eyes. She couldn't see where she walked, but she trusted him with everything, even her life.

"You're not looking, are you, woman?" he teased.

"I couldn't peek even if I wanted to."

"Close your eyes and keep them closed until I tell you to open them."

"What are you doing? Where are we?"

"You'll see soon enough. Are your eyes closed?"

She nodded.

He peeled his hands away from her eyes and whirled her around to face him. "Now keep them closed."

"Okay." She opened them into slits when the rustle of his clothes told her he had moved away somewhere behind her.

In the direction she faced, there was nothing to see except a vast starry night and lines of headlights flying past on the main road in the distance, visible in short spurts between the spindly groves of pine trees.

The quarter moon hung in the sky, shedding a thin blanket of light over the beautiful rural terrain.

A wispy cloak of dust from their recent sojourn down the dirt road still lingered in the air. Behind her, a swath of light provided minimal illumination, but she couldn't determine its source. She had only a general idea of where they were.

"Where are we? Old McDonald's Farm?" She asked when a melancholic round of cattle lowing interrupted the quiet.

She sucked in a breath when opulent strings of music and the smooth and sophisticated strains of Ella Fitzgerald filled the night.

At the sound of his rustle of clothing, she closed her eyes.

Arnold stepped behind her, wrapped her in his arms, and hummed the tune of "My One and Only Love" in her ear.

They swayed in the shin-high grass, and from somewhere a note of lilac scented the air. It was a perfect moment.

Arnold took her hand in his, lifted it over her head, and twirled her as though they were on a grand ballroom floor. When the spin stopped, they were chest to chest.

Her heart thumped and she was breathless, but in a good way.

They were in a field, and she wasn't sure whose, but in the moment she didn't care. All that mattered was Arnold and her.

Behind them on the ground was a tablecloth with a floral pattern, on top of which was a wicker picnic basket.

"I thought we might have dinner under the stars tonight," Arnold said.

"Oh, it's lovely." She nestled closer into him as the song moved into another that perfectly set the romantic tone.

Not a single day passed that she didn't thank the Lord for giving her such a wonderful life with such a wonderful man.

She could have danced non-stop until dawn, so it was with reluctance that, half an hour later, she pulled away when he led her to the food spread.

"It's nothing fancy." With a bashful grin, he opened the basket and pulled out a plastic bowl covered with foil that contained fried chicken. "I didn't make it. Colonel Sanders did."

A smile tugged at her lips as they unloaded mashed potatoes and gravy, biscuits with a jar of her mother's spicy apple butter, and coleslaw. For dessert, he offered Oreo cookies that he had painstakingly wrapped in plastic wrap and secured with heart-shaped stickers.

She placed a can of Tab beside her plate and placed the other beside Arnold's.

The food that was supposed to be hot was cold, and the food that was supposed to be cold was lukewarm, but Alice barely noticed as they laughed and talked about everything and nothing.

***

<u>Present Day</u>

"Bucky! Get your tail in the house right now!"

Alice jumped, jolted back to the present time by their neighbor screaming at their yippy two-pound chihuahua.

"Bucky! I ain't going to tell you again. Get in here!"

She wanted to jump up, rush to the fence, and tell the piece of trash neighbor to shut her yap, but tonight, for once, she wasn't in the mood for a verbal sparring. She and the tramp always jumped on each other's throats at every opportunity, but tonight she wanted peace more than a rumble.

"Fine, you little beast, have it your way," the neighbor screeched. "Don't come clawing on the door later wanting in. We'll see how you like sleeping outside all night!"

Alice laughed a second later when the door slammed shut. The hussy was spitting mad, and she loved every minute of it.

When the serenity of the moment returned, her mind went back to the long-forgotten memory of the past that she had just recalled. At one time, Arnold and she had been happy together, yet she had somehow managed to put it all out of her memory. "Oh, Arnold, you old coot. I love you, yet I hate you."

Ahava stepped out of the shadows of the night. Her locks of brunette hair sparkled under the moonlight's rays. The Father had tasked her with keeping watch over this human since the day she was born. She didn't like seeing Alice on a path that would lead to her destruction if she didn't change her ways, but she refused to give up on her. While the humans had breath there was still time for redemption.

She knelt in front of her charge with a knowing smile. "You've been through so much pain in your life that you've forgotten how to love. That love is still hidden in your heart. We just need to find it again."

Sané, the fallen angel also tasked with keeping an eye on Alice, stepped past Ahava and put his hand on Alice's shoulder with a grin devoid of warmth. "She's too far gone. You'll never win her. She's ours."

Ahava looked at his hand and brushed it away from the human. "Saul of Tarsus hated the followers of Jesus. He killed as many of them as he could to stop the spread of the Gospel of Christ. He soon found out that nobody could stop the spread of Truth, and that even a vile murderer like himself could find mercy in the eyes of the Lord. He became the Apostle Paul and went on to spread the Gospel to an entire world. His words still spread the Gospel centuries later." She flashed him a brilliant smile. "I think if we can win the Apostle Paul, then we still have a chance with this soul too."

Chapter 20

When the rumble of the truck sounded in the distance, Arnold bolted out the door and onto the porch as fast as his feeble legs could carry him.

The semi gleamed in the sunlight as it made its way down the street and turned into the driveway. It was the most beautiful thing he had ever seen.

The truck came to a stop, the engine died, and the man from the truck lot jumped to the ground just as Arnold's pal, Earl, bounded from across the street to see what the racket was all about.

"What in tarnation is this?" Earl asked with excitement.

Arnold sucked in a deep breath of air tinged with a hint of diesel fuel. It was one of his favorite scents.

"Are you hitting the road again soon?" Earl asked when Arnold didn't respond.

Arnold shook hands with the delivery man. "I appreciate you bringing her to me."

The man shrugged. "No problem. We've started offering delivery services for our best customers. Plus, sometimes it's nice to get out of the office for a while."

Arnold ran his palm over the smooth fiberglass.

"We had it washed and waxed, and the interior detailed, so it will shine like a new penny for you." The man looked over his shoulder when a Chevy truck pulled in the driveway behind the rig. He handed the keys to Arnold. "That's my coworker to take me back to work."

Arnold thumbed the key with pride. He didn't realize until now just how much he missed being on the road. Most people dream of the day they can retire and stop living their lives according to another man's timeclock. Obviously, those people had someone to retire with who didn't detest their presence.

He whipped his wallet from his back pocket, pulled out a hundred-dollar bill, and pressed it into the man's hand. "Thanks for coming all the way out here. Take this and buy you and your coworker a nice lunch on me."

The man's eyes widened at the unexpected tip, and he pushed it away. "You don't need to do that. It's part of the service we provide."

Arnold stuffed the bill into the man's shirt pocket in a moment of rare generosity of spirit. "The Main Street Tavern is the best lunch place in town. I highly recommend that you boys stop by if you have time before heading back to work."

The man hesitated then gave an appreciative nod. "It's not necessary but thank you for your kindness."

"Tell Mabel to give you both a huge piece of chocolate meringue pie," he called after the departing man.

"Holy cow, that's a nice truck you got there," Earl said as the men backed out of the driveway. "I guess you're itching to hit the road again."

"I can only take being here with the old ball and chain for so long."

"Can't say I blame you," Earl chuckled. "I wouldn't want to be stuck here all day with Alice either."

Arnold gave him a dirty look. "Like Pauline's any better."

"No disagreement there," Earl nodded. "She spends all day at your house then comes home in time to go to bed, and I wouldn't have it any other way."

Arnold leaned against the truck and crossed his arms. "What happened to our lives?"

"What do you mean? Our lives ain't that bad."

Arnold shook his head. "I'm talking about our wives. We want to be around our wives as little as possible, and frankly, the feeling is mutual where they're concerned. This isn't how our lives were supposed to end."

"It's called forty years of marriage, my friend. After forty years of living with the same person, what do you expect? It's normal."

"I've known people who were married for sixty and seventy years, and they were happy their whole lives. It doesn't have to turn out this way, and I want to know what they did right that I did wrong."

"You need to talk to a shrink about that, not me. I'm an old fool who knows nothing. If you don't believe it, ask Pauline. She'll tell you."

"Are you and Pauline..." He paused, unsure if he wanted to ask such a thing. "Are you and Pauline happy?"

"Pauline hasn't been happy since the seventies."

Arnold scoffed at the answer. "Don't give me that bull. You guys go dancing at the VA Hall almost every weekend, and at least once or twice a month you go out to dinner."

"If that's your measuring stick for happiness, then I guess we're happy," Earl said. "Sure, we do those things, but ask me how much time we spend together the rest of the month."

"When's the last time you remember being happy with each other and not just tolerated each other? When did the good times end?"

Earl took nearly a minute of pondering before he looked at Arnold. "Honestly?"

"No, tell me a big fat lie."

Earl ignored the scathing sarcasm. "Pauline and I never had what I would consider one of those lovey dovey marriages like many people claim to have, but when all those women started coming to your house to play cards all day every day, things started going downhill for us."

"I guess it's hard to have strong marriages when our wives would rather be together than with us."

"Pauline's always been a give 'em heck kind of woman, and I knew that when I married her. Unfortunately, her rough edges get worse the older she gets. I guess mine do too, so I don't have much room to talk. Pauline's my lot in life, and we've learned to deal with each other."

A deafening racket interrupted their unusually earnest discussion, and they both turned to watch a band of motorcycles race past. "As hard as it is to believe," Arnold said when the silence returned, "Alice and I were truly happy at one time. Like, 'we can't live without each other' kind of happy. It's hard to believe we've turned into what we are now."

"I think it's a more common story than you think. People work hard to give the impression of a perfect life, but most of them have cruddy lives just like the rest of us."

"I've been content with our sorry marriage for years because I was never home, I suppose. Now, for some reason, I hate it."

"If you guys used to be happy, and now you're not, you might want to ask yourself what changed."

Chapter 21

Arnold tossed his suitcase onto the bed and threw in everything he needed for an extended trip. Now that the truck was in his possession the urge to get away was unbearable. Even though it had only been months since his last trip, it seemed as though years had passed as he tried to recall everything he needed to do before heading out again.

He didn't have a job lined up, and he didn't know where he would go, but getting away from home was all he needed right now.

Though he rarely used it, he dug his cell phone from his bedside table, plugged it into the charger cord, and turned it on. He had contacted the transportation company that he contracted through and informed them of his ability to take on jobs, so he hoped to hear from them soon.

He lifted a stack of white tank tops from one of the drawers and laid them into the suitcase, followed by a stack of work shirts.

"What're you doing?" Alice snarled from the doorway.

"Feeding the ducks," Arnold snapped back. "What does it look like I'm doing?"

"Looks like you're running away from home."

He grabbed socks and threw them into the suitcase. "Can't imagine why I'd want to leave the little slice of heaven we've built here, can you?"

"Are you really going somewhere?"

He thew another batch of socks into the suitcase and glared up at her when one pair bounced out and rolled across the room. "I'm busy, Alice. What can I do for you?"

She flipped him the bird and launched into a proliferation of obscenities. "You don't have to bite my head off. I was just asking a question."

When she bolted down the hallway toward her own room in a state of offense, he rushed to the door and slammed it shut, hard enough to send her a clear message. He didn't want to see or talk to her right now, and maybe never again.

A few seconds later, she slammed her door with just as much ferocity, which brought him a self-indulgent smile.

Once he was packed, he dropped onto the bed in a snit. How dare Alice get angry at him for having an attitude when she basically had told him she wished he had died.

He ravaged her with a mental barrage of the filthiest words he could conjure. Though he could cuss up a storm with little provocation, even he couldn't out cuss his dear little Alice.

He snatched up the Bible Aunt Deborah had given him. "Lord, Aunt Deborah says that You talk to her through the Bible. Maybe You could give me something to help me through all this crap I'm going through."

He snapped it open and read aloud the first verse he encountered. "A young man was following Him, wearing nothing but a linen sheet over his naked body. They seized him, but he pulled free of the linen sheet and escaped naked."

He looked up at the ceiling and frowned. "With this body, I ain't running nowhere naked."

He flipped back a few more pages hoping for a more relevant verse. "If only you would be altogether silent. For you, that would be wisdom." He looked toward Alice's room and flipped her a double bird. "That's a word for you direct from God Himself."

He flipped forward and read aloud. "It is better to live alone in the desert than with a crabby, complaining wife." He couldn't help but smile. "Are you saying I need to move to the desert, Lord? Because sometimes the barren desert would be more hospitable than living with Alice."

"No one with crushed or severed genitals shall be admitted to the assembly of the Lord." He slammed the Bible closed and tossed it to the foot of the bed. This wasn't working the way he thought it might. "So much for the Bible giving me a little direction. I don't care what Aunt Deborah says, that book is plumb weird."

***

1971

Alice placed her undergarments in the suitcase next to Arnold's. Though they had been married for several months a blush still tinged her cheeks at the thought of him seeing them.

She burst into laughter when he sneaked up behind her, wrapped her in his arms, lifted her into the air, and pressed animated kisses to her neck.

"You almost ready to go?" he asked when her laughter subsided.

"I think I'm ready, but I want to doublecheck and make sure I haven't forgotten to pack something."

"You know, Salt Lake City has these groovy little things called stores, and rumor has it we can buy things if we forget something." He rubbed his stubbled cheek against hers in a playful manner.

"We can't afford this little vacation as it is. Why waste money on things we already have?"

"I don't want you worrying about money. I've got it covered."

She leaned down and pressed a kiss to the tip of his nose. "I don't need you to coddle me. We're married now, and married people do crazy things like worry about money."

"I've been putting a few extra dollars aside for the past few months so I could surprise you with a weekend away, so there's no need to worry about money. We're good."

"We may be good, but why spend our hard-earned vacation money on more toothpaste when we already have some here? We need to spend smart. That's all I'm saying."

"It's vacation. We're not supposed to spend smart. We're supposed to throw it around and have fun."

She closed the suitcase with an exaggerated sigh. "Throw it around? Not in this house, we don't."

"Wait, wait, wait." He opened the suitcase back up and used his finger to lift the edge of a fancy bra and panty set he had never seen. He glanced up at her and crooked his eyebrow. "Have mercy, what's this?"

Embarrassed, she patted his hand away. "Stop it."

"I'm pretty sure we can't afford ... that," he teased.

She patted his face with her fingers. "Don't worry, my love. Like you, I have my ways."

He grabbed her in his arms when she shrieked at the sound of a crack of thunder that interrupted their playful banter. "Don't be scared," he whispered. "I'll always protect you."

***

<u>Present Day</u>

A roll of thunder shook the house and brought him out of his memories.

He flipped over in bed and watched as lightning danced on the walls through the parts in the curtains. With a deep sigh, once again, thoughts of how far his marriage had slipped riddled him.

"Lord, are you there?" He knew He wasn't. How could a non-existent God be there to listen to him? Still, it was worth a shot. "Alice hates me. Have I messed things up so much that I can't fix it?"

Lutis stood beside the bed. "He's there, child, if you would just believe."

Fraush stepped next to Lutis, glared at him, and shook his head.

Chapter 22

Hyacinth and her best friend Sheri meandered through Marci's Closet, the local high-end boutique.

Sheri made a mad dash for a knee-length black dress with large white polka dots. The arms were flared and at the waist was a white ribbon belt. "Oh, my word. Isn't this gorgeous?"

Hyacinth rolled the soft fabric between her fingers. "It's beautiful." She flipped around the price tag and grinned.

"What's the damage?" Sheri asked.

"You don't want to know."

She braced herself for a few seconds before flipping up the tag. Her eyes bugged out, and she let out an exaggerated sigh. "Thirty-seven hundred bucks!" She slipped the dress back onto the rack. "Why do we do this to ourselves? Why do we come to these expensive boutiques when we know we can't afford anything?"

"Because it's fun to torture ourselves with beautiful things that are just outside our reach."

"Fun for you, maybe," Sheri pouted. "I'll never be able to get that dress out of my mind."

"You could always let Mastercard buy it for you and pay him back later."

Sheri shook her head. "If I can't afford it, I refuse to put it on credit. I know too many people who get into financial trouble that way. I'm not going there."

Hyacinth placed her arm around her friend's shoulders. "That's my sweet little responsible friend."

"Can you imagine walking into any store and buying whatever hits your fancy? It must be nice."

"It must be nice, but hey, we have Jesus, so there's that."

"I love Jesus, but I really want that dress. I could save up for it, I guess, but by the time I have that much money, it would be so last season."

"Honey, if I ever spent three thousand bucks on a dress, I'd wear the dumb thing until it fell apart, trends be darned."

"What do you say we get ourselves out of here before I find the stairs to the roof and fling myself to an untimely death?"

"I don't think this place is big enough for stairs to the roof, but I can see if they have a really tall ladder."

Sheri looked at her and laughed.

"Come on, honey." Hyacinth dragged her toward the door. "Let's get out of here."

On the way, Sheri stopped and grabbed a metallic silver leather slingback. "You remember that pantsuit I bought at—"

Hyacinth put her hand to Sheri's mouth and changed her voice to mimic that of a flight attendant. "Put down the shoe and make your way to the nearest exit."

"But—"

"Drop it."

Sheri took a final glance at the shoe, blew it a kiss, and set it back on the display. "Being poor sucks."

"You're not poor, you just don't have unlimited funds to spend on things you don't need. There's a difference."

"Besides, who needs nine-hundred-dollar shoes, right?"

"Is that how much they cost?"

"I don't know," Sheri shrugged. "I didn't have the heart to look but, in this store, I wouldn't doubt it."

Outside, a solid breeze caused a rustled whisper to blow through the tree leaves in the outdoor shopping center and carried with it the savory scent from the pizzeria a couple of doors down.

"Honey, if you really want the dress, I'd love to buy it for you," Hyacinth said when her friend cast another look at the boutique. She had more than enough money in the remnants of Jenner's trust fund to buy her a hundred such dresses.

Sheri waved her offer away. "Not in a million years."

Hyacinth almost argued with her about it but knew it would be a fruitless exercise. Instead, she jerked her head toward the restaurant as they strolled past. "How about we drown our sorrows in a thick crust pizza with extra cheese?"

Sheri flung open the door with a sassy flair and gestured Hyacinth inside. "It's the second-best thing and much easier on the budget."

Though pizza had been Jenner's favorite meal, Hyacinth could always take it or leave it. Today, the heavy scent gave her a forlorn sense of nostalgia for the husband she hadn't seen in months. In the past when they had eaten out, they always took turns choosing restaurants, and this place was his choice of dining options with a frequency of at least two times a month.

As they shuffled their way through the lunchtime crowds toward an empty table on the far side of the dining room, Hyacinth turned at the sound of someone shouting her name.

Given the mayhem of the all-you-can-eat buffet, she had a hard time discerning who had called to her. She tossed her purse onto the booth seat and slid in beside it.

She glanced up when the business proprietor, who also went to their church, rushed to the table with a grin. "Ellen!" Hyacinth pushed out of the booth and giggled when the sixtyish woman nearly plowed her down with an effusive bearhug.

"Oh, honey, how wonderful to see you." She patted Hyacinth's back.

"How have you been?" Hyacinth asked when the woman finally pulled away. She ran her fingers over the woman's hair. "I love the auburn. It's very chic."

"Last year, I said I would move into my sixties and accept all the gray that the good Lord gave me, but once all the color wore off and I realized just how much of it I had, I was quick to make a hair appointment."

"It looks wonderful." Hyacinth slid back into the booth.

"I've been meaning to send you a card, and maybe call on occasion after—you know—but you know how it goes," she said with an apologetic shrug. "Life."

"It goes so fast I can barely keep up."

"Jenner was such a wonderful young man. I miss seeing you and him around here ever since the Lord took him home." Tears flooded into her eyes, but she swept them away as though they were a pesky nuisance. "It was a beautiful service."

Hyacinth clutched her hand. "I'm so sorry I didn't get to see you that day. It was so—"

"You had so much to deal with that day," the woman brushed aside the apology. "Anytime Jenner came in here he brought such a light with him. He was an amazing man."

"Thank you. I think so, too."

The woman gave Hyacinth's hand a final squeeze then brushed her hands down the front of her apron in a nervous gesture. "Listen to me, prattling on when you ladies are here for a nice lunch. The server will be right over to take your drink orders."

"It's always so nice to see you, Ellen. You're a dear, and Jenner and I think the world of you." As soon as she said the words, she froze. Sometimes she still found herself referring to him in the present tense even though logically she knew he was no longer here.

Sheri reached across the table, gripped her friend's hands, and offered an encouraging smile. "Do we want the buffet?"

Hyacinth glanced at the long lines and shook her head. "I don't feel like fighting the hordes for a few pieces of pizza. Would you mind if we ordered from the menu instead?"

"That's exactly what I had in mind." She whipped up the menu and glanced over it then dropped it back to the table and punched it with her fingertip. "I know this sausage, onion, and mandarin orange pizza sounds weird, but what do you think?"

Hyacinth twirled the menu around, read the description, and gestured with her hands. "I'm of the camp that pineapple belongs on pizza, so I think it sounds just disgusting enough to be good. Let's go for it."

"I overheard some teenagers at church raving about it. My palate isn't much more refined than that of a teenager, so it can't be that bad if they like it."

When the server placed a side salad and soft drinks in front of each of them, Sheri gave her friend a tight smile. "How hard is it when people bring up Jenner out of the blue like that?"

"It depends on the day," Hyacinth shrugged. "Some days it doesn't bother me at all, but if it's an especially emotional day it can be tough. Either way, I know people mean well."

"I don't know how you've handled such a monumental loss so well. Girl, I'd fall apart."

Deep in thought, Hyacinth twirled the straw around the rim of her drink before responding. "I know for people who don't have the Holy Spirit in their life, they truly won't understand this way of thinking, but the promises of God through scripture really do help in times of loss. When grief tries to overwhelm me, I always remember the Apostle Paul saying in Corinthians that, for a believer, to be absent from the body is to be present with the Lord. Even though I miss seeing Jenner, it's impossible to be buried under grief when I know he is literally in the presence of the Lord right now. For me, that is an immense peace in my heart."

Even as her friend spoke the words, they brought immediate warmth to Sheri's heart. "Nonbelievers hate us for believing in something they don't, but oh, if only they knew how much they were missing because of their unbelief. I can't imagine going through life without, as the hymn says, such a blessed assurance."

"That assurance doesn't mean we don't grieve, but it means we don't grieve as the world does, without the hope of seeing our loved ones again. That's how I get through it from one day to the next."

After lunch, as they strolled through the outdoor shopping center, someone grabbed Hyacinth's arm from behind. Surprised, she whirled around to see who was there. "Well, hey, Janie."

Janie bore into her with a stern gaze. "I need to talk to you."

Chapter 23

The vibration of the rig's diesel engine rumbling beneath him was a sensation to which he was well accustomed. Years of listening to the engine was probably why his hearing wasn't as good as it used to be. To most people, the combination of the noise and vibrations would be insufferable for any amount of time, but to him it was welcome, like a visit from a good friend. "Plus, if I go deaf, I won't have to listen to Alice yammer on." He was probably the only person in the world who would consider such an ailment as a blessing.

It was the early morning hours, and his body hadn't wanted to get up, which was surprising since the early hours never used to bother him. He had gone soft during his time of recuperation.

He had only been gone from the house for a whopping ten minutes, and already the comfort of having only his presence to deal with washed over him. If he ever again considered retiring, he would look back on the past few months of being home with Alice and think again. As far as he was concerned, he would die in this truck hundreds, maybe even thousands of miles away from Alice. Most people dreamed of spending their last moments with their loved ones, but not him. If he never had to see Alice again, it would be too soon.

The town dwindled behind him, and trees whizzed past with occasional sparkles of light from beat-up homes tucked into the woods.

He held up both hands and flipped the bird to the retreating town. "Good riddance to every one of you."

Even though the truck was new to him, it was a year old, and somehow it still managed to retain the new car scent that everyone loved. How it was possible, he didn't know, and he wondered if the dealership had a new car scent that they sprayed in the vehicles.

As he left the squalid Iowa town where he had been born and raised and merged onto the interstate, his thoughts went back to Alice, and he grinned in satisfaction. He had left town without telling her. The only way she would know he was gone was when he never came out of his room for the day. The thought gave him pleasure. Leaving without telling her was, in his opinion, the same as giving her the bird. She would be furious, or on second thought maybe she wouldn't care in the slightest. Maybe having the house to herself again was what she wanted.

He had walked down the hallway with two suitcases in hand and a duffel bag slung over his shoulder. He considered sticking his head in her room to tell her he was leaving. As his hand clasped around the doorknob, though, he shook his head.

He went to the kitchen with the intention of leaving a note beside her vintage glass ashtray—the only place where she'd never miss it, because heaven knew the hag would miss a meal before missing a cigarette. He tossed the pen and pad to the table with another shake of his head. "Let the hateful old biddy find out I'm gone when she finds out."

Once again, as he headed out into the world, the sorry state of his marriage hit him in the gut more powerfully than he wished to admit. What happened to us? It was a refrain that filtered through his mind more often than usual lately. Did he suddenly have stronger feelings of love toward her? Not really. If he had to attach a label to what he felt, nostalgia is the only word he could use to describe it.

***

<u>1971</u>

He sneaked into the bathroom to rinse his face and brush his teeth in the quiet of the early morning hours. He held his breath as he gently closed the door to keep from waking his queen. He frowned when it squeaked just before it latched closed. The squeak wasn't noticeable during the day but could wake the dead during the slumbering hours.

Time and again, he made a mental note to buy some oil to stop the pesky sound, but it never entered his mind again until the same time the next morning. His wife deserved to live in a home where the doors didn't squeak. Today would be the day he'd purchase what he needed to make the door fly open with nary a sound.

They didn't have money for such purchases. What little extra money they had left over after bills, which was usually embarrassingly little, he would rather spend on something nice to upgrade their pit of a house that had long ago seen better days.

As a bachelor, the sad little home had been plenty for him, but now that he was married, he wanted to give Alice more. Moving into a nicer home wasn't an option, so giving the place a few cosmetic touches was the best he could do.

He hated being poor. Alice deserved more than he could give her, and he often wondered why she had married a character like him. It wouldn't have taken her long to find someone better. Someone who could give her the life she deserved. Someone who could afford oil for the door hinges.

Though they had little money to spare, Alice had found a way to brighten the dreary room with a couple of pink ruffled towels that were there for décor purposes only, not for practical use. She had placed them on a towel rack next to the shower, atop the bland, beige-colored everyday towels.

His boss had allowed him to bring the pitiful remains of a can of yellow paint that would have been thrown away. It was only enough to paint two of the four walls in the bathroom, but he was surprised at how so little did so much.

He rinsed his toothbrush and placed it in the cup next to hers in the medicine cabinet.

He hated leaving her to go to a blasted job that he hated, where he got no respect. Where the boss treated him as a common low-paid laborer and nothing more.

Leaving a beautiful woman to spend all day with a bunch of smelly men who were stuck in the same dead-end job as he was depressing.

He slathered Powder Fresh Ultra Ban roll-on deodorant under his arms and forced his mind away from the drudgeries of work. There was no sense in dwelling on it sooner than necessary since he would be their slave from 8 to 4.

He pomaded his hair, combed in a hair part of precision, and looked at himself in the mirror. "Looking good, old boy." He winked at himself, flicked off the light, and moved to the kitchen for a bowl of Bran Flakes.

They had scrimped and saved their dollars for the past month, and last weekend they were able to purchase enough material for Alice to make curtains to hang in the kitchen window to replace the tacky and dilapidated window blinds that contained several broken slats.

"Honey, let's not buy material. Let's buy store bought curtains so you don't have to make them yourself," he had said as they approached the fabric area of the department store that was packed with bright bolts of fabric.

She moved to the farthest corner of the store, to an area of marked down clearance materials. "Why buy them when I can have the satisfaction of making them with my own two hands?"

He gave her a playful scowl. "Have you ever sewed anything, much less curtains?"

"They're curtains. It's hardly rocket science." She picked up a roll of blue floral chambray that was frayed at the edges.

To him, it looked faded and older than Methuselah.

She caressed the material between her fingers before placing it back on the shelf.

His gaze roved over the display of fabrics, none of which appealed to him.

She took down a bolt of fabric that had a blinding array of orange, white, and yellow flowers with green leaves. "This will brighten up the kitchen, don't you think?" She looked up at him with an expectant gaze.

"Well, if you're going for bright, I suppose that'll do it."

"You don't like it?"

"If you like it, I like it."

She shook her head. "I want you to be happy because you have to look at it every day, too."

He glanced over his shoulder at the full store. "If you insist on making them yourself, why don't we at least look at the newer patterns before we decide?" He loved her frugal nature, but it hurt his pride to think that their curtains would be made of everyone else's castaways.

"There's no need to pay full price when the clearance fabrics are just as good. They may not be as trendy as the newer stuff, but who cares about trends? Anything is better than that gross miniblind we have now." She ran her fingers over the fabric then plunked it in the shopping cart that Arnold pushed. "I'll put it in here as a potential."

Next, she picked up a pink and brown swirling pattern that was just as bold as the previous and held it up for his consideration.

"I like it," he nodded.

She dropped it in the cart then picked up fabric with brown, orange, and white interlocking circles.

"Please, dear Lord, no," he said before she had the chance to turn around and show it to him.

She giggled and placed it back on the shelf.

"Unless you like it?" he said, suddenly feeling bad for hating on something that she possibly liked. He would take burlap potato sacks hanging in the windows if it was what she really wanted.

"Is there anything here that catches your eye?" She picked up a roll of orange, green, and white flowers on a sky-blue background.

"Actually..." He rushed to a display an aisle over and picked up a bolt of white and pale blue sunflowers and gray pansies on a background of cornflower blue. "This is kind of nice, do you think?"

"It's gorgeous, but it's full price."

"Alice, my dear," he laughed. "We're not swimming in money, but we can afford to pay full price if we find something we really like. Even if we go a little over-budget, it won't kill us."

She shook her head and took down another bolt of fabric from the clearance section, this one a yellow cloth with dainty purple flowers. "This will work nicely with the walls, don't you think?"

At her determined expression, he placed the full-priced roll back on the shelf with a sigh. "Don't forget, we're painting the kitchen walls soon so get whatever you like." The fact that they both knew paint for the kitchen was several more months of saving down the road went unsaid.

"But aren't you supposed to paint the walls then coordinate with curtains?"

He leaned in and gave her a devious smile. "I say, let's go crazy and be rebels."

***

<u>Present Day</u>

If someone had told him that years down the road he would think of something as trivial as picking out kitchen curtains in the early seventies as the highlight of his romantic life, he would have called them a liar to their face.

His mind churned in rage at the chain of events that had led to the derailment of their lives. At Alice for living so far in the past that her life in the present is nothing but bitterness and hatred. At himself for not being a bigger man and keeping his family unit intact against all odds.

As the sun crept into the horizon and splashed shades of orange into the sky, he raised his eyes upward. "God, if You exist, tell me what to do to fix my marriage. I've wasted so much time being angry at her. I don't want us to die mad at each other. No matter how hard I try to be nice to her, she won't give an inch."

Even though there was no history to prove that his prayers would be answered, he prayed the words from sheer desperation.

Lutis sat in the passenger seat, keeping a watchful eye over his charge. "Keep praying. The Father hears you."

Amicus materialized in the space between the human and Lutis. "These humans. Why do some of them not understand the need to turn their hardened hearts to the Father before it's too late?"

"We're working on putting the right people in his life who can steer him in the right direction."

"He already has his Aunt Deborah, a precious child of the Father, who has spoken into his life. If he won't listen to her, to whom would he listen?"

"She's the obvious choice, but sometimes family is too close. Somewhere out there is someone who can speak the truth to him, and he'll hear and accept it."

A low rumble of laughter floated from behind them.

Amicus turned and looked deep into the shadows at Mondaci's beady and red-glowing eyes.

Chapter 24

Hyacinth unplugged the vacuum cleaner from the wall and wound the power cord around the hand grip.

The doorbell sounded through the house with a jarring peal.

She grimaced and glanced at the clock on the wall. "She's fifteen minutes early." She dropped the cord, swept her hands through her hair, and headed for the foyer.

When the door swung open, Janie stood on the porch wringing her hands.

Hyacinth gave her a bright smile and gestured her inside. "How's it going, sweetie?" She closed the door and led her visitor into the living room where the vacuum cleaner still stood in the center of the room.

"Sorry, I'm a little early," Janie said.

Hyacinth waved away the apology. "Don't be silly. I'm glad to visit with you for a while. How sad is it that we go to the same church every Sunday, yet we rarely do more than wave at each other from across the sanctuary?" She tugged on the vacuum to pull it to the storage closet then stopped when Janie burst into tears.

She pushed the vacuum aside, rushed to the stricken woman, and grabbed her in a tight hug. Janie had a harsh edge to her personality, so the unexpected show of emotion took Hyacinth by surprise. "Oh, honey, it's okay. What's going on?"

Janie settled into the hug for several seconds before pulling away and wiping her tears with the sleeve of her blouse. "Jeez, how embarrassing. I'm so sorry."

Hyacinth gestured toward the kitchen. "At times like this, I find that oatmeal scotchies and Diet Coke are just what the doctor ordered. What do you say?"

"Perfect." Janie chuckled and stood to her feet. As she slid into a kitchen chair, she glanced around the room. "Your house is beautiful. I've never been here."

"It's home sweet home." Hyacinth dropped a platter of cookies and two tall glasses of ice on the table. "Dig in while I grab a couple of Diet Cokes from the fridge." She scowled and looked over her shoulder. "I don't mean to insinuate that you need a Diet Coke, but I can boil water to make iced tea if you prefer that."

"Girl, these hips need all the help they can get. Diet Coke is fine." She snatched a cookie from the platter and closed her eyes as she chewed. "I've never had an oatmeal scotchie. They're fabulous."

"I'm not the best baker, but cookies are my specialty. Unfortunately, as you can see by my hips, I've never met a cookie I didn't like." She sat at the table across from Janie and looked her in the eyes. "So, how's life been for you lately?"

"Oh, you know." Janie shrugged as though suddenly deep in thought. "If I could hurry and get done with school, life might be fun once again. Full-time school and part-time work are, as my grandma used to say, for the birds."

"Are you almost done with school?"

"God willing, two more semesters and I'm done."

"Remind me what your degree is? Business Administration, right?"

Janie nodded. "For years I wanted to be a nurse like my mom, but by the time college rolled around I realized I didn't like people well enough to be a nurse. Then I wanted to be a veterinarian for a short time, but I learned that I like most animals as well as I like most people. At least with a business degree I can hopefully hide away in an office somewhere and stay away from everyone."

"Yeah," Hyacinth giggled. "Nursing takes a special kind of person, and you kind of need to like people."

"I know it's horrible to say, but I really don't like people."

"I don't know. There's always one of those people in every crowd, but I think most people aren't so bad."

"Yeah, I suppose." Janie rubbed her hands over the dessert plate then stood and went to the kitchen island to pick up a picture of Jenner and Hyacinth. "How're you doing, you know, with everything?"

"I have good days and bad days, but the Lord has helped me through it."

Janie placed the picture back on the island. "I'm such a … a freaking witch," she exclaimed without turning around.

"What? Girl, what are you talking about?"

Janie whirled around to reveal tears that rolled down her cheeks. "I was horrible to Jenner before he … before he …." She sniffled and yanked a paper towel from the dispenser and wiped it under her nose.

Hyacinth gave her a compassionate look. "You and Jenner had your issues, but there's no need in—"

"No," Janie shook her head. "I was horrible to him, and he didn't deserve that. He was a great guy."

Roga circled around her and stared with hardened eyes. "You were justified in treating him the way you did. Stop worrying about the dead."

Hyacinth patted the table. "Sweetie, come sit down."

Janie dropped back into her seat and stared at the platter of cookies that no longer looked appealing.

Roga paced back and forth behind the table.

"What happened in the past is done. Don't give guilt or any other negative emotions a place in your life."

"I've heard the saying a million times, to love the people around you because you never know if they'll be gone tomorrow," Janie sighed. "I always thought it was a stupid saying to emotionally manipulate people, but now I know better. Other than grandparents and other old people, I've never personally known anyone who died. Now that Jenner's gone, it hits home a little harder. It's not just a saying, it's true."

And other old people? Hyacinth fought to suppress a smile. Spoken like a true young adult who has barely lived long enough to witness the real atrocities of life, like death. It wasn't lost on her that Janie wasn't much younger than she, so why did she seem so much younger? "I guess the saying is a little cliché, but I think it's still a perfect attitude for life. None of us are promised tomorrow, so why not treat everyone you encounter as though you know it?"

Janie released another deep sigh. "Yeah, well, too little, too late, huh?"

"What happened that you disliked him so much?" She shook her head. "You don't have to answer if you don't want. I'm just curious."

Janie thrummed her fingers on the tabletop. "It's hard to say because he never actually did anything to me. I just didn't like him. He thought too highly of himself because he had his own group and was a travelling worship leader."

The statement startled her because Hyacinth saw him as one of the humblest people she'd ever met. She would never say so though, because she didn't want to diminish Janie's feelings on the matter. Right or wrong, people were allowed to feel what they felt.

"I guess you knew he and I dated for a few weeks back in the day before you two were married, and he made the comment once that he hated that some broad at our denominational Singing Nationals competition beat him in the solo category. According to him, he was way better than she was, and not only that, but he was also more anointed, too." Janie shook her head. "I mean, come on, what a lame thing for someone to say. Then one time he announced to the youth group that he couldn't talk to anyone prior to singing a church special because apparently talking to people would shatter his so-called holy anointing." She slapped her hand on the table for emphasis. "Sorry, but if your anointing can be disrupted that easily then perhaps you were never anointed in the first place."

Roga pointed at Janie and laughed. "And he called himself a Christian? He deserves for you to hate him."

"That's a pretty pretentious thing for someone to say," Hyacinth agreed. "Don't you think people deserve grace for things they said and did when they were young and stupid?"

The comment made Janie crack a smile. "I'm sorry. I shouldn't say things like that since Jenner's gone."

"I disagree. Let's talk and get it out into the open. I'm not Jenner, obviously, but maybe talking about it will help you let it go."

"How petty am I? Still thinking and getting angry about things that happened years ago when we were still teenagers in high school. If I saw anyone else acting this stupid, I'd kick their butt and tell them to get over themselves."

Hyacinth reached across the table and grasped Janie's hands. "Jenner was hurt by your often abrasive behavior, but he would be the first person to not only forgive you but also he'd tell you to forgive yourself."

"Are you crazy!" Roga bent down and snarled into Janie's ear. "You're supposed to forgive him?" He glared at Hyacinth then returned his attention to Janie. "What a goody two-shoes"

"Yeah, forgive him," Janie scoffed. "Because that's so easy to do."

"Forgiveness is rarely easy because we're flesh and blood human beings, and forgiveness isn't in our nature, but as Christians it's what we're called to do. The Bible is clear on that. If we don't forgive others of their sins, then God won't forgive us of ours."

"What happens when we don't want to forgive?"

"When that happens, it's our flesh talking. That's why Galatians tells us that those who belong to Christ must crucify the flesh and walk instead in the Spirit."

"What does that even mean?" Janie snapped. "Crucify the flesh and walk in the Spirit? It makes no sense."

Lord, speak Your words through me so this soul can hear You and Your truth. "When we talk about the flesh, that means our physical flesh and blood bodies and anything that is hostile to God or things in our life that don't submit to the truths that we're taught in God's Word. Struggling with the flesh is something that every Christian will deal with until we're complete in righteousness. In other words, when we die. As we grow in Christ, our spirits become more attuned to God and the truths written in His word."

"I love the Lord, but that sounds like a bunch of religious malarky," Janie said.

"It's truth straight from God's word."

Janie looked across the room and suddenly wished that she hadn't come here. She wanted absolution, not a sermon.

"Sinners have no problem doing things like lying, cheating, or submitting to offense. When He saves us from our sins, we become a new creature in Christ. As we grow in Christ, the Holy Spirit takes root in our lives, and we become more sensitive about things like lying, cheating, and being offended and causing offense. When the Holy Spirit convicts us, even though we still may not want to crucify the flesh, that's when we must walk in the Spirit and do it anyway."

Janie stood and glanced down at Hyacinth with a weak smile. "Thanks for letting me stop by and for talking to me. I acted like a total hag to Jenner every time I saw him. Everyone knows it. I can't apologize to him, but I can at least tell you that at the heart of it, I—" Her voice crackled with emotion, and she wanted to crawl away and hide in embarrassment. She cleared her throat and tried again. "I know it makes no sense after the way I treated him, but I really did love him, and I apologize for the way I treated him."

Roga kicked in her direction. "You love him, huh? You treated him worse than most people would treat a mangy dog. You're a pathetic excuse for a human. How dare you even think of asking for forgiveness. You're weak!"

Hyacinth stood and placed a hand on Janie's arm. "Thank you for telling me that. It means a lot to me. It would mean a lot to Jenner too, so promise me you won't let guilt of the past eat away at you. If you give the enemy a foothold in your soul, he'll take it and even more. If the Holy Spirit has convicted you of something, repent of it, stop doing it, then move on. That's how we gain victory over that liar called the devil."

"Liar?" Roga went to Hyacinth, wrapped his spindly fingers around her throat, and looked her in the eyes. "I'd kill you right this instant if I could."

Nitasah stepped behind the demon. "She's ours. You don't have authority to touch even a hair on her head."

Roga spun around and waved a finger in Nitasah's face. "We'll see about that."

"What if I know I need to forgive but don't want to?" Janie asked.

The pain and searching in the woman's eyes brought a tender ache to Hyacinth's heart. She knew what she needed to say but hesitated to do so.

"Tell them the truth even when they don't want to hear it. Plant the seed of truth in her hardened heart," said Nitasah.

She steeled herself and plowed forward with all the gentleness she could muster. What good are Christians who don't have the boldness to tell the simple truth? "If a person truly doesn't want to forgive, especially one who claims to be a Christian, then I'd say that person needs to examine their heart because they're probably not of the faith."

"Whatever." Janie gave Hyacinth a quick hug then made her way to the front door. "Maybe we'll see each other at church soon." She flung the door open and stepped onto the porch.

"I love you, sweetie. I'm always here if you want to talk," she called out, but Janie was already halfway across the yard.

She stood on the porch and watched as the woman backed out and sped away without as much of a glance. "Lord, I spoke Your truth into her life. I pray that You'll soften her heart so she can receive. Help me to be Your hands and feet, and to take every opportunity to direct the lost to You."

Chapter 25

After two days of driving to nowhere, Arnold found himself in a small town nearly an hour outside of North Carolina. He clutched his coffee cup and stared out the window, lost in thought, at the cars that zipped past the hole-in-the-wall restaurant that buzzed with customers.

"Can I get you anything else, doll?"

He looked up at the waitress who had blazing red, wild hair. He couldn't tell if it was a bad hair day or a trendy style. "I suppose I shouldn't, but how about a second piece of that pecan pie?"

"We only live once. That's what I always say," she cackled. "How about a fresh cup of coffee to go with it?"

"Sure, thanks."

Behind the counter, she plopped another piece of pie on a plate and brought it to him then topped off his coffee. "Anything else, sugar?"

He shook his head then changed his mind when she turned to leave. "Excuse me, Miss?"

She trounced back to the table with an amicable smile.

"You look like a youngster who knows the ways of the world."

"My word, I ain't been called a youngster in years, but I guess if you consider a washed up and haggard forty-one-year-old as young, then, honey, I'll take it."

"If I wanted to find someone, how would I go about doing it?"

She squinted her eyes and gave him an appraising look before answering. "I guess it depends on who you want to find and why. If you're looking for a hitman or a pretty little thing who charges by the hour to help the night pass a little faster, then I'm afraid I can't help you."

The sparkle in her eyes told him she was teasing, so he gave her a little sass in return. "There ain't no pretty little things out there who would take my money even if I was paying."

"Oh." She waved the comment away with a giggle. "Who do you need to find? You can find just about anyone on the internet these days. It's a little scary if you ask me."

"I don't know," he said, suddenly wishing he hadn't brought it up. "I was in the hospital several months ago. How would I contact them?"

"Oh, honey, that's easy. Just Google the hospital and give them a ring."

"I don't have a Google and don't plan to buy one," he snipped because that's what crochety men do.

"It's a search engine," she corrected in a playful tone. "You don't have to buy it. You use it to look up information you want to know." She whipped her cell phone from her apron when it became clear he wasn't a techy sort of person. "What's the name of the hospital?"

"I don't remember exactly, but it was in North Carolina and had an angel in the title."

He leaned in and watched as her thumbs flew over the screen of her phone. After a few seconds, she looked up with a triumphant grin. "Angel Medical Center in Franklin?"

It astounded him that finding something could be that simple. It would be impressive if he didn't hate modern technology. "Maybe. That sounds about right."

"Florence! Get your tail over here and pick up your order before it starts growing cobwebs," a man behind the counter bellowed.

"Put a lid on it, you old grouch," she bellowed back.

She glanced up at Arnold, cracked a grin, and pulled an order pad from her apron then ripped out a page, scrawled a number, and slid it across the table. "Here's the number. At a quick glance, it's the only hospital with the word angel in the name, but I'm at work and don't have time to spend a lot of time searching."

He picked it up and stuffed it into his shirt pocket. "Thank you for helping a clueless old man."

"My pleasure, honey. Anything else you need?"

"Florence, I'm not telling you again. Your order."

She whipped her head around. "I heard you, and I said to keep your pants on. I'll be right there."

"I don't need anything." He gestured toward the counter. "Go get your order. You don't want to lose your job for helping an old geezer like me."

"Honey we've been married for sixteen years. If he fires me, guess who'll come home to his clothes scattered all over the county?"

***

Back in the rig, he dug his cell phone from his duffel bag and punched in the phone number the waitress had given him. "Yeah. I was in the hospital there a few months ago. I wondered if you could tell me how to get into contact with someone."

"I'll see if I can help," answered the friendly voice on the other end.

"I don't know exactly who I'm looking for."

The conversation fell silent for several seconds. "Sir, if you don't know who you're looking for, I'm not sure how I can help."

"All I know is the person's first name is Jenner."

"I need more than a first name, sir."

He'd been on the phone for less than thirty seconds and the conversation was already going nowhere fast. "See, that's the problem. I don't have a last name to give you."

"I don't know any doctors with the name Jenner. Is it a staff member?"

"It was another patient. He ... he died." The words left him feeling hollow. *I killed someone. I didn't mean to, but I killed someone.*

Fraush sat in the passenger seat and watched the interaction with interest and wondered what the human was up to.

"I'm sorry, but I can't give information on patients, sir. That would be a HIPAA violation."

"I won't tell anyone if you won't," he said with a hopeful tone.

The voice at the end of the line released a chuckle of amusement. "Even if I were willing to break the law to give personal information on another patient, which I'm not, I still couldn't do it without a full name."

"Maybe you're not the one I need to speak with, but if I could give my patient information to someone there, could they look it up and see who was involved with the same accident as me?"

"Someone here might be able to find them that way with a little sleuthing, yes, but HIPAA laws still won't allow anyone to give you such information. I'm sorry."

Arnold swiped his hand over his face in frustration. The woman was just doing her job, but everyone bends the rules at some point or another, so why couldn't she be helpful this once? He blew out a quiet breath to calm himself. Lashing out would result in nothing but a dial tone at the other end of the call. "I understand you have rules to follow, ma'am. If I give you my information could someone there at least see if you could find out who the other person was? Maybe I can give you my phone number and you could ask someone in this Jenner person's family to call me? It's not a common name so surely he can't be that hard to find."

Yeah, right, he mocked himself for suggesting it. I was responsible for making someone a widow. Why would she call me back? Probably she wouldn't, but he had to try.

"I'm just the switchboard operator. I'll transfer you to someone who could tell you if it's possible."

Half an hour after explaining his medical visit months prior to a higher up in the facility, he hung up the phone with a smidge more hope amid promises from the hospital to contact the victim's wife and pass along his contact information.

"No guarantees you'll get a callback," the executive had said, "but we'll do our best to pass on your information."

It was far from a perfect scenario, but it was better than nothing. He gripped the steering wheel with his hands and clenched his eyes shut. "God, I know I'm coming at You with a lot of stuff lately, but I need Your help even though I'm a worthless son of a—" His eyes popped open, and he cringed. "I guess I shouldn't be saying those kinds of words while I'm praying to You, but Aunt Deborah says You know what's in our hearts even before we speak it, which means I'm caught anyway."

Fraush growled so loudly that it would have frightened any human who had the ability to hear it. "Stop praying to a powerless fairytale who doesn't exist. You're alone in this world, and there's no help for you." God existed. Of course, He existed, but oh, how easily the lie rolled from his tongue. His lies were made easier by humans who were weak and susceptible to deception.

Arnold squeezed his eyes closed again. "The person I killed, God? I need to talk to his wife and ask her forgiveness. Please, if You're there and hear me at all, please make her want to talk to me. A couple of minutes is all I need."

"God ... Doesn't ... Exist ... You louse!" Fraush stomped his feet against the floorboard as he launched a stream of profanities. "You're a hopeless murderer. Deal with it."

Arnold opened his eyes and dropped his hands into his lap. "I'm a murderer. Why would God listen to me, much less answer my prayers?" His eyes flooded with tears that he didn't bother to wipe away. "I'm alone in this world, and I'll die a murderer that no one, not a single person, not even my wife, cares about."

Fraush leaned back in the seat and coughed out a maniacal laugh. "That's right. You're a loser."

Lutis leaned between the seats and placed a hand on the human's shoulder. He couldn't stand watching his charges struggling under the weight of such delusion. "Aunt Deborah loves you, and whether she knows it or not, Alice loves you too. Don't listen to the lies of your enemy. God does exist, and He loves you so much more than any human ever could. Learn to trust in Him and believe."

Tears streamed down his cheeks and soaked into his shirt. "I'm a murderer. I may as well take vengeance on myself and take my own pathetic life." An eye for an eye, a life for a life. It was only fair.

Fraush's deafening laughter filled the cab of the truck. "Yes. Kill yourself and do everyone a favor."

"Do not take vengeance on yourself. It is the Lord's to avenge," Lutis shouted amid the rowdy laughter.

"Shut up, Lutis. He's not even a believer. He belongs to us, not you," Fraush said.

The ting of metal against metal proliferated the heavenly realm as Lutis unsheathed his sword. "Say another word and see what happens, demon."

Fraush chuckled. "You really think you have authority over me? Fine, then, do as you will."

Lutis pressed the cold steel into his neck before releasing it and re-sheathing it.

Fraush's body shook with unrestrained taunting laughter. "Yes, that's what I thought." He pivoted and looked Lutis in the eyes. "That human is ours and always will be."

Arnold tossed his head back and spewed a haunting cry of pain from a deeper place than he had ever known existed. His body spasmed as he wept bitter tears.

"The Father always hears you, child, even in your most hidden pain. Call out to Him, and He will answer you."

Chapter 26

A lice stubbed a cigarette into the overflowing ashtray then lit another.

It dangled between her lips as she dumped the butts into the trash can, rinsed it, and placed it back on the table, ready for tomorrow's card games.

She glanced at the clock beside the door that led to the back porch. It was a few minutes short of midnight.

It didn't dawn on her until she passed Arnold's door that she hadn't seen him a single time today. She walked past to her own room then went back and knocked on the door. "You in there? I haven't seen hide or hair of you today. If you're dead, I ain't sleeping under the same roof as a corpse all night."

When he didn't answer, she thumped the door with her foot. "You in there? Answer me."

She pushed open the door to an empty room and crudely made bed. "Arnold?"

Confused by his absence, she checked every room in the house, even her own. She rambled a slew of profanities. "Where in tarnation are you?" She growled as she made her way to the rotary phone. "Pauline, Arnold ain't over there with Earl, is he?"

She listened and pursed her lips. "He's not? Well, I don't know where he is then."

She nodded when Pauline set the phone down to talk to her husb and."Earl said what?" She gritted her teeth as she listened.

"Okay, thanks." She slammed the phone onto the cradle and muttered another round of obscenities as she flipped through her address book and dialed.

When Arnold answered, the familiar hum of the diesel engine confirmed Earl's story. "You left town without even botherin' to tell me?" She pelted him with more filthy words.

"Woman, if you called to be vulgar, I'll hang up on you. Don't think I won't."

"It's common courtesy to tell your wife when you leave town." Her words were laced with the acidity of unadulterated hate.

"Yeah? Well, it's common courtesy to not tell your husband you wish he had died." Arnold said with matched venom.

Her vision swam with fury. "Are you coming home soon?"

"Maybe I will, maybe I won't."

She gripped the phone and shook it in front of her then slammed it back onto the cradle. "Good riddance," she screamed into the empty house.

Minutes ago, she was ready to drop into bed but now her blood pumped through her body with such wrath that sleep wouldn't come for hours.

She went to the living room, kicked one of Arnold's shoes across the floor, and crashed into the recliner that she rarely used.

Outside the window, the moonlight spilled to the Earth, washing the landscape in a silvery haze. Her loony neighbor from two houses down walked past with her Great Dane.

***

<u>1971</u>

It was nearly midnight and Arnold rocked back and forth in a squeaky rocking chair. It surprised him when a neighbor walked past with a rat-sized dog on a leash.

"Hey, Arnold." The woman waved at him as she passed.

"What're you doing out so late by yourself, Susan?"

She pointed at the dog who started yapping the minute Arnold made his presence known. "This little demon rules the roost. When he wants out, he goes out."

"Don't get too far from the neighborhood. There's a lot of crazy people in the world."

"Tell Alice hi," she called over her shoulder as she disappeared into the shadows between streetlights.

The screen door screeched open behind him then slapped closed.

Alice wrapped her hands around his neck from behind. "I don't like you working so many hours and getting home so late."

He craned his neck and pressed a kiss to her warm lips. "It's only for a few weeks, and we could use the extra money."

She ruffled his hair with her fingers then sat in the rocker beside him. "I don't like that you work yourself so hard. We don't need the money that much."

Her face was half hidden in the shadows, but she was still the most beautiful woman he'd ever lain eyes on. He laced his fingers through hers and they lapsed into an easy silence.

Pinpricks of light sparkled on an inky sky while cool breezes whispered through the trees.

When a forlorn train whistle from the distant tracks echoed through the night, Arnold broke the silence. "Cooler weather should be here within the next few weeks."

"Mm," Alice responded.

"Our first Christmas is coming up."

She rolled her head to the side and looked at him with a sleepy smile. "We were together last Christmas, silly."

He gripped her hand a little tighter. "Yeah, but last Christmas you weren't my wife."

She dropped his hand, cleared her throat, leaned up to the edge of the seat, and fixed her eyes on his. His hair fluttered in the breeze, and her heart fluttered in her chest. She had never loved a man as much as she loved this one sitting beside her.

"What?" he asked with an amused smirk.

She glanced down at a leaf that skittered across the porch and fell down the edge to the ground. "I have news," she whispered.

"Was that scoundrel Nixon impeached? Because I'd sure hate to hear that," he chuckled.

"Mom and I went to the doctor today."

His heart ratcheted up a few paces and he moved closer to her. "Is Marilyn okay?"

She nodded. "Mom's fine."

He leaned back in the seat with relief. "Thank the Lord. Cold and flu season is making the rounds. People her age need to be careful."

"People her age?" Alice laughed. "She'd be thrilled to hear that."

A blush warmed his cheeks. "I didn't mean—"

She slid out of her seat and kneeled in front of him. "I'm pregnant. You're going to be a daddy."

His breath caught in his throat as the words penetrated his consciousness. His face brightened with a grin. "Preg ... you're having a baby?"

She pressed her hands to his face. "*We're* having a baby."

Tears of joy flooded his eyes. "A baby," he whispered.

She nodded.

"Is it a boy?" he asked in a hopeful tone.

"It's way too early to tell."

He pushed out of his chair and stood to his feet, covered his mouth with his hands, raised his fists in the air, and screamed his loudest whoop.

She rushed to her feet with a laugh and pressed her fingers to his lips. "Sshh. It's late. You'll wake the entire neighborhood."

He swept her off her feet, carried her into the yard, and spun her in circles. "I don't know how we'll feed and clothe it, but this is the best night ever."

***

<u>Present Day</u>

A chill made its way up her spine.

She stepped out of the cold house and into the tepid night. A songbird warbled a sad song while an ambulance siren blared across town. She was completely alone, in every sense of the word.

She had worked so hard to bury the past. The daydream brought with it a heavy cloak of melancholy.

As newlyweds, they had barely scraped by financially, yet they had been happier than they'd ever been. They had each other, and that was all they needed.

A baby on the way? They couldn't afford to bring another human being into their happy circle, yet somehow it brought the greatest joy they had ever felt.

She gazed up at the sky and shuddered as a coyote wailed into the night. "It was a lie. Every bit of it was a lie. We weren't happy. We were ignorant and naïve."

Ahava, glowing with a soft light, approached her from behind. "It wasn't a lie. You and Arnold were happy, and you can have that happiness again. You don't have to spend the rest of your life estranged from each other."

Alice bristled at the sound of music so light she wasn't sure she heard it. She moved to the end of the porch toward the sound.

Their widowed next-door neighbor, whom they rarely spoke to because they had nothing in common with such a religious person, sat on the porch listening to a small radio.

Alice listened for several minutes, but the wind only carried snippets of the music her way. She was about to head back to her chair when the woman stood to her feet and raised her hands into the air.

Taken aback by the strange behavior, Alice lingered a little longer to observe.

The woman's crackling and aged voice rose to the heavens. "A wonderful Savior is Jesus my Lord, He taketh my burdens away."

"That woman's outside late at night singing out loud to no one? She's crazier than I am." The last thing she wanted to hear was a Jesus song, yet her feet wouldn't move her away from the scene.

"He holdeth me up, and I shall not be moved, He giveth me strength as my day." She waved her hands in the air and turned her face to the sky. "Father God, I pray for my neighbors tonight. May they slumber under the peace of Your almighty hand of protection. Provide for their every need, and if anyone doesn't know You, bring them into my path so I may show them the way."

"Psh," Alice scoffed. "Crazy loon needs to be locked up in an institution."

As soon as she finished her prayer, the woman broke back into singing. "He hideth my soul in the cleft of the rock that shadows a dry, thirsty land. He covers my life in the depths of His love and covers me there with His hand."

Alice flipped her the bird. "Here's a hand for you, you old biddy."

She whirled around, reentered the house, and slammed the door behind her.

Chapter 27

"I'm such a witch." Janie's leg bounced like a livewire under the table. She picked up her Styrofoam cup and slurped down several gulps of her carrot and green apple fresh pressed juice. A hint of ginger gave the drink the perfect amount of spicy bite.

"Is that a moment of self-revelation or are you seeking confirmation?" Nancy giggled.

Janie gave her a sarcastic scowl, flipped her the bird, then lapsed into a flimsy grin.

"You know I hate it when you make that vulgar hand sign," Nancy reprimanded. "How many times do I need to have this conversation with you? For Christians, cursing with your hands is just as bad as cursing with your words."

Janie raised both hands and repeated the gesture.

Nancy picked up her drink then slammed it back down. "Honestly, I don't know why I even bother with you. You'll never change, will you?"

"What?" Janie asked with a breezy expression. "Oh, don't be a goody-two-shoes. You know I was just kidding."

Felicia gave her a good-natured pat on the back. "Do you not know what the Bible says about such things? 'Lay aside all filthiness and naughtiness, and receive with meekness the engrafted word, which is able to save your souls.'"

Janie hugged her close with a playful grimace and stared across the table at Nancy. "How'd we get so lucky to inherit such a puritan into our little group?"

"Honey, I'm only a puritan compared to you." Felicia pushed her away with a chuckle. "You know you love me though."

"You won't go away, so I might as well love you."

Given Janie's intense dislike of her just a few short months ago, the words caused a warmth to rush through Felicia's body. Though they were far from best friends, Janie at least made a pretense of being genial. "Why are you a witch? What'd you do this time?"

"I went to Hyacinth's house yesterday."

Nancy's eyebrows raised. "Really?"

"Don't act so shocked," she snipped. "I've always liked Hyacinth."

"How did it go?"

"I was afraid she wouldn't want to talk to me, but she acted like I was her long-lost best friend."

"Hyacinth is nice to everyone. She's a salt of the Earth kind of gal. She would never turn anyone away," Nancy said.

She didn't know why, but the words irritated her. "Unlike meanie little me, you mean?"

Nancy shrugged. "That's not what I meant at all, but you said it, honey."

Janie raised her hand, but instead of extending her middle finger like she wanted, she clenched it into a fist and dropped it to her lap.

Felicia nudged Janie's thigh with her own. "Way to go, girlfriend." She glanced at Nancy with a mischievous grin. "Look at her, resisting the devil one middle finger at a time."

"It's just a finger. I don't see the problem with it."

"It's the nonverbal equivalent of a four-letter word that even sinners shouldn't say, much less Christians. If you don't see the problem with that gesture, you might pray and ask the Holy Spirit to reveal it to you." The words could start a squabble of epic proportions since Janie didn't like anyone pointing out her less than exemplary Christ-like behavior, so she kept her words soft.

Janie sighed and fixed her with a harsh stare. "I know it's a bad gesture, and a habit I need to work on kicking. I'm not stupid. I just wish people would stop ticking me off every time I turn around."

"Be not quick to become angry, for anger lodges in the hearts of fools." Felicia held up her hands in surrender. "Try a little harder not to take people's bait. That's all I'm saying."

"I don't know if that's from last night's fortune cookie or from the Bible but stop quoting stuff at me all the time. It's annoying, not to mention pretentious, if I'm being honest."

Felicia fluttered her eyelids in innocence. "When we quote scriptures, we're not being annoying. We're holding each other accountable and helping to refine each other into better believers. We're iron sharpening iron, if you will."

Iron sharpening iron. She had no idea what that meant but presumed it was another obscure Bible quote. "Just so you know, you're baiting me now." Though she could easily erupt, she gave Felicia's cheek a playful pinch and smiled. "How about we nip that in the bud before my patience runs out."

Nancy jumped in to steer the conversation to safer territory. "Fine, truce. Let's change the subject back to Hyacinth. What did you girls talk about?" After all the drama between Janie and Felicia, it was nice to see Janie at least attempting to be a more decent person.

"I've been thinking about Jenner a lot since he died. I feel guilty for always treating him so badly. I know I'm probably the last person he thought of when it happened, but I can't help wondering, what if in his last few moments something mean I said flashed through his mind? I'd hate to think that in his final moments, me being a witch was something he relived." She turned her attention to a baby that screamed across the fancy juice bar. She took another sip of her juice. "Not gonna lie. Next time I'd rather have a chocolate malt than this overpriced fresh pressed stuff."

"I don't know how it works, but I hope the Holy Spirit only lets us remember the good times in our last moments. Either way, Jenner is a forgiving guy."

"Yes, I know," Janie snapped. "Jenner was perfect and saintly and ... blah, blah, blah. I swear, just one time I'd like to hear you people talk less about how perfect he was and more about how he liked to kick puppies."

Jenner would never kick anyone, and especially not a puppy, but Nancy wanted to sidestep that landmine of a conversation. "I hate that I haven't tried to check on Hyacinth since the funeral. How is she?"

"She seems fine. I hadn't been there ten minutes before she started preaching at me about forgiveness and walking in the Spirit." She shook her head. "I swear, hanging out with all you people is like being in church every minute of the waking hours."

"Did you at least feel better by the time you left?"

"No, I don't feel better. Have you not been listening to me? I feel horrible for the way I treated him."

"Sweetie, don't let yourself get bogged down with guilt," Felicia said. "Guilt never helps."

Moisture popped into her eyes before she could stop it. She dobbed a wad of napkins to her eyes and tried to pull herself together. She hated showing emotion in front of anyone, especially her friends. She was a hard-nosed personality and that's what people expected out of her. She looked up, first into Nancy's eyes then into Felicia's. "How am I supposed to ask a dead person to forgive me? Am I supposed to feel this guilt for the rest of my life? I'm such a witch."

Felicia grasped her friend's hand even though she knew she would probably hate it. "The Bible does teach that if we've offended someone, we are to go to them and ask for forgiveness, but that's not always possible for any number of reasons. I think talking to Hyacinth was probably a good step in the right direction, but ultimately you can repent to God and ask His forgiveness. If you can walk in His forgiveness then learn to forgive yourself, I think you'll find that the guilt will lessen with time."

Janie rumpled up her napkins, tossed them to the table, and stood to her feet. "I've had enough of these healthy juices. Anyone want to go to the ice cream shop and blow their diet with me?"

"Girl, I thought you'd never ask." Felicia jumped up and tossed glasses and napkins onto the plastic tray.

Outside, next to the car, Janie pulled both women into an unexpected tight hug. "I love you two broads. I don't do mushy, feely, but thanks for putting up with me and my cranky ways."

Chapter 28

Light from the images on the television screen flickered on the walls of the rig's sleeper unit.

It was almost midnight, and he was bone tired, yet sleep continued to elude him, a problem he rarely had. He moved past one channel after another in search of something that would help to dull his mind into sleep.

Despite how much the truck salesman had tried to explain it, he still didn't understand how the marvels of satellite television worked. What he did understand, though, was that it would probably cost him an arm and a leg. His plan was to discontinue it after the trial period ended, but now that he had at least fifty channels to occupy his time late at night, he reconsidered. It might be worth every penny.

He stopped on an episode of *Charlie's Angels*. Back in the day, it had been his and Alice's favorite television show, and it brought with it memories of them squeezing onto the couch and cuddling together as they watched every weekly episode. Thanks to the wondrous technology of satellite television, he could binge one episode after the other.

Halfway through an episode, he picked up his phone, scrolled through the contact list, and stopped at Alice's name. They hadn't spoken in days and though part of him felt justified in prolonging the marital estrangement, the other part, for a reason he couldn't imagine, wanted to hear her voice.

For several seconds his thumb lingered over the call button, but he tossed the phone across the bed instead. It tumbled across the mattress and came to rest a couple of inches from the wall. "I'll be jiggered if I'll call on a hateful old hag who doesn't even want to hear from me."

He flicked off the television and turned on the radio. Maybe a little music would usher him into dreamland. He rolled past several music channels and paused at the cathartic voice of a man whose vocal cadence was oddly comforting.

"Welcome to Worship Radio, where—"

"Ah," he groaned aloud. "You can't go five channels without being lambasted by a religious zealot."

"Tonight, I'm reading uplifting Christian fiction stories set to beautiful musical scores. It is sure to uplift your spirit. As I read, allow yourself to drift into a perfect place of peace," the man encouraged. "You can log onto our website anytime to listen to the story in its entirety if sleep overtakes you."

Irritated, yet intrigued, he set the remote aside and nestled into his pillow as the opening strains of a musical interlude filled the truck.

***

1971

Arnold gripped the steering wheel as they sat in the parking lot.

"What's wrong?" Alice looked over at him and tried not to break into laughter. "You look like you're about to march before a firing squad."

"We're about to go into a church. It might as well be a firing squad."

"I used to go to church when I was younger. I enjoyed it from what I remember." She rubbed her hands over her tummy with a dreamy smile. "Wouldn't it be wonderful to go to church as a family and to raise our child with a religious belief that they can carry through their entire life?"

He pasted on a tense smile. "Sure, if that's what you want."

She glanced over at the small white clapboard church with the tall steeple and stained-glass windows. It looked like the image of every cozy church she had ever seen. "No, sweetie, it can't be what I want. It needs to be what we want."

Stay home on Sundays and sleep late. That's what he wanted, but he would not voice such an opinion for fear of squelching her enthusiasm, even on something as useless as church attendance.

He reached over and placed his hand on her stomach. "Let's get in there and raise this tyke in the fear and admonition of the Lord."

Pebbles on the gravel parking lot crunched under their feet as they strolled hand in hand toward the rural Baptist church.

Yellow daisies that lined the building's foundation waved in the breeze, and the scent of recently cut grass hung in the air.

They paused at the door before entering. Arnold cut his eyes over at Alice. "It's not too late to catch brunch over at the diner."

"We don't need to spend money on brunch. Besides, I've got a roast in the oven back at home. That'll be way better than some greasy spoon." She squeezed his hand. "The hardest part of going to a church for the first time is finding the courage to walk in. Once we're seated, it'll be fine. You'll see."

It was the last thing he wanted to do, but he pushed open the door and stepped inside. Before he could close it, a woman rushed in their direction and thrust a bulletin of announcements at Alice. "It's wonderful to have you."

She looked each of them in the eye followed by vigorous hand-shakes. "This is your first time to join us." It was a statement, not a question.

"Yes," Alice said.

"I'm so happy that you chose to worship with us." The woman laced her arm through Alice's and led them through the small foyer and into a modest sanctuary where a coiffed woman played the organ. "Reverend Hallford looks like a linebacker, but he's as soft as a kitten."

When the woman paused to hug another woman, Arnold leaned in and whispered into Alice's ear, "It sounds like a dadburn funeral in here with that organ."

"If you're not here to meet anyone, I would love it if you two would sit with me during worship." Their friendly host looked at them with expectant eyes.

"We don't know anyone here and would be delighted to sit with you," Alice nodded. "Thank you for being so kind and thoughtful."

"It's my pleasure. Why, that's what we do in the house of the Lord." She led them to the fifth row on the piano side and gestured them in. "I'll be at the door to greet people for the first ten minutes of the service then I'll come join you."

As they sat, nearly every person in the building approached them with effusive greetings, including hugs, which Arnold could have done without.

When a toddler boy streaked past their pew chasing after a screech-ing girl, Alice squealed and clutched her stomach. "Aren't they precious? One of these days that will be our kids running the aisles."

Kids? Plural? The thought of multiple kids made beads of sweat pop up on his forehead. There was barely enough money to keep him and Alice in the basics, yet she dreamed about adding multiple kids to the equation.

The organ music amplified in volume and soon the piano joined in. In Arnold's opinion, it only slightly improved the sound of the music.

Everyone in the sanctuary found their seats and raised their voices in a rousing rendition of a hymn he recognized, Rock of Ages.

When the music concluded, the pastor stepped up to the podium and preached on the topic of 'if God is good, why does He let believers suffer?'

"What did you think of it?" Alice asked as they drove home.

"It was okay. They were nicer than I expected."

"You expected the church people to not be nice?" She asked in a teasing tone.

"I don't know what I expected." As he drove, the pastor's words rolled around in his mind. "The sermon was interesting."

"It's been a while since I've been to church, so I'm glad he chose that topic to preach about."

"I've always wondered why God allows bad things to happen to people in general, but especially to good people who believe in Him. When he pointed out the scripture where Job asked his wife how they could accept the good things from God but not the troubles—I never thought of it like that."

"I liked the scripture in Romans, when he said that we should rejoice in our sufferings because suffering produces hope and character. I'm going to write that verse down and keep it where I can always see it. I tend to feel sorry for myself when something bad happens. It never occurred to me to count it as joy. Having joy during bad times, the concept seems so backwards, doesn't it?"

"Everything about religion is backwards, but after hearing that sermon today, it made me think that's not always a bad thing." He glanced at his favorite diner. "How about we sneak in and splurge on lunch?"

"Let's save our money and have lunch at home."

He gritted his teeth as he drove past. He hated not being able to take his wife out for Sunday lunch along with the rest of the good church people. Alice deserved better than him and his meager offerings.

"That last scripture he read brought tears to my eyes," Alice said.

"I don't remember which one that was. Remind me."

"The one about the day when God will wipe away all our tears. So many things break our hearts in life. I can't imagine not feeling pain or crying ever again. Isn't that a wonderful thought? Today's sermon is one I'll never forget."

He brought her hand up to his lips and kissed the back of it. A day when there would be no pain and suffering? It was a nice thought, but he would believe it when he saw it.

***

<u>Present Day</u>

Arnold rolled over in his sleep as the melodic sounds of radio music filled the early-morning hours. "God will wipe away all your tears," he muttered in his sleep.

Lutis sat in a dark corner of the rig, keeping a close vigil over his watch.

Mondaci snarled in the dark then bent down and whispered into the human's ear. "How can God wipe away your tears when God doesn't exist." As soon as he said the words, he cut his eyes over to the Protector Warrior and smirked.

Arnold's head thrashed back and forth on the plushy pillow.

Lutis stared at the Enemy Traitor. "My enemy tells lies about me ... God, be faithful and destroy them."

"Nice scripture," Mondaci said. "Too bad the human is too big of an idiot to recognize such things."

"The scripture wasn't for him. It was a reminder for you. One of these days God will destroy you and all your evil contemporaries. You will burn in eternal Hell for all the lies and deceptions that you've sown among humanity."

The words caused a chill to race down Mondaci's spine, but he refused to even flinch in response. He could lie to weak humans all day long, but in the end, his destiny was of pain and torment forever.

"That may be true, but I'll do my best to obliterate as many humans as I can in the time we have left. When my cries rise from the ashes of the torturing, sulfurous flames of Hell, his cries will be there beside me."

Chapter 29

T he day was warm and sultry, and Hyacinth's heart soared at the sounds of playful laughter amid the gentle splashes of water in the pool.

"Laughter has been missing from this house for so long. It's wonderful to have it back," she said to Sheri. As she said the words, her heart dipped inside of her. Jenner was in a far better place, but guilt at enjoying life niggled at the edge of her conscience.

"Mm," Sheri answered with a sleepy grunt from behind sunglasses that half covered her face.

Hyacinth reclined back in the lounge chair and allowed the sun rays to drench into her skin for a few minutes before she pulled the oversized umbrella back over her.

***

A Few Years Ago

"I've always dreamed of visiting here." Hyacinth's gaze studied the emerald waters, the azure sky, and green foliage of the lush Fijian island. "I still can't believe we're finally here."

Jenner swam behind her in the infinity pool and pulled her to him in a tight embrace. "The view is spectacular." He pressed gentle kisses to her neck as he spoke.

She turned around to face him then jerked her head to the side. "Did you see Mr. Hunky over there in the blue swimsuit? Hubba hubba, right?"

He dropped his mouth open in mock offense and floated away from her. "If you want Mr. Hunky, I'll not stand in your way."

She grabbed his feet and pulled him back. "I didn't say I wanted him. I'm just enjoying the view."

He dropped his feet to the pool bottom and nodded toward a woman in a string bikini that covered nearly nothing. "In that case, I guess you don't mind if I enjoy the view, too?"

Hyacinth took his chin in her hand and turned him away from the woman. "How about we focus on the palm trees and leave the flesh and blood views to all the single and looking."

He rested his forehead on hers. "Mmhm, that's what I thought." He pushed away from her toward the ladder. "I'm headed out of the pool for a while. One of those mango mint smoothies is calling my name."

"You've had three of those in the last two hours."

"We're on vacation. I can have as many as I want." He pushed out of the pool and dried himself with a towel.

A woman pushed a toddler passed Hyacinth in a pool float, and her eyes nearly flooded with tears at the sight of the child laughing, kicking his legs, and slapping the water with his hands. She longed to have a child of her own one day.

"You want me to grab you one of those disgusting banana smoothie things you like while I'm at the bar?" Jenner's words brought her out of her musings.

"Sure, why not?" She didn't need the extra calories of yet another smoothie but would get back on track once they were back in the realities of Cape Kennington. Vacations were for splurging, and that's what she intended to do.

When Jenner slid back into the water with their drinks, they marveled at the vividly colored squawking parrots that lined the tree limbs and the pelicans that swooped with grace over the waters in search of their next meal.

Despite the tropical heat, Hyacinth nestled closer to him. "I love home, but wouldn't it be wonderful to live here in such a beautiful place?"

"It's nice for a visit, but I don't think I'd want to live here." He placed his half-drunk smoothie on the edge of the pool, picked up his cell phone, and swam a foot over to the impressive waterfall at the end of the pool that was rife with rocks, palm trees, thick ferns, and colorful tropical flowers. He nodded for her to join him. "Let's get a picture in front of the waterfall."

It took several attempts to get just the right angle, but they finally took a picture that was worthy of framing and social media brags that would make his friends and family green with envy.

As they snapped a few last-second pictures, a tsunami of water flooded over them and soaked his iPhone.

"What the—" He whipped around just as a smiling girl's head popped out of the water in a wave of giggles. "Scram, you little brat. You got my cell phone—"

Hyacinth smacked his arm and gave him an evil eye. "Be nice. She's just a kid having fun."

He snarled his nose then turned back to the girl as guilt washed over him. "Hey, kid. That was a nice splash. I'll give you twenty bucks if you can make an even *bigger one*."

***

<u>Present Day</u>

She sucked in a deep breath and bolted up in her chair then wiped away water that rolled down her face.

At the sound of raucous laughter, Hyacinth turned and glared at the pool. "Lucas Harold Perkins! Did you just splash water all over me?" She screeched. As she patted a cotton towel over her skin, she couldn't be too mad because in the heat of the day it felt nice.

Camden gave him a rough push. "Yeah, Harold. Why'd you splash her like that?"

"I didn't splash you," Lucas pointed at Camden. "He did it."

"Nunh uh." Paige ran to the edge of the pool and pointed at Lucas. "He splashed you."

Camden shot her a playful glare. "Why you gotta be such a tattle-tale, you wretched little sea urchin?" He pulled her into the pool, and he and Lucas pretended to try to hold her under the water.

She rewarded them with a bevy of screams of delight.

"You boys better stop that roughhousing in the water or you'll all get tofu for lunch."

She shook her head when, not to her surprise, they all ignored her. "If you accidentally drown the kid, guess who gets to explain it to her parents?" She bent over and scrunched her drippy hair with the towel.

"Those two boys are a handful, let me tell you." Sheri stirred her iced tea with a straw then took several healthy swigs. She glanced down at Hyacinth's cell phone. "Honey, your phone is ringing."

"Grab it for me, will you?"

She snatched it up and glanced at the screen. "It's just a phone number and I don't recognize the area code."

"Go ahead and answer. My parents are on a cross-country drive. They'd probably call on their cellphone if they needed anything, but you never know."

She swiped her finger across the screen and answered it. "Sure, hang on just a minute." She muted the phone. "It's a hospital. Angel Medical Center?"

Hyacinth bolted up and tossed the towel onto her chair. "Angel Medical Center? That's the hospital everyone was taken to after the bus accident. What do they want?"

Sheri shrugged. "Do you owe them money?"

"Not anymore. The insurance money paid off all the medical bills."

She nearly cried at her friend's anxiety-stricken expression. "Don't worry about it, hun. I can tell them you're not—"

Hyacinth stretched out her arm and wriggled her fingers. "It's okay. I'll talk to them."

Sheri cradled the phone close to her chest. "Are you sure? You look like you're about to cry."

She wriggled her fingers again. "It's fine. Jenner died there so I hoped to never hear from them again."

Sheri gave her a cautious stare before handing over the phone.

"Hello?" She glanced at Sheri then at the pool where Camden sat at the top of the tall curvy waterslide with Paige between his legs. When he released and they sped off, Paige screamed with glee all the way down until they landed in the pool.

"Yes, this is she."

Sheri split her attention between the pool and Hyacinth.

"Hm hm."

"Okay."

"Yes, I see."

When Hyacinth's face scrunched, Sheri leaned up in her chair. "What's going on?" She mouthed.

Hyacinth looked away and massaged her forehead with her fingertips. "I understand. Can you hang on a second?" She placed the phone on mute and released a deep sigh.

"Honey, what's wrong?" Sheri whispered. "Is everything okay?"

"It's the hospital." The words came out as though she were in a trance. "The man who was in the semi-truck accident with the bus wants to talk to me."

"What?" Sheri's eyes bugged in disbelief. "The man who killed—" She reached out for the phone. "Let me talk to them. I'll tell them exactly where that horrible man can go."

Hyacinth blinked and shuddered as though finally coming to her senses. "Why would he want to talk to me?"

"I have no idea but hang up that phone right now. Honestly, the nerve of him to think it's okay to reach out to you like this, and the nerve of the hospital for calling you about it."

"The police investigation didn't find him complicit in the accident. He was as much of a victim as our people. Maybe he's struggling and needs someone to talk to—someone who understands."

A startled expression carved onto Sheri's face, followed by a hardened one. "Or maybe he's a sleaze who's looking for someone to scam. Seriously, hang up. You owe that man nothing."

Hyacinth turned her attention to the pool where Lucas, Camden, and Paige sat in the shallow end shooting each other with water guns. Paige's happy squeals gave her a burst of happiness.

She stared at the screen for another few seconds then unmuted the phone.

Chapter 30

"It's your play, Pauline. Stop dawdling." A choking plume of cigarette smoke hovered around the dining room table.

"Keep your britches on, old lady. I'm thinking," Pauline snapped. The snippy retorts were typical for their group, and no one thought anything about it when it happened.

Alice pushed away from the table with an exaggerated sigh.

Pauline held her cards closer to her chest. "Keep your eyes off my business."

Alice gave her arm a soft pop as she walked behind her. "I ain't got no use for looking at your cards, so pipe down."

In the kitchen, she pulled out a platter of quartered wedges of smoked bologna sandwiches on white bread, sliced tomatoes, Vidalia onions, a mountain of radish discs, and crunchy iceberg lettuce.

She slapped the platter onto the buffet table in the dining room, disappeared into the kitchen and came back out with bags of chips. "It was my turn to cook today, but I ain't been feeling so well lately, so it's sandwiches or nothing."

Nadine placed a couple of sandwich wedges on her plate. "You couldn't at least spring for something fancier, like ham or turkey instead of bologna?" She teased.

"Eat it or not. It's all the same to me." Alice glanced around the table. "Iced tea alright with everyone? Or I can make a fresh pot of coffee if anyone wants that." Without waiting for a response, she brought out four frosty glasses filled to the brim with ice and a pitcher of tea with condensation rolling down the sides.

When their plates were full, Alice slid back into her seat and popped a radish into her mouth with a sigh.

Pauline tossed her cards face down on the table and looked at her friend with compassion. "What's going on with you? You seem more sluggish than usual."

"I ain't been resting too well. Sleep don't come as easy as it once did."

Helen nodded. "Lost sleep. It's one of the hundred things that sucks about getting old."

Nadine slung her cards to the table with a sly smile. "I haven't pooped in over a week, and Edward has the nerve to complain that I'm not as nice as I used to be. I swear, no one tells you all this stuff when you're young and pretty."

Pauline cackled. "When you're young you think the golden years are sitting on the porch with the man you love reminiscing about the olden days, but it turns out its nothing but crippling arthritis, constipation, praying you don't pee your pants every time you sneeze or cough, and to make matters worse, your kids suddenly start telling you what to do."

"I got some interesting news today," Nadine said in a mocking tone. "Our good for nothing son called to let us know they're expecting another child. I swear, him and that worthless floozy of his needs to have a kid about as much as the Antichrist does."

"Maybe it'll calm them down and make them into respectable people," Helen said.

She let out a sarcastic laugh. "If the first three kids didn't turn them into decent people, I doubt a fourth will bring positive change."

"That son of yours is about as unbalanced as a mental ward. Those poor kids of his don't stand a chance at a normal life," Alice muttered as she bit into her sandwich. "You may as well go ahead and reserve all four of those kids a suite at the state penitentiary. That's where they'll probably end up."

***

1971

Alice meandered down the aisles of the thrift store down the street from their house. Since they only had one car and Arnold needed it to get to work, the thrift store was a close place to get out of the house during the day.

She pushed the rickety shopping cart around the store and stopped to look at a goldish-orange yellow jumper with vertical brown diamond patterns. It would look good with a brown turtleneck sweater.

The tag pinned to the shoulder strap priced the garment at four dollars.

The hem was frayed, but she could rip out the seam, trim it, and re-stitch it. She was no seamstress but with minimal work it would look as good as new.

She chewed her bottom lip as her gaze took in every detail of the dress. It was inexpensive compared to the same garment brand new in the trendy stores, but something could pop up before the next pay day that they needed more than this outfit.

She placed it back on the rack with reluctance and made her way down the aisle. She loved Arnold, and he did his best to assure they had everything they needed—and they did have everything they needed—but it was times like this when she wished they could have more than needs.

Why was Arnold so resistant to her getting a part-time job to help make things easier for them?

She looped around to the next aisle and tried to put the jumper out of her mind, but when two women's laughter drifted from the other side, she darted around, grabbed the garment, and placed it in her cart.

At least this way no one could buy it out from under her until she made up her mind one way or the other.

To avoid the temptation of further impulse buys, she left the clothing section and went to the newly added small non-perishable food section where any impulse buys would benefit the entire family, not just her.

She passed the accessories department and a long necklace with dark green, orange, and gold glass beads grabbed her attention. "That would look groovy with the jumper," she muttered under her breath. She draped it over the jumper and her heart clutched in her chest. As she suspected, it coordinated perfectly.

Despite not needing to, she tossed it into the basket.

Half an hour later, she meandered to the front of the store and stopped just short of the check-out registers. She held up the dress and necklace and tried to talk herself out of them but shoved them back into the cart and moved into the line.

Arnold, as he always did when he suspected she wanted something they couldn't afford, would have told her to get the outfit and not think another thing about it. His well-meaning generosity toward her many wants were why it fell to her to be the frugal one of the family.

She placed her few grocery items on the counter next to the register then held up the dress one final time.

"Oh, honey, do yourself a favor and splurge. You deserve it," the cashier said.

Surprised, Alice glanced up with a timid laugh. "Am I that transparent?"

"This isn't my first time around the block. I recognize the 'should I, shouldn't I' look in your eyes."

"We haven't been married all that long. I try to be responsible with our money."

The woman stuck out her tongue and groaned. "I hate doing the responsible thing."

"Tell me about it." She took a split-second look at the clothing and necklace then plopped them onto the counter. "Do it quick before I change my mind."

"Atta girl." The woman held up the dress and folded it neatly with a regretful shake of her head. "Why do I never see the good stuff until someone comes through the line to buy it?"

Riddled with guilt, Alice fished out her wallet and passed a twenty-dollar-bill over to the woman. "You're welcome to it. I really shouldn't spend the extra money."

The woman stuffed it into a sack with an amused laugh. "Honey, look at you then look at me. I'd look like a can of busted biscuits. I couldn't get these hips into it even if I wanted to." She handed over the change. "Have a blessed day."

Alice stuffed the bills and loose change into the zipper part of her purse. "You too." She pushed the cart to the corral and headed for the door then went back to the register. "I'm so sorry," she whispered to the woman who stood with her back to the door reading a paperback novel.

The woman looked up, startled, then glanced at the space surrounding the cash register. "Oh dear, did I forget something?"

"No, no. Nothing like that." She stared down at the floor then back up. "Do you know if they have need for part-time help here?"

"I don't know if they're looking for help, but they need to." She pulled a thick pad from beneath the register and yanked off the top page. "Fill this out and bring it back. My name's Marnie. I'll put in a good word for you."

***

<u>1971- Later That Day</u>

After dinner, they snuggled on the couch to watch *The Sonny and Cher Comedy Hour*. The show didn't hold her attention like it usually did, so she slid from beneath his arm and stood. "I'm a little thirsty."

"Grab me something while you're in there?" he asked without removing his stare from the television screen.

She added ice to two glasses and poured in sweet tea. She took a sip, pulled the folded job application from her purse, and stared at it for several seconds. "It would be nice to bring in a few extra dollars to help us out." Deep in thought, she tapped the paper then rushed across the kitchen and pulled an ink pen from one of the drawers. Her heart thudded in her chest as she filled in the requested information. Having something to do for a few hours a week while Arnold was at work was a pleasing thought.

She was so focused on filling out the information that she jumped when Arnold kissed the top of her head.

"Where's my tea, woman?"

She pointed at his glass. "Sorry, I got distracted and forgot to bring it to you."

He took a gulp then turned to pilfer in the cabinet. "Do we have anything sweet to eat?"

"There's graham crackers and Nilla Wafers in the other cabinet." She stood and rushed across the kitchen. "How about I make you some graham crackers with peanut butter? I even have a few chocolate chips to sprinkle on top." She pulled a plate down from the cabinet and grabbed the jar of peanut butter.

Arnold took the peanut butter from her. "I'll make it. You sit down and rest."

"You worked all day. Go enjoy the show. I'll bring these to you."

"Honey, I don't expect you to wait on me hand and foot like you do. Let me make our snacks and bring them to you for a change."

She leaned in and pecked his lips. "You work all day. It's the least I can do." She patted his rear then gave it a playful squeeze. "Now scoot out of my kitchen."

He grabbed his glass and drained it then picked up the paper she had been fussing with when he walked in. He glanced over it then looked up. "What's this?"

"What's what?" She glanced over her shoulder, shrugged, then went back to slathering thick layers of peanut butter on the graham crackers. "It's a job application."

"I know being a working woman is the thing these days, but I thought we decided you weren't going to?"

His crestfallen expression made her sad. She rubbed her hands on the dishtowel. "I know it's important for your pride that I don't hold a job, but it's the modern thing to do. Times have changed. Women want to work and make their own money and contribute financially to the family."

"It's not about my pride. Having a boss to deal with is no fun. They don't treat the people under them very well, and they get away with it because there's no one to tell them they can't. I don't want you dealing with people like that." He shook his head. "They're just ... bosses aren't nice people. There's no need to put yourself through that if you don't have to."

"I can deal with mean people, and I can always quit if I don't like how things go."

He lowered himself into a kitchen chair with a sigh. "We only have one car. How do you plan to get back and forth from work?"

"The thrift store down the road is close to our house. I can walk."

"Absolutely not. I won't have my wife walking the streets at all hours like a cheap floozy."

"It wouldn't be that way. The store doesn't open until nine in the morning, so I wouldn't be out at all hours of the day."

"What happens when it rains or snows? What happens in the winter when the days are short? It's a dangerous world out there and people are crazy. I don't want you walking home in the dark."

"When the weather's bad I'll bundle up and carry an umbrella." She pressed her hands to her stomach. "Wouldn't it be nice to have a few extra bucks coming in for the next few months until the baby is born? We need a lot of stuff to get ready for him ... or her."

"I'm the man. I'm supposed to support my family. I won't have my wife out there working a job. We may not have a lot of money, but we're not derelicts."

She put her hands on her hips and glared at him. "Maybe I'm not asking your permission."

It was their first time to disagree on something like this, and her attitude annoyed him, but he kept his voice soft. "There's a lot of sickos out there who would love to run across a pretty little thing like you walking across town by yourself."

"I realize that, but if they hire me, I could walk there in less than ten minutes."

"A lot could happen in ten minutes."

"A lot could happen no matter where I go. I've been walking to the thrift shop at least a day or two a week since we got married and nothing has happened yet."

"You're walking around town and not telling me?" He pressed his fingers to the bridge of his nose and took a deep breath.

"I'm not out there walking around town," she huffed. "I go to the thrift store and back. I can only sweep and mop so much in a day's time, and soap operas don't do it for me like it does for other women. I get bored out of my mind sometimes and need to get out of the house for an hour or two."

"I understand that it gets boring around here, day in and day out, but I don't want you walking anymore. If you want to go somewhere during the day just let me know. You can drop me off at work and drive wherever your heart desires."

"Fine," she said with exasperation. "If I get the job, it'll only be part time during the day while you're at work. I could drop you off on the days I work then pick you up and bring you home at the end of the day."

He went to the counter and snatched up a couple of graham crackers. "I already told you, my wife ain't getting no job."

***

<u>Present Day</u>

Boisterous laughter brought her out of the daydreams of a life that she hadn't thought about in years. She and Arnold hadn't realized it then, but despite the lean times they had been living the best times of their lives.

Their bank account contained more money now than ever, yet they didn't have each other. They lived in the same house together, yet they had been estranged for years.

With trembling hands, she lifted a cigarette to her lips, lit it, and sucked in a lungful of smoke. She picked up the deck of cards and shuffled them. She needed a task, even a simple one, to chase away the ghosts from the past.

Chapter 31

It was Sunday morning, and breakfast was out of the way. As Arnold weaved through the morning traffic on his way to the interstate onramp, a tall and regal building perched on a hillside captured his attention.

"Good News Tabernacle." He shook his head, but an unexpected longing pierced his heart. He hated church and especially Christians, so why was his heart drawn to such things?

At the last second, he made his decision and switched lanes, cutting off several cars in the process. He drove through the stoplight that turned red halfway through it.

A cacophony of angry horns erupted around him.

He smiled, held up his middle finger, and waved it in every direction. That was what he thought of the world and everyone in it.

Lutis watched the human with a grim expression. "That's an abhorrent gesture that never helps a situation."

Fraush's laughter filled the truck. "Shut up, Lutis." He turned his attention to the human. "It's a hand gesture. Who cares?"

Guilt flowed through Arnold's mind, so he dropped his hand to his lap though his mischievous grin still lingered. "You're getting soft in your old age," he grumbled. "It's a stupid hand gesture that no one probably even saw. Who cares?"

"From the abundance of the heart the mouth speaks," Lutis said. "That includes offensive gestures."

Fraush released a deep sigh and made the same gesture, directed toward Lutis.

Lutis pulled on the handle of his sword. "Do it again and you lose a hand."

As he drove through the intersection, the church's long driveway loomed to his right and cut through the hillside. He slapped his blinker and turned onto the driveway that was lined with lush green trees. Vibrant flowers filled the area between the entrance and the exit.

As he neared the parking lot, he snickered at the welcome sign. *Welcome to your place of rest and restoration.*

"Welcome to your place of judgement and intolerance," he scoffed. "That's what the sign *ought* to say." He navigated the rig to the back of the lot where several vacant spots remained and pulled into them.

He gazed over at the massive building and the streams of people in their Sunday finery disappearing through the entrances. "Why are you here, Arnold? You have nothing in common with these people." He whispered a profanity. "You don't even believe in God so why bother coming to places like this?"

He placed his hand on the gearshift to leave but something in his heart wouldn't allow it. He was drawn to a place that he hated with all his being.

"There's a small church just down the road," Lutis said. "They're built on a strong foundation of Biblical truth."

"Or maybe you can shut your mouth and let him choose for himself." Fraush growled.

"Maybe a smaller church would be better." Arnold shook his head. "If I'm going to walk in the doors of a church, I'd rather do it in a place like this where I can hide in the crowds."

He opened the door, jumped to the ground, placed his hands on his lower back, and bent backwards then to each side to stretch his muscles.

With an internal groan, he made his way toward the building. As he walked, he couldn't believe how massive the place was.

Sprinkled around the pristine cobblestone parking lot were different fruit trees whose limbs burst with apples, pears, and cherries. "I wonder if you get arrested for taking an apple on the way out?"

He crept inside the building to the gushing welcome of a door greeter.

"Welcome back to Good News." The man in his fifties, dressed in a suit with an untucked shirt and pants whose hems were several inches up his ankle, gave him a warm smile.

"I ain't never been here before."

He reached out his hand. "Well, I have the honor of welcoming you here for the first time then. What brought you to us? Let me guess. You saw Dr. Hansley on television, didn't you?"

"Dr. Hansley? Never heard of him."

"You've never heard of Dr. Hansley? My word, did we just crawl out from under a rock?" The man gave him a friendly pat on the arm. "Feel free to walk around and acquaint yourself with our beautiful facility."

"It looks more like a Las Vegas shopping mall than a church."

The man gazed around the place with a gentle nod. "It's amazing, isn't it?"

Pretentious is more like it. "I'm not into religion, but I have some questions about it. Could I talk to the pastor after church?"

The man gave him a knowing smile. "So many of his fans come here to talk to him. Unfortunately, he doesn't have time to visit with people, but we have experienced counselors who would be happy to speak with you." He held up an iPad. "I can schedule you with an appointment right now."

So many of his fans? Who did he think he was? Elvis? The man's words, appearance, and cocky demeanor caused an immediate and fierce dislike to fester within him. "An appointment? You mean the pastor of the church doesn't have time to talk to people?"

"Dr. Hansley would love to speak with everyone." The man's eyes narrowed in apology. "As you can see, this church holds over ten thousand people, and that doesn't count the millions from all over the world who watch our services online. We have many qualified counselors who can speak with you about anything."

"If I wanted to talk to a counselor, I'd find a mental health clinic," Arnold spat.

"I'm afraid that's the best we can do." The man's lips tightened with displeasure as he focused on the iPad. His finger slid down the screen as he spoke. "Shall I make you an appointment with a counselor? It looks like we can fit you in for this coming Thursday afternoon. I just need to know the nature of the visit so I can pair you with the most suitable counselor."

"Maybe I don't want to discuss the nature of my need with a door greeter."

The man gave him a sensitive smile. "I'm a professional who understands the need for utmost discretion. As you can imagine, I've heard it all, from pregnancy crises, to homosexuality, to financial woes, to salvation. Honestly, I've heard it all."

"Maybe I should have gone to the church down the street. Maybe the pastor there would have time to talk to someone."

"Perhaps so, sir." The man snapped the cover back over his iPad. "Let me know if you change your mind."

Arnold stepped around him and walked deeper into the church. To his left was a bookstore with a 10-foot-tall television screen of a man, he presumed it was the pastor, pointing inside. A dialogue bubble over his head said: *Come inside to buy my newest #1 New York Times Best-Selling novel*!

On the other side of the door was an identical television with the book's cover with text that read, *Stop living in poverty! It's not God's will for your life. Claim it NOW*! Next to the book scrolled one glowing review after another.

Next to that was a lavish coffee bar where hundreds of people gathered to drink coffee and eat pastries.

The Good News Media Store was next. On the walls were televisions broadcasting a worship team singing amidst light and smoke shows that rivaled any rock concert he'd ever seen. A blinding digital billboard proclaimed: *Grammy-Award Winning Good News Worship Team! Get their newest album NOW! Autographs the first Monday of every month from 6:00 p.m. to 8:00 p.m.*

"Autographs? Psh. Who are you, freaking Madonna?" He could already tell, even without meeting a single soul, that he didn't like any of these people. His mind jumped to the sermon he'd stumbled across several months ago about the dangers of being a carnal Christian. He wasn't sure what separated a carnal Christian from any other, but in his eyes, these people reeked of carnality.

It was funny how random sermons somehow made their way back to his mind at the strangest times. Tired of these peoples' nauseating backslapping, he made his way to the stairwell and upwards into the farthest reaches of the fourth-tiered balcony.

He no more than sat when the building went dark. The deafening crowd noise died in an instant. A deep baritone voice from the darkness made him jump in his seat.

"Please make welcome, Grammy-Award Winners, the Good News Worship Band."

The stage lights lit, and he had to close his eyes against the stabbing glare. When he could finally open them, seven men and women stood in jeans and t-shirts, without shoes, their hands thrust into the air. They bounced up and down to the beat of the obnoxious rock music.

"Is this the circus or a church?" Arnold blurted. "There's nothing sacred about this music."

The woman next to him shot her head around and glared at him.

It shocked him that anyone could hear a word he said under the ear-splitting pulsating noise.

He'd never been a fan of church, but he would take a rousing round of good old-fashioned "Bringing in the Sheaves" over this musical drivel.

When the music stopped nearly forty-five minutes into the service, his relief that it was over was immediate but short-lived. A woman on the worship team shouted into her microphone. "God wants you to know that He rages in the heavenlies with righteous anger. Many among you are filled with pride because you say you belong to Him while your neighbor doesn't. I tell you, you lie when you say these things, and God detests a liar. He decrees that your Muslim brothers and sisters are a child of God. Your Hindu brothers and sisters are a child of God. Your Tao brothers and sisters are children of God. It matters not whether you call him God, or Allah, or Buddha, followers of all are a child of God."

The woman next to him raised both of her arms and shouted. "Amen!"

Traitor angels positioned around the sanctuary bristled with excitement.

"Yes, oh yes! Amen!"

Arnold looked at the woman next to him like the lunatic she was.

Similar exultations of agreement rang through the auditorium.

"Regardless of the religion you follow, you are a child of the highest God, thus saith the Lord." The woman speaker on stage went slack as though the words had taken their toll on her. She fell to her knees then lay prostrate on the ground and wept.

Istus rose in stature in the middle of the sanctuary. His gaze fell on a frail-looking older man who sat on the main floor with his head bowed in prayer. "Speak words of truth with boldness, man of God."

The man looked up, stood to his feet without hesitation, and worked his way to the aisle as fast as his arthritic knees would carry him. The Holy Spirit had impressed a word on His heart, and it may not be popular, but he had to deliver it. "Buddha is not the one true God. Allah is not the one true God. The one True God does not look kindly on your lies. There is no God other than Him. Thou shalt worship no god other than Him. Jehovah, the God of Abraham, Isaac, and Jacob is the only true God, and the only God worthy of your worship."

The pastor snapped his fingers at his security detail, pointed at the man, and slashed his fingers across his neck.

They rushed toward the man, grabbed his arms, and pushed him toward the exit doors.

"Only those who call upon the name of the Lord Jesus Christ shall be saved! There is a generation who is pure in their own eyes, yet they are not washed from their filthiness. Know the truth and do not be of that evil generation."

Odi shuffled after the guards grinning from ear to ear. "You are a liar." He turned to one of the guards. "He is a liar. Shut him up now."

"Shut up, old man, if you know what's good for you," hissed one of the security guards.

"Speak the truth of the one true God and in doing so you'll set the people free," Istus shouted. His voice thundered through the heavenlies.

"He is the way, the truth, and the life. No man comes to God except through His Son Jesus Christ. There is salvation in none other than Jesus Christ. There is no other name under Heaven by which you must be saved except Jesus Christ. God gave His only begotten Son that whoever believes in Him shall be saved!"

The guards pushed the man into the lobby then into a high-backed seat. "Sit here and don't say another word, old man." The main guard looked at one of his underlings. "Call the police and have this man arrested. We want him punished to the fullest extent of the law." He turned and glared at the old man. "We extend no mercy to troublemakers."

When the underling didn't move, the guard's eyes bulged. "Now!"

The man turned and dashed away.

He glared at the old man one more time then motioned for all the men except one to follow him. He snapped his fingers at the remaining man. "Don't let him out of your sight until the police arrive." He turned on his heel and disappeared back into the sanctuary with his entourage close behind.

Istus placed his hand on the man's shoulder. "Well done, good and faithful servant. You were obedient in speaking the truth, and the heavenly Father is pleased."

He stepped to the door and looked back into the sanctuary. Traitor demons and Warrior angels buzzed around the room.

The pastor stepped to the podium with a serene and apologetic smile. A hulking demon twelve-feet tall towered behind him with an evil sneer. "Sometimes enemies of the truth slip into our congregation like wolves among the sheep," the pastor said. "Don't let the lies of the enemy steal you from seeking the experiences for which you came here today." He turned to the music leader and raised his hands to heaven. "Lead us back into worship."

Chapter 32

Arnold was never so glad when the final amen of the church service was muttered. Those people had whooped and hollered, jumped up and down, and screamed out loud at every other word the pastor said to the point that he needed to get into the truck for some peace and quiet. "Crazy people." He melted into the crowd that pushed into the stairways and elevators that led away from the fourth level balcony.

Refusing to wait in line forever for an elevator, he pushed into the stairwell with a heavy sigh.

A woman beamed up at him with a grateful smile as he held open the door for her. "Oh my. Wasn't that a marvelous service?"

"If you like noisy chaos and mayhem then I suppose it was okay," Arnold snarled.

"Hmph." The woman scrunched her nose at him, lifted it into the air, and whipped away from him.

"I've been to a Packers game full of drunk cowboys that was more reverent than this church service." It was an unnecessary jab since he'd already clearly offended the dear Christian woman, but he took the opportunity with relish.

The woman turned and glared at him. "The flowing of the Holy Spirit is beautiful and not to be mocked."

He glared back at her but kept his mouth shut. These people were as crazy as mental patients so there was no need in continuing the verbal altercation.

It took forever to make his way down to the main level, and by the time he did he was even more irritated than usual.

The main lobby was packed, and he couldn't move in either direction without bumping into someone. Rather than fight the unruly fray, he moved toward the sanctuary to wait for the mass exodus to thin out.

At the entrance to the music store, he recognized several people from the worship team who stood just inside the door greeting people with effusive smiles, signing autographs, and posing for selfies with the enamored masses.

"These Grammy-Award-Winning nobodies think awfully highly of themselves," he mumbled. When the crowds thinned by a fraction, he made his way over to the coffee bar.

The lighted sign depicted so many options that it was overwhelming. Hot coffee, iced coffee, frozen coffee, Ethiopian coffee, Tanzania Peaberry coffee, Sulawesi Torafa Coffee, Japanese tea. "Good grief, whatever happened to good old Folgers?"

More than fifteen minutes later when it was finally his turn at the counter, his emotional state was steaming more than an espresso. "I'll take a coffee," he said to the smiling, zebra-striped haired man with a nose ring whose pants clung to his chicken legs so tightly that he looked like a ridiculous caricature.

"Of course. What kind of coffee?"

"Just a plain old coffee," Arnold blustered. "None of that frou frou pansy stuff. A plain old drip coffee."

Taken aback by Arnold's brusque behavior, the man nodded and pushed a coffee cup across the counter a minute later.

Arnold slapped a five-dollar bill on the counter, accepted his change, and whirled around to leave, ignoring the tip jar. "Four bucks for a black coffee. You people are bigger crooks than a politician."

"Cream and sugar are on the cart to your left," the man behind the counter called after him. "God bless you, sir."

"If I wanted cream and sugar, I would have ordered a pansy coffee." He retreated into the main lobby which was much emptier now. He turned toward the doors when a flurry of activity caught his eye on the far side of the room.

Mr. Superstar Pastor breezed into the lobby flanked on all sides by stoic security guards.

The President of the United States wasn't this protected, he thought.

People lined up in the area to wave at him as he passed by.

Arnold's annoyance ratcheted back up. Was there no one in this church who didn't think too highly of themselves? Despite his annoyance, he moved closer to the lines of people.

"Oh! Dr. Hansley!" A woman screeched.

The murmur in the room increased to veiled excitement. Arnold couldn't believe the way these people acted. If the man in their midst was the Pope, he could understand the excitement, but this pastor was, in the grand scheme of things, a nobody.

The longer he stayed in this church the more convinced he became that these people were idiots in the purest form of the word.

He sucked in a scalding mouthful of the coffee and nearly spat it to the floor. He managed to get it down despite the burn. A profanity unleashed through his mind, and it took a lot of self-control to keep from verbalizing it. Did the circus freak barista run it through the flames of the Lake of Fire before pouring it into the cup and handing it over to him?

As the pastor inched his way toward the center of the lobby, Arnold noticed how people clustered closer yet kept their distance.

"We love you, Dr. Hansley!" A man called out.

"Hello, hello, hello!" The pastor waved in all directions.

Arnold wondered if he had received waving tips from the Queen of England.

He pelted his fans with a cheesy smile of dazzling teeth that were so abnormally white they appeared to almost glow. His blazer was creamy white, and his denim jeans were a perfect match to the blazer. The only color he wore was a shirt in a blushy shade of pink that was unbuttoned halfway down revealing a smooth chest. His brunette hair was blow dried and styled in a flawless pompadour.

"These people are strange." Arnold turned toward the exit. He was eager to get away from the freak show. Had church always been this weird or had it, like many other things, become a casualty of the modern age? He had a pretty good idea.

"Excuse me?"

The voice rose above the fray, but he kept his momentum toward the door.

"You there? Excuse me."

Arnold couldn't imagine the person was inquiring after him, but he turned and glanced over his shoulder as he walked.

The pastor stared straight at him.

Unsure of what to do, Arnold paused.

The man gestured for Arnold to step closer.

Arnold didn't move a muscle. He wasn't a peasant under the man's feet, and he didn't care to be treated as such. If the man wanted to talk to him, he could be the one to make the move.

The man bore into Arnold with an uncomfortable stare for several seconds before he smiled and took a few steps in Arnold's direction.

The four security guards hovered in tandem around the preacher's movements. They reminded him of a nonsensical Laurel and Hardy movie.

The pastor stopped a few feet in front of him, but the security detail didn't budge from their protective perimeter. "You've never been here," the pastor said.

With the thousands of people who attended this church, Arnold didn't know whether to be impressed or perturbed by the man's proclamation.

"Nope."

The preacher's focus lasered in on him, and Arnold could imagine how a bug under a microscope felt. His heart thudded in his chest.

"You're not a believer."

Again, it was a simple statement, not a question.

"What makes you say that?"

He offered a knowing smile. "God tells me what I need to know."

In his imagination, Arnold flipped him the bird. Is God telling you what finger I'm holding up? "I don't know if I believe or not. I haven't decided yet."

"I believe, Lord. Help my unbelief."

Arnold didn't understand what the words meant, but he took a few steps toward the man. "I don't know how to believe in God. I want to, but I don't know how."

The men tightened their stance around the preacher, and one of them extended his arm toward Arnold. "Step back, sir."

When Arnold made no effort to move, the man's voice rose. "I said step back, sir. Now."

Arnold locked eyes on the preacher. "I need help from someone. How do I believe like everyone here believes?"

"I told you, and you do not believe. I do works in my Father's name, but you do not believe because you are not one of my sheep."

The words might have been in a foreign language for all Arnold got out of it. "I don't understand what that means."

"Come back and visit one of my miracle crusades. When you witness my many signs and wonders, then you'll believe." The preacher gave Arnold a condescending smile then took a few steps back. The guards moved with his every step like soulless automatons.

Mondaci stood between the preacher and Arnold. He glanced around at the heavenly beings stationed around the massive room. A few of his enemies, angels of light, stood scattered around but mostly the place was choked with his own cohort of dark spiritual beings.

"Liar!" Lutis glared at Mondaci then stepped in front of the preacher until they were nose to nose. "You call yourself a man of God, but you're a man of lies, just like your father, Satan, the father of lies. You are a false prophet spreading false doctrine to spiritually weak people who don't know scripture well enough to call you out for what you really are."

A crooked smile crept across Mondaci's leathered face. He clicked his tongue several times at Lutis. "Name calling. Such an ugly business, really."

The preacher gave Arnold a final genial nod then turned to walk away. "Blessings, brother."

"Wait," Arnold called after him. "I don't know what that means. I just want to know what it means to be saved. Can't you tell me now?"

The preacher took several more steps before turning and raising his arms in front of him with his palms turned upward as though receiving unseen adulation. "Brother, you may visit our Counseling Rooms every day until eight p.m. to learn how to be saved."

"I don't want a counseling room. I want to talk to you."

The preacher dropped his hands, cocked his head to the side, and raised a hand in a motionless wave. "Be well, my brother."

Arnold was confused as the man and his security moved across the lobby and disappeared into a barricaded hallway. *All I want to know is how to be saved so I can believe.* An intense hatred for the young pastor boiled within him. *I thought preachers were supposed to help you when you needed it. I thought they were supposed to answer your questions. I thought they were supposed to tell you how to be saved.*

A woman slipped beside him with a dreamy look in her eyes. "You're so blessed that he spoke with you personally," she gushed in a whispered tone. "I've gone to church here for five years, and he's never said a word to most of us."

Numb with confusion and anger, he turned to the woman. "What are miracle crusades?"

"Oh, his crusades are wonderful. He never preaches at them, but who needs preaching when there's such heavenly music, right?" She gave him a knowing smile. "He speaks miraculous words and people are instantly healed. They walk out of wheelchairs and toss aside their crutches because they no longer need them. He hovers his hands over people's heads, utters a language that God gave only to him for their own special communion, and miraculously delivers them from demon possession. I'm convinced that Pastor Hansley is a prophet. We place him right up there with Jesus himself. The church elders encourage us to consider him as a type of deity, and I for one believe that he really and truly is."

"He does miracles but won't have a simple conversation with me about getting saved? Even Jesus told people how to be saved when they asked him, didn't he?"

"Don't take offense. He's a busy and important man of God."

"If he's too busy to tell me what I want to know, maybe you can tell me?"

The woman pointed to the far side of the lobby. "We lay people are not encouraged to have such important conversations with each other. The Counseling Rooms are in concourse C. There you will find professionals who can provide the help you need."

No longer than he had been here, he already hated the phrase counseling rooms. "What did he mean when he said that about, 'Lord I believe, help my unbelief?"

She waved his words away. "I don't know for sure what the words meant, but the staff in the counseling rooms can explain it to you. I urge you to come to one of his miracle crusades, though. If you see his many miracles and still don't believe, in my opinion, you're a lost cause."

"I don't need healing from anything, so what good is a miracle crusade for me? I need to know why I have such a hard time believing that God exists. How do I learn to believe in God like you believe in Him?"

"Stay around long enough and, I promise, you'll see enough miracles and signs from Dr. Hansley that you'll believe in God whether you want to or not." She placed her hand on her chest and tears filled her eyes. "If I hadn't seen Dr. Hansley's signs and wonders with my own eyes, I'd still be lost in my unbelief."

Lutis glared at the grunting traitor angels that moved around the woman. "Only evil and adulterous generations seek after such signs. No sign shall be given but the sign of Jonah. Don't seek miraculous signs. When you seek God in Spirit and in Truth, you'll find Him."

Before Arnold could press her further, the woman turned and zipped across the lobby.

Lutis hated to see humans under the control of the evil one, and even sadder to him was that many of them didn't even realize it.

As she breezed away, a dark figure clung to her spirit in a vicious death grip of delusion.

Lutis spoke with a loud voice. "You don't need to be a professional counselor to minister salvation to your fellow humans. Go ye into all corners of the world and preach the gospel to every creature. That is the Great Command of Father God."

The creature that clung to the woman turned, looked at Lutis, and broke into laughter.

Chapter 33

Arnold scampered out of the church in an angry huff. "What's the point of a church if you leave more confused than when you arrived?" He muttered as he heaved himself into the rig.

He started the engine to get the air conditioner flowing then glanced up at the sky. "You don't exist, do you? You're just a make-believe God that people have concocted to make themselves feel less alone in this world."

Out of nowhere, tears spilled from his eyes and trailed down his cheeks. "We're all alone here. When we die, there's nothing more." His voice quivered with emotion, and the revelation punctured his heart.

As he watched out the window, the parking lot cleared. A few well-dressed stragglers darted across the stretches of parking lot and ducked into the few cars that remained.

When a white limousine that sparkled under the harsh rays of the sun pulled around the building, his anger multiplied. He didn't have proof that it was the pastor, but who else at the church would have the pompousness to arrive and leave via such an extravagant vehicle.

It slipped past a car with its hood up. The woman, dressed in a gauzy, flowy dress that fluttered in the breeze, watched as the limousine drove past.

"What kind of piece of trash pastor drives past a woman who's broken down in the church parking lot?" He pulled the truck into gear and for a brief second considered stopping to help her, but like the limousine, he drove on past. "Why should I care about her if the preacher doesn't?'

Guilt pricked at his consciousness as he pulled to a stop before merging onto the busy intersection. He took a final glance in the rearview mirror. The woman had a phone to her ear.

Someone will be there to help her soon. She'll be fine.

***

An hour into his drive with no destination in mind, rural scenery flew past at dizzying speeds. His cell phone rang, startling him out of his reverie. It was scary to think that he had driven so many miles without the slightest consciousness of anything he had done behind the wheel. "Keep this up, and you'll kill another innocent bystander."

He pulled onto the interstate's wide shoulder and picked up his phone that had stopped ringing seconds before. The screen displayed a number that he didn't recognize, so he tapped on the voicemail icon and listened. His mouth dropped open and went dry.

"Mr. Collins? My name is Hyacinth Alekson. You don't know me, but Angel Medical Center called me. They gave me your number and said you needed to talk to me. You can call me back at 555—"

He scrambled to grab an ink pen from the dashboard then glanced around for even a sliver of paper to jot down the number. He cursed aloud at the cleanness of the rig. There wasn't a piece of paper in sight.

The woman ended the message before he found a box of travel-size toothpaste in his toiletry case. He opened the cardboard box and flung the toothpaste back into his bag, but it bounced out and rolled under the driver's seat. He pounded the wheel with his hand, stamped his feet on the floorboard, and unleashed a stream of obscenities.

He took several deep breaths to calm himself then pressed the play button to listen to the message again. He scribbled the phone number but the ink in the pen wouldn't flow. With another curse, he touched the top of the pen to his tongue then yanked it back and forth across the cardboard. Nothing.

He cursed and flung the pen across the cab of the truck. When it landed on the passenger seat within reaching distance, he grabbed it in a rage and flung it across the cab again.

This time it landed on the floorboard and rolled to a stop within an inch from the door. He glared at it, flipped it the bird, then snatched another pen from the dashboard.

For the third time, he played the message and scrawled the number.

He jumped in his seat when a fellow truck driver flew past and blared his horn. It sounded like a discordant trumpet that could wake the dead.

It was probably a well-meaning gesture of hello from one trucker to another, but Arnold wasn't in the mood for niceties. He held up his middle finger and kept it up until the truck was a blip on the horizon.

He took several deep breaths then punched in the number before it dawned on him. All he had needed to do was click on the phone number to return the call. All the madness of the failing ink pen would have been avoided if he had used his head for something other than, as his grandmother used to say, an empty hat rack.

Alice would have told him how stupid he was, and she would have been right. He was a stupid man, and even he knew it.

His gaze locked onto the display of numbers and his hands shook. Her voice had sounded nice enough, but what if she hated him? What if she told him what she thought of him. What if she had a mouth like

Alice and called him everything but a white boy? How much had the hospital told her? Did she have an inkling of who he was? He hoped so because he hated to be the one to break it to her that the strange man calling was the one who had murdered her husband.

He stared at the numbers for a few more seconds then hit the call button before he could change his mind.

***

Hyacinth had just flicked on the television and tuned it to an easy listening station when the phone rang. She glanced at the screen and recognized the number.

Why this man wanted to speak with her, she couldn't imagine, but she squeezed her eyes shut against the anger that bubbled beneath the surface. Her husband would be alive were it not for this man on the other end of the phone call. "Lord, I thank you for the abundant mercy and grace that You've shown in our lives. Despite my anger and grief, help me to treat this man with the same mercy and grace that You've shown me."

She slid her finger across the screen before the call ended. "Hello?" Her voice, usually calm and steady, was passive and tense without any of its convivial flair.

"Mrs. Alekson? My name is Arnold Collins. I was ... you wouldn't know me, but I was in the hospital while you and your friends were there."

The poor guy. His voice sounds as stressed as I am. She cleared her throat, surprised by the sudden surge of emotion that threatened to spill over. She closed her eyes and whispered another quick prayer. The last thing she wanted was for her emotions to break in front of this stranger. She pushed herself to sound normal and light even though it wasn't how she felt. "Of course, Mr. Collins. How may I help you?"

"Do you ... did the hospital explain to you who I am?" There was an extended silence, and he wondered if the woman had hung up on him, not that he would blame her. If the tables were turned, he would hang up on himself.

"They told me you were in the diesel truck that collided with our ministry bus."

Ministry bus. The words pricked his spirit. He had forgotten it, but he remembered someone at the hospital telling him that the bus was a traveling gospel group.

"I heard that your husband ..." he paused to choose his phrasing because to say the word 'died' to a grieving widow seemed offensive. "I heard what ... what happened to your husband. I can't tell you how sorry I am."

He slapped a hand over his mouth and begged himself not to cry. He took several deep breaths then continued when she didn't attempt to speak. "I know I'm the last person you want to talk to right now—probably ever—but I couldn't live with myself if I didn't at least try to reach out and apologize for ... for what happened that night."

"Mr. Collins."

Her tone was so friendly that it emboldened his resolve not to cry.

"A heavy wooden beam was laying across a dark road. No one involved could have known what was about to happen. The police were very clear about that."

No, I fell asleep behind the wheel. He wanted to scream until his words soaked into the widow's mind. She needed to know the kind of person she was talking to. If I hadn't fallen asleep behind the wheel maybe I would have seen the beam and averted an accident. Even if the bus had still hit it, maybe it wouldn't have been fatal if only one vehicle had been involved.

"Maybe." His lack of truthfulness only added fuel to the fire of hatred that he felt for himself. He was at a loss for words. He didn't know what to say to this woman because no words would ever tame the grief that she would live with for the rest of her life.

Lutis leaned in and whispered into the human's ear.

Arnold's eyes bulged open at his next thought that came out of nowhere. He shook his head. He couldn't believe such a thought would ever occur to him. "Well, I guess that's all I wanted to say. I know it'll never be enough, but I'm sorry for your loss, and I'm sorry I did it to you. If God exists, I hope you and He can both forgive me one day."

"There's no need to punish yourself, Mr. Collins. You—"

"Please, I'm not a fancy man. Call me Arnold."

"Arnold, don't punish yourself. You're a victim just like we were. Don't let the enemy beat up on you like that."

I'm not a victim. You're the victim because I made you one. He sucked in a breath and held it for several seconds as he battled to keep his composure. "Thank you for being so kind. I don't deserve it," he finally said.

"How are you doing after the accident?" She asked.

How am I doing? She wants to know how I'm doing? "I had a minor broken leg and was laid up for several months. Other than that, I had a few fractured ribs. It's been a long process of rehabilitation but I'm back on my feet, except I'm even slower now than I was before." A hollow, awkward laugh tumbled from his lips, and he hated himself for it. Her husband was dead and buried and I'm complaining about being slow on my feet?

"That's wonderful news, Arnold. I'm glad to hear that all turned out so well with you."

Again, the line fell silent, and he didn't know what to say, so hanging up seemed like a good option. He called to apologize, and he had done it. There was nothing else to say.

"I ... I suppose I should let you go."

"It was wonderful to hear from you, Arnold. Thank you for calling."

He wanted to end the call but was reluctant to do so. "Mrs. Alekson, you have no reason to do this, and I wouldn't blame you if you didn't, but would you care if I came to see you?"

The silence that stretched on the other end was all the answer he needed.

Hyacinth's breath caught in her throat, and she feared her lungs would collapse under the weight of the words he'd just spoken. "I ... well, I—"

"It's all right ma'am. I should have left well enough alone and not asked. Thank you for taking the time to talk to me. You have a great day."

Nitasah appeared next to Hyacinth and placed a hand on her shoulder. "The Father has a plan, child. Trust Him."

She didn't understand why, but she rushed the words before the line went dead. "Mr. Arnold? Do you know where Cape Kennington, North Carolina is?"

"I've heard of it but have never been there."

"It's a small coastal town. If you want to come here, I'll be happy to meet with you." Even as she said the words, she couldn't believe she had agreed to it.

"Are you sure?"

"You're welcome here anytime. It's a small town but there are plenty of hotels."

His head was spinning. What are you thinking, Arnold? What are you going to say when you get there? What will you do and say? "I can be there in two days."

***

Hyacinth hung up the phone and stared at it for several seconds. "Dear Lord, Hyacinth. What have you done?"

Nitasah looked down on his charge. "No fear, child. Your Father has a plan. Be obedient."

Chapter 34

The moon was high in the sky, and its rays highlighted the trees with a silver light.

His eyes were heavy with sleep, and he sighed a breath of relief when the rest area loomed into view.

Once the rig was parked under one of the lot's protective puddles of light, he slipped into the sleeping area and nestled under the sheets. Before he could drift off, Alice popped into his mind.

They hadn't spoken since the day she had called him upon realizing he was gone. His plan had been to make her call him when she wanted to talk, but it was clear that wouldn't happen. Despite his sleep-muddled mind, he picked up the phone and pressed "1" on the keypad.

He almost hoped she wouldn't answer then grimaced when she did.

"What?"

"What? That's how you answer the phone these days?"

"Only when it's someone I don't want to talk to."

"So now you wish I was dead and that you would never have to talk to me again?"

She didn't answer, and it took everything in him to not hang up on her. He needed to make things better, not make them worse. "You still playing cards?" He didn't care one way or the other, but it was a neutral topic of discussion that mattered in her world.

"The girls left around half an hour ago." Her words were ice cold, but it was better than nothing.

He glanced at the alarm clock that was built into the wall and chuckled. "Since when do the card hags leave before midnight?"

"The game was over, and it was too late to start another."

"What did you ladies have for dinner?"

"Pauline brought a spinach and mushroom quiche."

"That sounds interesting," he said.

"It was disgusting. After two bites I swapped it for a ham sandwich."

"Everyone else liked it, though?" It was a banal conversation, but it was good to talk.

"Where are you?"

"In the back of the rig about to go to sleep."

She broke into a series of racking coughs. They ended with her gasping for breath, followed by the familiar flick of a cigarette lighter, followed by the sound of her sucking in another lungful of tar. "Where'd you say you are?"

"In the back of the rig and trying to go to sleep."

He flinched when she pounced on him with an assortment of curse words. "I meant what state are you in?"

For the love of God, could you talk like a woman for once? "When I left Iowa, I went down through Missouri and into Arkansas. Now I'm in some scrawny town in Tennessee that God himself doesn't even know exists. I should be in North Carolina within a day or two, depending on how quickly I try to get there."

"Hm."

The verbal response told him she couldn't care less. "I went to church last night."

She broke into mocking laughter but had to stop to endure another full minute of coughing. "Did you find religion all of a sudden? I thought I knew you better than that."

"I ain't found no religion," he spat. "Don't you ever think about the days when we were married and went to that little church?"

"I ain't given church a single thought since the last time we darkened the doors of one. I try to block those months of insanity from my mind."

Over the years he hadn't given church a thought either, but part of him wondered if there was anything to it. Could it improve their lives if they gave it another chance? As bad as he was, could God ever see him let alone save him? He shook his head to dispel the unwanted thoughts. Church was nothing more than a crutch for the religious masses. It was his goal to wash the wispy thoughts of church from his mind. "You would never consider trying it again?"

He held the phone away from his ear when she lapsed into another prolonged coughing spell. When she returned and made no effort to answer the question, he let it go because he already knew her thoughts on the matter.

"I guess I should let you go," she said after a prolonged pause of neither of them knowing what to say next.

He wished her goodnight and hooked the phone to the charger cord. "Lord, how did our life go so wrong?"

***

<u>1971</u>

Dinner was over and despite her unwillingness to have him help with the dishes, he was determined to help anyway. As she washed, he rinsed and dried.

"I got some good news at work today," Arnold said.

She looked up at him, and his face beamed with pride. He wasn't overly handsome in the classic sense because he was too thin, at least in her opinion. Men in her family had always been on the larger side, not necessarily obese, but "big boned" as people liked to say. Still, she thought he was plenty handsome with his squared and chiseled chin and sharp cheekbones. "That's wonderful. What kind of news?"

He coughed into the crook of his arm then ducked his head as though telling his news embarrassed him. "I got a promotion today."

She sucked in a deep breath. "Oh, my word, Arnold, that's incredible. Why did you wait until now to tell me?"

He shrugged. "I thought I'd wait until after dinner."

She passed a plate over to him and gave him a quick peck on the lips. "I'm so happy for you."

"Don't get too excited. I'm not the vice president or anything like that. Once old man Wallace retires in a couple of weeks, you'll be looking at the Head Packer."

"The journey up the corporate ladder happens a step at a time. One of these days we might even own the place."

Her enthusiasm made him laugh. "I'm not smart enough to own the place, but I guess you never know."

She removed her soapy hands from the water and touched his nose. "You're just as smart as the next guy. Never sell yourself short." It was her turn to laugh at the sight of a pillow of billowy suds on the tip of his nose.

He wiped the suds away with the crook of his arm. "The promotion comes with a raise."

She plunged her washcloth into a beverage glass and swished it around for several seconds then handed it to him. "I suspected it might."

"It's only a two percent raise. If we save the pennies for an entire year, we might be able to fill up the car one time if we're lucky."

"No matter how small, if the Lord blesses us, we'll accept it with gratitude."

Not long after starting church she had begun adding religious talk into their conversations. It didn't bother him, but it always took him by surprise.

She sprayed both sinks with water, then he wiped them with his drying towel.

As he put up the last of the dishes into the cabinets, she brought a tray of store-bought cookies from the pantry and placed it on the table. "In case we have a sweet tooth later."

He danced a silly jig, ending with a wiggling of his hind end. "My sweet tooth is already howling. We'll have them while we watch television?"

She gestured him toward the living room. "Be careful with the crumbs."

He gave her a playful nod and made his way to the living room, but she grabbed his arm. "I also have a little news."

He glanced down at her tummy with a lopsided smile. "Is it a boy?"

"I still don't know the gender."

His lopsided smile disintegrated into a snarl. "Twins?"

She swatted him with the dishtowel then turned to drape it across the oven handle. "It has nothing to do with the baby."

He dropped the cookies, grabbed her in his arms, lifted her off the ground, and twirled her in circles. "Have I told you lately how happy I am that you're my wife?"

"That's sweet and thank you. I love you, too." She wriggled her feet until he placed her back on the ground. He smothered her with kisses then released her, backed away, and bent to pick up the cookies he had dropped. "What's your news. Lay it on me."

She ran her fingers through her hair and chewed her lip. "I … I got a job today."

"What do you mean you got a job today?"

His voice wasn't mean, but it wasn't light and fluffy like it had been seconds earlier.

"I applied for that job at the thrift store, and they called today and said the job was mine if I wanted it."

He cut his eyes up at her. "I'm sure it was fun to apply, but I hope you told them thanks but no thanks."

She crossed her arms across her chest. "I accepted the job."

He dropped the cookies onto the table with a deep sigh and scrubbed his hands over his face in frustration. "I told you that I don't want my wife working, especially now that you're pregnant. I don't want you on your feet all day, dealing with bosses who don't treat you with the respect you deserve and customers who treat you even worse."

His words came out muffled, but she heard every word.

He dropped his hands to his sides. "You call them tomorrow and tell them you appreciate their offer but that you're not accepting the job." He picked up the cookies and carried them into the living room.

She followed close behind. "Don't be so stubborn, Arnold. We could use the extra money, and you know it."

"I got a raise. We'll be fine."

"Yes, but we could do better than fine if I could bring in a paycheck too."

He shook his head. "I said no. We've done fine until now and we'll continue to do fine."

"I want to work, at least until the baby arrives. Once the baby's here, maybe I'll quit and be a mother full time."

He placed a hand on her arm and gave her a gentle smile. "I appreciate you wanting to help, but a man is supposed to take care of his wife. I want to take care of you, so let me. I agree that we could use more money until the baby arrives. Maybe I could get a few extra hours at work."

"No, I don't want you working yourself to death. What's the point of having a husband if you're always at work and we never see each other?"

"I'd rather work myself to death than see you working. I'm a man. That's what I'm supposed to do."

"That's not what you're supposed to do," she argued. "We're supposed to work together. It doesn't make sense to work yourself ragged when I can take a job for a few hours a day and be home by the time you get here. It's still a little extra money, and you don't have to overwork yourself. It's a perfect solution."

"I don't want my wife working," he snapped. "How would it look if my wife had to take a job to help support the family? End of story."

She put her hands on her hips and stared him down. "It's the seventies, not the fifties, and I have no intention of being a pearl-clutching housewife for the rest of my life. I'm not asking, I'm telling. The job starts next week, and I've accepted it."

Chapter 35

"You did what?" Sherri's eyes snapped with disbelief.

"What else was I supposed to say?" Hyacinth shrugged.

"What else were you supposed to—" Sheri picked up a novelty lamp shaped like a mushroom then set it back on the shelf. "For heaven's sake, Hyacinth, that man could be a rapist, a serial killer, a cat burglar, or something really sick."

"Is there anything sicker than a rapist or serial killer?" Hyacinth teased.

Sheri picked up the mushroom lamp, looked over it again, and placed it into her shopping cart. Not only was it fifty percent off, but it would also be a perfect quaint addition to her bookshelf in the living room next to her dancing fairy figurines. She pointed a finger at Hyacinth. "I'll tell you what you should've done. You should have thanked him for his call and for the thoughtful apology, hung up, and not given him another thought."

"We live in a day and age where people, especially women, must be overly cautious about things. I get that, but you didn't hear his voice. He sounded so broken."

"I hate that for him. He was a victim of a senseless tragedy just like you guys were, but it was inappropriate for him to call you in the first place, and doubly inappropriate for him to ask for a personal visit." Sheri shot her a disgruntled look. "You're a single woman now. You can't let strange men come around when they call you out of the blue. There's a lot of bad people in the world."

"Thank you for giving me a state of the world address." Hyacinth clicked her tongue in annoyance all the while knowing that her friend's concerns were valid. "It's not like I invited him to my home. I plan to meet him in a public space, like a restaurant."

"I vote for the lobby of the police department."

Hyacinth fingered the gems of a jeweled tree trinket. "Why does everyone treat everyone in the world like they're an enemy? We all need to be careful, I agree, but most people are decent. I can't explain it, but I don't think he has bad intentions. I think he needs someone to talk to."

"If he needs someone to talk to, let him get a counselor like everyone else in the world."

Hyacinth pursed her lips, heaved her shopping cart forward, and bolted across the store.

Sheri blew her bangs off her forehead in frustration then chased after her. They rarely argued and when they did it usually blew over quickly, but still she hated it. "Honey, hold on. Don't be mad."

Hyacinth picked up and examined a stretchy bracelet with lavender and clear faceted beads, pushed it onto her wrist, and turned to Sheri. "I'm not angry. I'm ..." She paused in search of the right words. "I don't know what I am." She pushed the cart a few more paces forward.

Sheri pointed at her wrist with a wry smile. "You have to pay for that, you know."

Hyacinth glanced at the bracelet, rolled it off her wrist, and placed it in the cart. "I know I have to pay for it," she snapped, then looked away, laughed, and turned to face her friend. "This is so not worth arguing about."

"I'm not trying to be hardnosed about it. I just want you to be careful. He may be the nicest guy in the world, but we don't know that. Maybe I'm overly cautious about this but inviting him here makes me nervous. That's all I'm saying."

"Your concerns are valid but there's nothing I can do about it now. I was anxious about it when he first asked, but I told him he could come, and I feel okay about it."

"Fine. If you feel okay with having a strange man around, go ahead. I can't stop you if it's something you want to do, but wherever you meet him, Joseph and I will be there to watch out for you."

Hyacinth placed her hand on Sheri's arm. "I'm okay with that. In fact, I'd appreciate it."

"Well, good," Sheri puckered her lips in a faux pout. "Because we're doing it whether you want it or not."

"Knowing you guys are there will make me feel better. Thank you." She nodded toward the cash register area. "You ready to get out of here?"

Sheri nodded and followed her. "You need to meet him in a public place that's well lighted and that has lots of people."

Hyacinth glanced over her shoulder as she placed her purchases on the counter. "Oh shoot. I was thinking about meeting him in the dark alley behind the adult video store."

Sheri picked up a stuffed animal owl and chunked it at her. "Nobody likes a smarty pants."

Chapter 36

The house was silent and though her skin was cool, a sheen of sweat covered her face. Alice rolled over in bed and glanced at the alarm clock, whose hands glowed softly in the dark.

Her lower back was sore, so she slipped from beneath the covers as quietly as possible to keep from waking Arnold.

The nagging lower back pain had been present for several days but she attributed it to the hours on her feet working at the thrift store and lugging around bundles of merchandise. It was her first job, so being on her feet for hours at a time combined with so much bending and stooping would undoubtedly create unusual body pains that would get better with time.

Arnold and she had squabbled when he saw her in the kitchen one evening taking over-the-counter medication to alleviate the dull pain. Just as she had swallowed the pills, fear flooded her mind. Was it okay to take medicine when she was pregnant? When she mentioned the back pain, Arnold had told her it was her own fault for taking a job instead of staying at home like a woman should do.

His words resulted in their first major argument. She had told him that she was a modern woman and would work if she wanted and that he could deal with it or not.

He hadn't spoken to her for the rest of the night, but they kissed and made up just in time to head off to bed.

As she stood to her feet now, she paused for a few seconds when Arnold stirred then settled back down.

She padded to the bathroom in the new pink slippers edged with satin piping that Arnold had bought for her at the local discount store. They were pretty, and the gift was thoughtful, but they were too dainty for her preference.

The squeak of the faucet handle was louder than usual as water tumbled into the sink basin. She splashed cold water on her face then pressed a towel to her skin.

She released a deep breath as she draped the towel over the towel rack and arranged it so that the edges were lined up with perfect precision. She needed something—she didn't know what—so she raised the bathroom window and sucked in several breaths of cool air.

Nausea moved its way up into her throat, but she swallowed down the sensation. All she needed was a cold or the flu on top of a new pregnancy.

The pain in her back increased to a searing flash. She squeezed her eyes shut and clutched the windowsill with her hands. "Lord, something isn't right. Please help this to pass." The prayerful words were strange to her even as she uttered them.

Though they had attended church on a mostly regular basis for the past few weeks, prayer was a foreign concept for her. It wasn't something she usually did but now seemed as good of a time as any to give it a shot.

Another pain sliced through her back and this time it extended into her abdomen with such ferocity that it took away her breath. She bent over and grasped her stomach. Is something wrong with the baby? She didn't know, but the thought of anything happening to their unborn child was more excruciating than the physical pain itself. "Lord, please protect my baby. Please."

An unconscious whimper worked its way out of her at the sensation of an immediate need to use the bathroom. With measured and careful movements, she lowered herself onto the commode. Her eyes widened at the unexpected sight of a thin, ghastly red rivulet that had made its way down one of her legs.

She pressed her fingers into the stream and brought them back up. Her fingertips were bright red and glistening. She clutched her gown then covered her face with her hands and moaned. "Lord, no."

She grabbed the edge of the sink as a wave of unbearable dizziness nearly toppled her to the ground. She held herself up as a series of shakes racked her body.

When she stood back up twenty minutes later, the water in the toilet bowl was jewel red and contained a clump of tissue the size of a lemon.

She slapped her hands over her mouth to stifle her cries. She wasn't a doctor, and knew precious little about pregnancies, but intuition told her what had just happened.

Arnold would be the first person she told, but for now she needed to grieve on her own. In numb disbelief, she stared at the clot of tissue that, with time, would have grown into her beloved first-born child. Was it a boy or a girl? Now she would never know.

Finding out she was pregnant had been the happiest day of her life, next to her marriage to Arnold. How do you survive the loss of your child? The words thundered through her mind as she wept. Should the loss feel this monumental and earth-shattering given how early in the pregnancy she was? All she knew was how she felt right now, alone in the middle of the night, and it was the worst emotional pain she had ever felt.

When her serious-at-the-time boyfriend, Paul, had broken up with her she thought her world would never again be the same, until she met Arnold, whose presence had healed her heart to the point that Paul rarely entered her mind.

This—losing her unborn child—was a hundred times worse than losing Paul. No matter how many people she lost in her life through death, she couldn't imagine it would ever feel as horrible as this.

She reached for the stainless-steel flush handle then yanked her hand away. Should she flush it, or would her doctor want to see it? Was it disrespectful, irreverent even, to consider flushing the unborn remains of a God-given human life down the toilet?

With a final shake of her head, she pressed the handle and cried as the remains swirled in the bowl and disappeared with a swishy gurgle of water. It was a sickening sound that she would never forget no matter how old she got. Would every flush of a toilet from now until the day she died bring her back to this moment in time?

She ripped a long strand of toilet tissue from the roll that hung on the wall and blew her nose. With a sigh she stepped into the tub, filled it with hot water, and added Calgon bubble bath. She stood as still as death while squishy bubbles covered her feet and ankles.

She glanced up at the ceiling, her eyes brimming with a fresh torrent of tears, overcome with shame as she mentally lashed out at the God who supposedly loved her.

How could a loving God give her the biggest desire of her heart—a child—then whisk it away from her in the middle of the night? God isn't a good God. He's vindictive and mean.

She lowered herself into the steaming water feeling even more guilt. The snow-white bubbles dappled with occasional pink spots mocked her and her loss.

Is it wrong to blame God, to label Him as mean and unfair just because things don't go as I planned? The words drifted through her mind as she slid deeper into the water.

Maybe it wasn't right to blame God.

Maybe all would be well again after a night of sleep that she was sure would never come.

Maybe then she could forgive Him.

For now, though, she was angry.

She hated God.

Chapter 37

Patches of stealthy green grass managed to grow amidst the brown and parched terrain. It crunched under her feet as she walked.

A warm breeze blew across her face, carrying with it the subtle lingering scent of a backyard barbeque. With her particular purpose in mind, the scent was inappropriate yet somehow comforting. It served as a simple reminder that no matter how important or small a person was, life carried on after their death.

Janie hugged an arrangement of white tulips and daisies close to her chest as she crested a small hill and made her way toward the fence line. The whir of traffic speeding past on the highway barely registered so far back in the cemetery.

On the other side of the fence, horses and cows grazed without a care in the world, and baby goats frolicked among their grown counterparts. Farther away, Miller's Lake, as the locals called it, even though technically it was a pond, sparkled under the setting sun.

Before she was close enough to read the name on the headstone, tears flooded her eyes. She took in a deep breath as Jenner's name came into view.

An assortment of faded and dingy silk flowers lay at the base of the headstone, but bright new ones filled the concrete urns that flanked each end of it.

With her foot, she pushed the faded flowers aside and replaced them with her fresh ones. In this heat they wouldn't last long, but they were a gesture from her to Jenner, a token of the things that she could never say to him.

She sat on the ground in front of the headstone and arranged the flowers, not that presentation mattered all that much. Two days from now the fresh flowers would be wilted and rendered trash for the next person to pick up and discard.

"Flowers, like people, are like fog, here today and gone tomorrow. Isn't that what the Bible says?" She spoke to the headstone as though it were Jenner listening to her every word. "I don't know. I'm pretty sure it says something to that effect. I guess I need to do a better job of knowing what the Bible says."

She didn't move a muscle when colorful butterflies, at least twenty of them, fluttered into view around the headstone. She held her breath when one landed on her wrist for several seconds before lifting off and floating back into the group that continued to fly around the area.

Where had they come from, and where would they go next? Since dusk would be upon them soon, it wouldn't be long before they were hidden and quiescent until tomorrow.

The lowing of the cattle drew her from her musings. She brought her focus back to the headstone. "I know you can't hear me, but I needed to apologize for the way I treated you when you were still with us. I've come to realize that I'm not a very nice person sometimes." She flung her hands out in a dramatic fashion and laughed. "Okay, I'm not a nice person most of the time, but I'm trying to do better. I've even become friends with Felicia, and I never thought that would happen."

She stood to her feet, dusted herself off, then leaned down and touched the top of the headstone. "I hate that I wasted so much time on being mean when we could have been friends. Always be nice to people because you never know if today will be their last. Is that in the Bible?"

She shrugged her shoulders and backed several steps away. "I'll be back in a few weeks and bring more flowers with me. I love you, brother."

Her heart thudded in her chest as she turned and made her way back across the cemetery. When she crested the hill, the car with her two best friends standing beside it caused a rippling smile.

She picked up her pace and dashed in their direction. "Thank you, girls, for letting me do this on my own. It was stupid but something I needed to do."

Nancy grabbed her wrist and gave it a friendly squeeze. "It's okay. We've had a nice breeze, and it's so nice and quiet out here. The hills are beautiful—well, they would be if the drought hadn't killed them."

"Even though they're not as green as they should be, I still think they're beautiful," Felicia interrupted with excitement. "Oh, and you won't believe what happened. Nancy and I were talking and listening to eighties music when this huge group of butterflies flew right up to the car. There were tons of them, like hundreds."

Nancy leaned in and whispered to Janie with a sly grin. "It was more like thirty or forty."

Felicia waved the comment away. "They were so beautiful that it seemed like hundreds of them."

Janie almost told them that the same thing happened to her, but she decided to keep it between her and Jenner. She glanced back over her shoulder toward the grave and wondered if it had been the same butterflies.

"I did a Google search, and do you know what a group of butterflies is called?" Felicia paused and gave each of her friends a moment to consider the question.

"I have no idea." Though it had annoyed her at first, Janie found that she now loved her friend's effervescent personality and plethora of useless facts.

"A group of butterflies is called a kaleidoscope. Seriously, how fun is that?"

Before she could stop them, tears again flooded Janie's eyes. She pulled her friends into a group hug, something she rarely felt the need to do, and kissed them both on the cheek. "Thanks for always being my friend, even when I don't deserve it." She swiped her hand across her eyes and squared her shoulders. "In honor of Jenner, let's go to the Dairy Farm Drive-In and order the largest chocolate malt that money can buy."

Chapter 38

Arnold sat on a slatted park bench as the sun burst over the ocean in a dazzling palette of peaches, oranges, and golds.

He couldn't remember the last time he had stopped to enjoy a sunrise, especially one over the ocean. Being landlocked in Iowa made such luxuries impossible.

He had arrived in Cape Kennington in the wee hours of the morning, parked his rig in a public beach parking lot, and had awakened just as a blush tinted the sky.

The beauty of the sunrise took precedence over his caffeine addiction, but he needed a cup of coffee soon.

Tall beach grasses rustled and swayed in the breeze on either side of him, the waves pounded onto the shore, and as though by a silent stirring, a chorus of bird warbles filled the morning air around him.

The sounds coalesced into soothing echoes that lulled him into a rare sense of serenity. He was never one to enjoy the solitude of his own mental ramblings because thinking usually got him into trouble. In this place, though, he could sit here all day with perfect contentment.

Even rarer than his state of peace was the unavoidable smile that appeared when Ella Fitzgerald's voice floated toward him in a playful rendition of Mack the Knife.

He had no use for any modern singer. They were all trash as far as he was concerned, but the familiar strains of music from a bygone era caused an unexpected surge of happiness.

He stood and glanced over the beach grasses and found the origins of the music. A group of at least thirty geriatric men and women in colorful clothes that flapped in the wind did wobbly stretching exercises in the sand.

Most of them appeared much older than he, and yet another strange emotion welled within him. He wanted to be down there in the sand with them doing those stretching exercises. He didn't want to talk to anyone, and he surely didn't want to forge new friendships, but he longed to be with older, wiser people.

Never had he ever had the urge to be with other people. It was strange the unusual places his mind had taken him lately.

After watching the older people laugh and talk between attempts at stretching their limbs, he retook his seat. His alone time was short lived when a frail-looking man with a poodle on a leash appeared next to the bench. "You mind if I sit for a spell, partner?"

Arnold wanted to tell him to find his own bench, but he gave the man a half-hearted nod.

The man lowered himself onto the bench with slow, measured movements and a deep sigh. He secured the leash to the metal bench arm then watched as the poodle moved to the closest patch of beach grass and disappeared behind several thick tufts. He tugged on the leash. "Roxy, girl, don't you get in there and wallow in the dirt. You'll mess up your new hairstyle."

Arnold gazed from the corner of his eyes when the poodle came back out, stood between the two men, and gazed up at each of them.

The man thrust up his hip with what looked like effort and dug around in his pocket. His hand came out seconds later with several doggie biscuits. He handed one down to the dog, who accepted it with a tail-swish of excitement.

A poodle seemed like a strange pet choice for a man, in Arnold's opinion, but who was he to judge? The world would be a better place if people would be less judgmental and mind their own business.

"I've never seen you out here before," the man said in a friendly tone.

"It's my first time." Arnold kept the response short in the hopes that the man wouldn't keep up a conversation.

"I come here almost every morning to watch the sunrise. I used to come here in the wintertime, too, but the cold makes my arthritis flare and sometimes I can't make it out. I can still see it from my living room window, so I can bask in the beauty of the Lord's creation even when my joints won't cooperate."

The beauty of the Lord's creation. These Christians are like viruses, they're everywhere you turn. "Yep," Arnold answered.

The man pointed in the direction of the elders on the beach. "When I have a really good day, I join them for stretching."

The poodle jumped up and pawed at the old man's legs.

With a groan he leaned down, picked her up, and placed her on his lap. "Roxy here is a diva but good company for an old man like me. My wife loved her, but the Lord saw fit to take her home. It's tough on an old man to adjust to bachelorhood after decades of marriage."

"Hm. Sorry to hear that."

The man flashed him a warm smile and thrust his hand in Arnold's direction. "My name is Odell Willoughby."

Arnold gave his hand a quick shake then pulled away. "Arnold Collins."

"You from around here? I don't recall ever seeing you around town."

"I just pulled into town this morning."

"Vacation?" The man chuckled. "People love beach vacations."

Arnold wanted to get up and find another bench free of chatty people, but he didn't want to be mean to someone who would probably kick the bucket sooner rather than later. "I'm here to meet someone but I may stick around for a day or two."

"Are you widowed, like me?"

Jeez, you're a nosy old man. "My wife is alive and kicking, but we don't like each other very much. She likes for me to be away as much as possible.

The man nodded as though he understood. "He who finds a wife finds what is good and receives favor from the Lord. Proverbs 18:22."

Arnold barked a sarcastic laugh, and the poodle jumped in the man's lap. "A good thing? You ain't never met my Alice. That woman's mouth is cruder than any man's I've ever met. She ain't no gift from the Lord any more than I am. I guess in that way we deserve each other."

"We're supposed to love our wives as the Lord loves the church, according to Ephesians. Do you love your wife as Christ loves the church?"

The man already knew the answer, so Arnold shook his head. "At one time I did, but things change."

"As sure as the leaves turn in the fall, things in our lives will also change. It's a certainty, indeed."

Arnold twisted on the bench and looked at the man. "You're one of them Christians, ain't you?"

"I'm far from perfect but, yes, I'm a Christian." The man looked at him with sparkling eyes of humor. "I used to be a preacher back in the days before high blood pressure, glaucoma, and arthritis got a hold of me."

Lutis stepped behind the men and watched with a loving expression. He didn't turn at noises behind him because he already knew who it was.

"Lutis." The snarling voice belonged to Mondaci. "Fancy seeing you here."

Mondaci ignored his words and kept his gaze on the humans.

Snippets from the huge church he had visited came back to Arnold's mind with surprising clarity considering he hadn't given it a single thought since he'd pulled out of the church parking lot. "Do you think God loves everyone?"

"Interesting question that you ask. To help me give the best answer, what makes you ask that?"

"I visited a church recently. It's one of those big churches that has thousands of people, and apparently the pastor is famous. A woman singer started screaming during the music, and the music stopped. She said God loves Muslim people, and Buddhist people, and Islam people just like He loved those Christian people."

Odell's forehead scrunched in deep thought. "And you don't believe that, I presume, given the question?"

"If I believed in God, I would believe that He loves everyone, but this old man stood up and started yelling that there was no God other than the one true God of Abraham. He said only those who call upon the name of the Lord will be saved." Arnold chuckled at the remembrance. "The security guards didn't like what he had to say. They literally dragged the poor guy out of the sanctuary."

Odell nodded as the thoughts swirled through his mind in a jumble. "Believe it or not, this topic is quite controversial in the church."

Once again, confusion wrapped itself around Arnold's mind like a relentless boa constrictor. "How can God not love everyone? Isn't loving everyone what makes Him God?"

"God does love everyone, but he's also a God of judgment. He gives men free will to choose Him or not. For those who don't accept His offering of salvation then commit to living a righteous life according to His commandments, He will have no choice but to judge them to eternity in Hell."

"How can a loving God send people to Hell? That doesn't make sense."

"He's a loving God, but He's also a just God. He didn't create Hell for people, He created it as punishment for Satan and his followers who rebelled against Him. Even though He didn't create men for Hell, those who rebel against Him and refuse salvation are, likewise, sentenced to eternal judgment in Hell, just like Satan and his demons. What kind of God would He be for sending His own angels of rebellion to Hell but not send humans who rebelled in the same manner?"

Arnold shifted back in his seat and crossed his arms over his chest.

"Does that make sense?" Odell asked after several minutes passed in silence.

"I guess, but I don't like it. Sending people to Hell isn't loving. How can people like you call Him a loving God when He is anything but?"

"We don't have to like it, but it would be in all our best interests to accept God's mercy and grace while time remains. If you think of it in that way, God sends no one to Hell. People choose that eternal outcome when they refuse his gift of salvation, and when they live in defiance of His holy commands."

Despite the man's words, he still thought any God who sent people to burn forever was a crummy, no-good God. "So, all the Buddhists and Muslims and everyone else who uses their free will to worship another god are just out of luck?"

"That's why Jesus gave His followers the Great Commission. Matthew 28 instructs us to make disciples of all nations, baptizing them in the name of the Father, the Son, and the Holy Spirit, teaching them to obey everything that He commands. Mark chapter 16 tells us to go into the world and preach the gospel to all of creation. If people, after hearing the truth, choose false gods over the True God, then their punishment is an eternity in Hell."

"Who's to say that God's way is right, and everyone else's way is wrong? Maybe Buddha's way is the truth and Christianity is wrong. Or maybe Allah's way is the truth? Maybe there's more than one way."

"No matter what you're talking about in life, there's always only one truth. Versions of the truth are nothing but lies. The Bible says that no one comes to the Father except through His Son, Jesus, and that's the truth I stand on and preach."

Like most religious people, it never helped to argue with them. It was their way or no way, end of story. Arnold shook his head and brooded for several seconds. "We're back at the same question, aren't we? This conversation has fixed nothing. Who's to say that Christianity is the totality of truth, and that every other religion is a lie?"

Odell gave him a warm smile. "All I can do is tell you the truth and point you in the right direction. Just keep in mind that whatever you choose, you'll end up in one of two places—Heaven or Hell—so choose wisely."

Mondaci snarled his nose at the old man, raised his chin to the sky, and released a howl of anger. "Don't listen to that crazy old man. Whatever truth you choose is the right truth for you."

Arnold chewed his bottom lip as he absorbed all that was said. He was even more confused than before. If he wanted to shave his head and worship Buddha, who was this crazy old man to tell him he was wrong? How obnoxious to think that his God's way was the only way.

Though he couldn't get away from this man fast enough, he turned back to face him. "I know we will never agree on everything you just said, but I have one more question."

Odell patted him on the knee. "Ask away, brother."

"I don't believe in God, but I want to. How do you accept salvation when you can't figure out how to believe in the person who gives it?"

"How indeed?" Odell took a few seconds to prayerfully seek a way to answer the man's question. Though feeble in body, his mind was attuned to the scripture hidden in his heart. "This may seem like a cop out of an answer, but the Bible instructs us not to lean on our own understanding, but on God's. Pray to Him, admit that you have doubts, then ask Him to help you overcome them. Prayer will change your life in every way, even in areas where you have doubt."

Arnold puckered his lips in frustration. It was, indeed, a cop out answer. No one ever had an answer for anything. Their kneejerk response was always to pray, and it annoyed him.

"I wish there was an easy answer to help people immediately overcome their doubt, but I know no such words. Read God's word, obey what it says, and make His word the utmost authority in all aspects of your life."

Odell yanked on the leash to bring the dog back to him. "To be saved, Romans 9 says, 'if you confess with your mouth and believe in your heart that God has raised Jesus from the dead, you will be saved. It's really that simple. You don't have to clean yourself up to come to Christ. You can come to Him as you are, confess your sins, and believe that God raised Jesus from the dead as an atonement for your sins. When that happens, the Holy Spirit will begin the process of sanctification in your life."

Oh, great. Now I'm expected to believe that some man I don't even believe in, that I've never seen or heard, thousands of years ago died then rose from the dead. He was over this conversation, so he stood to his feet and thrust his hand down at the old man. "It was a nice talk, but I have to run." Without waiting for a response, he whirled around and darted toward the rig.

"Don't wait too long, Arnold," Odell called after him. "God's waiting for you to turn to Him before it's too late."

Chapter 39

Arnold fought to catch his breath as he absorbed the news.

When Alice collapsed into sobs, the sight broke his heart. He stood from his chair in the living room and swept her into his arms. Is our baby really gone? How can that be possible? The words hammered through his mind as he tried to console his wife of a grief that was inconsolable.

They weren't in a financial position to take on a baby, they both knew that, so maybe it was a good thing. Though it was a sentiment he would never say aloud, it was there in the back of his mind, offering, to him, an odd sense of peace. He hated that such a loss had been foisted upon them, but it was a loss he could handle. Alice would have a harder time getting over it, and he would be there for her for as long as it took.

"What did the doctor say?" he asked when her sobs quieted.

"I haven't seen him yet, but I called this morning first thing and told him what happened."

"Why didn't you wake me last night?"

She took his hand in hers and squeezed it. "I know I should have, honey, but I needed time to process what happened. Please don't be mad."

"I'm not mad. I just wish I could have been there to support you, that's all."

"I have a—" She sucked in a breath to get herself under control. "A beautiful crib came through the store the other day and my boss told me I could set it aside for us and pay for it over time. She even said we could—" she pressed a tissue to her nose and closed her eyes. "She even said we could keep it in the storeroom until we were ready for it."

"That was nice of them."

"I guess I'll tell them they can move it to the showroom since we don't need it anymore."

"Why don't you hold on to it for a while longer? We're still young, you know. We can be pregnant again in no time."

She tossed the tissue into the trashcan and yanked another from the box. "Oh, Arnold, I know you're right, but I don't even want to think about another baby right now."

"When you're ready, dear. That's what I meant."

She leaned in and kissed him then stood to her feet. "I guess I should whip up some dinner before it gets any later."

"Let's not cook tonight. How about I—"

She shook her head. "We don't have the extra money to go to a restaurant."

"Yes, we do. I stayed over for an extra two hours after work and when I was done my boss gave me twenty bucks to put in my wallet, and that's above the regular overtime pay."

She gave him a weak smile and lowered her head. The last thing she wanted was to cook, tonight of all nights. "We need to put that money back for a rainy day. There's no need in going out for supper when I have all the makings right here."

Alice was always the voice of reason in their life, and he usually succumbed to her will, but not this time. "As far as we're concerned, today is a rainy day. When he gave me the twenty bucks, I decided right then and there that I would splurge and take you out for dinner one night. It's Friday, and tonight's the night."

"I'm not all that hungry tonight and my eyes are swollen from crying all day. I'll agree to splurging for dinner, but can we save it for another night?"

"I'm sorry, I should have realized you might not be in the mood to go out tonight. We can go whenever you feel like it." He took her hand and led her to the couch. "Why don't you have a seat while I rummage around in the kitchen for a little dinner. I know you're not hungry, but you need to eat, at least a little."

She sat at the end of the sofa then jumped back up. "You've worked all day. I won't let you cook dinner."

He placed his arms around her and looked into her eyes. "When you married me, we became a team. I'm not as good a cook as you, but I can manage to get us a little food on the table. Let me do that for you, okay?"

"No, I can—"

Arnold placed his finger over her lips to shush her.

Her shoulders fell and she gave him a weak smile of gratitude. "My heart hurts too much to argue. I'll let you deal with dinner this one time."

"Will you eat a little bite with me?"

"I'll try."

"Good. You sit, and I'll call when it's ready."

She sat on the sofa, laid her head on the cushioned arm, and stretched her legs across its length. "Let's keep it simple. There's bread in the pantry and Virginia ham and cheddar in the refrigerator. There's a stash of Fritos in the cabinet behind the bag of sugar."

Hiding the good stuff from me, huh? "I'll come get you when it's ready."

Chapter 40

The clicking of her acrylic nails on the tabletop didn't enter her subconsciousness until the waiter placed a frosty glass of water on the table in front of her.

Hyacinth dropped her hands to her lap to keep them still then gave the man a gentle nod.

"We're still waiting on the rest of your party to arrive?"

She glanced around the dining room as she spoke to the waiter. "A gentleman, but I'm afraid I've never met him, so I don't know who I'm looking for." *Why did I say that? It makes it sound like I'm on a blind date.* "I gave him my name to check-in with the host, so he should find me fairly easily."

Be quiet and stop rambling. She took a sip of the water to give herself something to do.

"If a man comes in looking confused, shall I send him your way then?" The waiter teased.

"Go ahead and send them my way," she laughed.

He left menus with the promise that he would return soon.

Her heart was doing calisthenics in her chest. *Lord, I'm a nervous wreck about meeting this guy. I don't know what he wants but give me the grace to hear what he has to say.* Her gaze focused on the door when a man entered and looked around the restaurant. He had dark, perfectly styled hair, wore a suit and tie that looked expensive, and was incredibly handsome. Too handsome, in her opinion, and way overdressed.

She looked down at her dark blue jeans and blue and white striped blouse. She should have placed more thought into her apparel for this meeting.

Her hands shook, and she picked up the glass for another sip. She locked her stare on him as he made his way through the restaurant with a manly swagger then past her table, where he gave a vigorous handshake to another man dressed in a similar fashion. She breathed a sigh of relief that she wouldn't have to sit through lunch with such a handsome man.

To allay her anxiety, she glanced across the room to the bar where Sheri and her husband sat sipping soft drinks.

Sheri gave her a cheery wave followed by a thumbs up.

They were far enough away that they wouldn't be able to hear conversations but could see everything that happened at the table.

Though Hyacinth wasn't worried about anything bad happening in such a public place, speaking with the man who had been involved in the same accident as Jenner was a nerve-wracking experience.

She stiffened in her seat when an older man with salt-and-pepper hair, dressed in jeans and an oversized t-shirt, entered the restaurant.

He was the total opposite of Mr. Handsome from a couple of minutes ago, and something told her that this was her guy.

She watched as he spoke to the man at the podium, glanced around the room, then fell into step behind him.

When the host neared the table then paused and gestured for the man to sit, she glanced over at Sheri with a leery gaze. She sent up a silent prayer that Sheri wouldn't abandon her for a bathroom break then scolded herself for such a judgmental thought.

She pasted on a warm smile and stood to her feet when the man paused at the table. The poor guy looked as though he was just as nervous as she was, so she held out her hand. "Mr. Arnold?"

He nodded, gave her hand a cautious stare, then shook it.

She nearly gasped aloud at his crushing grip and was glad when he dropped her hand and glanced around the restaurant.

He was a big guy with broad shoulders and a scraggly face with wrinkles at the corners of his eyes. Though he was rough around the edges as far as looks went, she had an inkling that he had been a handsome man in his younger years.

She gestured at the table. "I'm Hyacinth. Won't you have a seat?"

He looked at the chair across from her with suspicion for several seconds, as though afraid she was trying to play a trick on him.

Finally, he took a seat. "I hope I don't embarrass myself. I ain't used to having dinner at such fancy places."

Hyacinth looked around the café. She had chosen it carefully because she wanted some place nice yet not so stuffy and elegant that it would make meeting a stranger even more uncomfortable than it already was.

"My husband and I love this—" She paused when she caught what she had said. She was so antsy that she was suddenly guilty of doing what she despised—speaking before thinking. "My husband and I loved this place. We loved coming here for Sunday brunch after church. Jenner was such a child at heart," she giggled. "Every time we came here, he had chocolate chip pancakes."

She pressed her lips closed and picked up her water glass. The last thing she wanted was to monopolize the conversation, especially given that he had asked for the meeting.

Determined to have better manners, she took a long drink of the water to give him an opportunity to speak. Her throat was parched, and the freezing liquid felt good as it tumbled down.

The silence was awkward for several seconds before he finally spoke. "Thanks for meeting with me. The last person you ever expected to hear from is me, I'm sure."

Since the statement was more than a little true, the waiter stepping up and interrupting was a welcome intrusion. She glanced over at Arnold. "If you like chicken fried steak, it's the best in town."

He picked up the menu and glanced over it. "Chicken fried steak sounds good. Mashed potatoes with steamed carrots and cauliflower—oh, and sweet tea if you have it, extra lemon."

The waiter nodded, scribbled both orders on his pad, and scurried across the dining room and through wooden swinging doors.

The silence between them was oppressive, so Hyacinth gave him a warm smile of encouragement. When he didn't return the gesture, she turned to the bar in search of Sheri's familiar face. She was tempted to wave her hand, to summon her friends over to the table to join them, but that would probably make what he wanted to say even more awkward.

He cleared his throat. "You must be wonderin' why I asked to meet you."

Chapter 41

His voice snapped her back to reality.

Heat flowed into her cheeks to realize that she had drifted off into other thoughts as the man spoke to her. She wondered how much of his introductory small talk she had missed with her rude inattentiveness.

"I wanted to tell you in person how sorry I am about what happened to your husband. You're too young to be a widow, and it's all my fault." It annoyed him when moisture collected in the corners of his eyes.

She cocked her head to the side with a friendly expression. "Mr. Arnold, I appreciate your apology but like I said on the phone, you were a victim just like all the rest of them. You have nothing to apologize for."

If I had been more alert at the wheel, maybe I would have seen the beam and averted disaster. "You don't have to answer if you don't want, but was your husband the only one who died?"

"My husband, Jenner, and the bus driver, his name was Tommy. They were the only ones who died. Jenner's best friends, Camden and Lucas, had minor injuries. One of the guitar players was in a coma for several weeks, and his condition was iffy for a while, but with lots of prayer he pulled through. Both of his legs were broken, and he had extensive facial fractures."

"I'd be obliged if you would give my apologies to all who were on the bus that day. I never meant anyone any harm."

"I will pass it along if that would make you feel better, but please don't beat yourself up over this. I promise, it was an unfortunate situation of you all being in the wrong place at the wrong time. The Lord always has a plan, even when we mere mortals can't understand it."

"You mean to tell me you think the Lord's plan was for your husband to die, and you're not mad as a wet rooster at Him?" His words flew out louder than he had intended. He closed his eyes for a couple of seconds to pull himself together.

Hyacinth glanced at the bar where Sheri and Joseph kept their attention on her table.

At Arnold's outburst, Joseph rose to his feet with a somber expression.

Sheri placed her hand on his arm to restrain him.

When he looked down at her and she shook her head, he sat back down.

"I didn't mean to raise my voice, Ms. Alekson. All this religious stuff—I don't know what I think of it."

"I apologize if speaking about such things makes you uneasy. I didn't mean to be insensitive to your belief system. Sometimes I forget that not everyone is as comfortable with it as I am."

"My wife and I used to go to church back when we first got married years ago, but we haven't been since—well, in a long time."

"What's her name?"

"Alice."

"Do you have children?"

He shook his head.

At his silence and subtle change of countenance, she suspected it had been the wrong question to ask.

"Do you have children?" he asked.

"It was our plan one day, but we never had the chance."

The waiter deposited their food on the table then slipped away.

Arnold looked down at the steaming plate of food that looked and smelled amazing, but he had no appetite.

Across the table, Hyacinth nibbled at the leafy greens of her salad and picked around the chunks of veggies and grilled chicken.

Though this woman was nothing like Alice, something about her reminded him of her when they were younger.

He scooped up a bite of the mashed potatoes but set it back down on the plate. "You're obviously a religious person."

"I prefer the term Christian over religious," she shrugged. "I get what you're asking, though, so yes."

He fiddled with the fork but couldn't force himself to take a bite. "Alice and I don't have the best relationship these days. We haven't for years." As soon as he said the words, he hated himself for uttering them. This woman's husband was dead because of him, and he had the nerve to complain about his marriage being trash?

"I'm sorry to hear that, Mr. Arnold. What do you think happened?"

The warmth and compassion in her voice startled him. How could she be so nice after he killed her husband? If the tables were turned, he probably wouldn't be as nice about things. He hesitated for a full minute, contemplating how to answer the question. "I've been a truck driver for years, and I like to stay away from home for as many weeks as possible before going back. Eventually, we grew apart."

"Unfortunately, that happens a lot in marriages."

"Did it ever happen with you and Jenner?"

"Thankfully, no." A thoughtful expression crossed her face. "We had our fair share of, shall we say, disagreeable moments, but we weren't married for long enough to grow apart."

"I've tried to fix our marriage since the accident, but she's not interested. Almost dying has a way of making you want to fix what's broken in your life."

"A lot of clarity comes with seeing your life flash before your eyes, I imagine."

"I've always heard that, but my life didn't flash before my eyes, so maybe I wasn't as near death as I thought. Maybe I need to find a way to make Alice's life flash before her eyes without almost killing her first. That might make her appreciate me more."

Hyacinth pushed her plate toward the center of the table and leaned forward. "I'm no expert in relationships, but can I give you some advice?"

"Sure."

"Reopen the lines of communication with each other. When you're sitting at home, try reminiscing together about the fun things from the past that you did as a couple. You'd be surprised at how remembering the past can bring you back together."

Yeah, that would work—if I could get her away from her card hags, he thought with a trace of bitterness.

"If you had a bucket list back in the day, dust it off and see what things you can do now that you didn't get to do back then. Is there a special place that you two ever dreamed of visiting but never did? If so, surprise her with a fabulous trip to France, or wherever. I know you still work, but now, in the golden years of your life, is the perfect time to do the things that you couldn't do when you were younger with less time and even less money."

"It sounds like a good idea," Arnold scoffed. "I can't even get her out of the house for an occasional dinner so leaving the country is probably out of the question."

Hyacinth snapped her fingers. "In that case, bring it to her."

"Say again?"

"If you can't get her out, start small by bringing it in to her. Go to her favorite restaurant, order out both of your favorite meals, and have a romantic picnic. Pull out the big guns by using your nicest china. Arrange it on the plates and make it look beautiful for her, then go to the florist and buy flowers to put in the center of the table. Be sure and tell the florist to keep the arrangement short. When you're trying to have a romantic dinner, it's no good to have tall flower arrangements. You want to see into each other's eyes."

He wanted to laugh and tell her that such things might work with other women but not with Alice. "That's an idea. I'll keep it in mind."

"It sounds like a simple thing but start dating her again. Take her out on real dates to do the things you used to do before you were married. The nostalgia of doing things you used to do could really help. Even better, you could try new things as a couple. Take her to the local art center and you guys take oil painting lessons or learn how to make your own pottery. If you both like animals, maybe you could volunteer at the animal shelter."

He gave her a half-hearted nod. Alice would never go for any of these things. "Yeah, sure. Thanks."

She reached across the table and grasped his hand in hers. "I know it sounds daunting, maybe even impossible right now, but if you guys have been estranged for years, it may take weeks or even months of persistence on your part. In the end it'll be worth it if it works, don't you think?"

He nodded his agreement. "It's worth thinking about."

"And Arnold?" She patted his hand then pulled away. "Don't underestimate the power of your touch. Do little things like kissing her before bedtime or in the morning after you wake up. If she's upset, take her in your arms and hold her for as long as you need to make her feel better."

"Oh sure. If I did any of that she'd think I was abducted by aliens."

"It may feel awkward at first if you guys have stopped doing such things, but trust me, there's no quicker way to win over a woman's heart."

"It's some great ideas. No wonder you and Jenner had a great relationship. I envy that."

"This is my opinion, but I think you should keep the gestures small in the beginning. Save the trip to France for down the road when things are less awkward. Contrary to popular belief, most women don't want grand gestures. Always remember, it was probably the small things that won her heart in the first place, and it's the small things that will keep her heart forever."

Chapter 42

When the waitress placed the ticket on the table, Hyacinth reached for it, but Arnold snatched it away before she could grab it.

Hyacinth unzipped her wallet and pulled out her debit card. "We can have them split the bill."

"I may not be the nicest guy on the planet at times, but my momma taught me that a woman never pays for her own meal. I suppose in today's backwards culture, picking up a woman's tab isn't politically correct, but I'm from the old school way of doing things. I hope that doesn't offend you."

"Unlike some women, I love that male chivalry isn't completely dead yet, although I fear it's on its way to a demise in the likes of the dinosaurs." She dropped the card to the table and slid it across. "I don't expect you to pay, though. We can have them split it."

He slid it back across the table. "You were nice enough to accept my request to meet with you, ma'am. As payback for the inconvenience, I'd appreciate it if you would allow me to buy your lunch."

"Yes, but you drove all the way here from—" She paused as she realized she knew very little about him. "—well, wherever you're from."

"I live in a little town in Iowa that you'd miss if you blinked while driving through it. So please, let me buy your lunch."

Her instinct was to argue, but the determined look in his eyes made his intention clear. She ducked her head with a bashful smile. "Thank you. I appreciate your generosity." She put the debit card back into her wallet and tossed it into her purse. "If you ever make it back this way, it'll be my treat."

The sentiment warmed his heart in an unexpected way. After all the traumas of their intertwined pasts, he had expected this woman to hate him, to treat him like the murderer he was, yet she exuded a peace and lovingkindness that he didn't understand.

After Arnold paid the ticket, and as they made their way out of the restaurant, she wiggled her fingers in Sheri's direction and mouthed a silent goodbye. Her visitor was a friendly older man. Though rough around the edges in a lot of ways, he posed no threat. She would be fine around him without her well-meaning chaperones.

After an hour and a half of the restaurant's cold interior she was glad to bask in the welcome heat of the sun. They strolled through the parking lot without a word, but it was a comfortable silence. "This is me." She pointed at a champagne-colored SUV with sparkling golden flecks.

Everything about her, from her graceful demeanor to the fancy way she dressed, to the glint of her smooth hair, and now to her vehicle, told him that she didn't hurt for material possessions. He wondered how a traveling gospel group, especially one so young, managed to have money, and he wondered if they were famous—at least as far as a gospel group could be. He pointed across the parking lot at the rig. "That's me over there."

Her gaze followed his finger and her mouth dropped. "The eighteen-wheeler?"

"That's me."

"It's beautiful. Can I see her up close?"

The question took him by surprise. He had never met a woman who was impressed by his rig, so he gestured for her to precede him.

She glanced over her shoulder at Sheri and Joshua who stood on the restaurant's sidewalk watching them with an eagle eye. When she gave them a casual wave, Sheri raised her hands as though asking, "what are you doing?"

Hyacinth whipped her phone from her pocket and sent a quick text message. You guys can go. He's a great guy, so no worries. xoxo

She snickered when, as expected, Sheri texted back seconds later. Are you crazy?? We're not leaving you here with a possible axe murderer! Where are you going??

With a smile, she shoved the phone back in her pocket. Dynamite couldn't blast her friend away, and she loved her for it even though her overprotectiveness wasn't necessary.

"Let me guess. Your girlfriend wants to know what in the world you're thinking, riding off into the sunset with Mr. Tall, Dark, and Handsome?" Arnold turned as he walked, and it didn't take long to guess that the couple looking in their direction were there with Hyacinth.

"Actually, she thinks you might be an axe murderer." Hyacinth laced her arm through his with a giggle as they neared the rig.

Her easy banter made his heart ache. How quickly Alice, the love of his life, had gone from a sweet woman just like this to what she was today. What he wouldn't give to have back even a wispy shadow of the past. A flirtatious grin or a teasing stare. He'd take anything, but that would never happen, and it was all his fault.

Hyacinth's arm woven through his gave a warm flutter in his heart. He waved away her teasing words. "Tell your friend that blood freaks me out. I'm too big of a wuss to be an axe murderer."

"Let's keep that between us and give her something fun to worry about." She reached out and ran her fingers over the rig's fiberglass body. "I've never seen one this close. It really is an amazing vehicle."

"And loud, too. After riding around in these things for years, I'm about half deaf." He nodded toward the door. "You want to sit inside?"

When her head jerked in his direction, her eyes were wide. "Can I?"

He jumped up onto the footrail, opened the door, jumped back to the ground, then held her hand and guided her into the vehicle.

His heart was as light as air when she squealed like an excited little girl and clutched the wheel in her hands. She bounced up and down in the seat as though she were driving.

He almost told her that the rig wasn't as rough of a ride as she depicted but kept the thought to himself.

She reached up over the door, frowned, then looked down at him. "You don't have a horn?"

He hopped up onto the footrail with a grin. "It's in the steering wheel like a normal horn. Older trucks had the pull cord, but most newer ones don't. You can have them specially installed, though."

"You should have one installed. That would be more fun."

As soon as she said it, he knew he would have one installed the minute he got home.

She looked down at him with a sly smile. "Can I honk it?"

"Sure, if you want." He glanced over his shoulder then back up at her. "It's pretty loud, though, so expect heads to turn."

She placed her palm over the center of the steering wheel, squeezed her eyes shut, and held her breath for several seconds before putting all her weight into it.

She jumped then screeched with joy when the ear-splitting foghorn filled the space around them then echoed back. "That was amazing. Do kids ever come up beside you and move their arm up and down?"

"Sometimes." He didn't tell her that when they did, he usually ignored them then flipped them the bird after they drove past. After today he would be nice to every little kid he saw on the road. If they wanted him to blow the horn, he would blow it twice.

He waited while she looked at and touched everything in the cabin. Usually, anyone who touched his stuff like that would have gotten a tongue lashing, but the short visit with this woman had scuffed out his rough side—or at least he hoped so.

Several minutes later when she held her hand down so he could help her back to the ground, he was disappointed. She was the first person in ages that he had clicked with, and he hated for it to come to an end.

"Thanks for letting me see inside your truck. I love it." She almost asked him if he would take her for a ride around the block, but that would be silly. Besides, Sheri would lay on the road in front of the tires before she'd let her drive off with a strange man. She patted the truck again. "Where are you headed next?"

"I'm not sure." He looked off into the distance where the ocean sparkled between breaks in the tree line. "I've been out of the loop since the accident. My next job doesn't start for another week, so for now I'm a man of leisure." As soon as he said the words, the idea struck out of nowhere. "Maybe I'll go back home and rest for a few days. That ought to make the wife happy." He released a rueful laugh.

She placed her hand on his arm and squeezed. "Go home and re-bond with Alice. You won her over once and I have faith you can do it again."

"I was younger the first time around. I worry that no amount of wooing will work."

"She still loves you or she wouldn't still be there. You just need to remind her what she's missing."

She can already see what she's missing. A fat slob with a cranky disposition. Even if he wanted to change, he didn't have the energy to put forth in doing it. "You don't know me that well, but can I give you a hug before I head out?"

She pushed on his arm with a playful smile. "I was going to steal one from you if you didn't offer."

His heart melted when she walked into his embrace and stayed there for several seconds. She smelled like a tropical island full of citrus and flowers.

When she pulled away, she dazzled him with a smile. "I'm so glad you called. I was anxious about what I would say and feel when I saw you for the first time." She patted her chest. "This was good for me."

He jumped up on the rig's foot ledge and looked down at her. "It was even better for me. Thank you."

"No more blaming yourself about what happened. You promise?"

"I'll try." He needed to come clean and tell her that he'd fallen asleep behind the wheel all those months ago and that his involvement in her husband's death was worse than a random beam in the road, but he didn't have the nerve to confess such a thing. Not to mention, what would happen to him if he told her, and she went to the police with his admission? Would they arrest him? Would he have to go through months, years even, of court sessions? It wasn't how he wanted to spend the last years of his life.

She held up her hand in a still wave. "Keep my phone number. If you ever find yourself back in the neighborhood, I'd love to see you again."

Really? She really wants to see me again. "You got it." He jumped up into his seat when she turned to walk away. "Hey?"

She looked over her shoulder and looked up at him.

"I know you need to go, but—"

"I don't have to go anywhere." She walked back to the truck and under its shade.

"What does it mean to be saved? Really saved?"

Mondaci and Fraush stepped behind Hyacinth.

"No!" Mondaci shouted.

She hesitated for only a split second before jumping up on the foot ledge and clutching for dear life onto the stainless-steel handle. "To be saved, God must first draw a sinner to His call. He convicts sinners by the power of the Holy Spirit. The moment a person confesses their sin, makes a deliberate decision to turn away from sin, and believes in faith that Jesus has saved him, then he is saved."

What does that mean, though? "That involves some fancy prayer, right? I ain't prayed a whole lot in my life."

"Jesus said that we are free to come to him just as we are. He doesn't want a fancy prayer with impressive words." She touched her fingertips to his heart. "Talk to Him like you're talking to me right now. He's always listening. You can even do it in your heart without uttering a single word. If He draws a sinner through his Holy Spirit, He'll accept them as His own."

He nodded and gulped over the tightening in his throat.

"Arnold, can I pray with you before you leave?"

Fraush rose in height until he was eye level with the woman. "If you know what's good for you, you'll turn around and walk away."

He glanced past the man in the driver's seat to Lutis who sat in the passenger seat.

"The seed's already been planted in his heart," Lutis said.

"Oh, big deal. How many planted seeds wither away, die, and never amount to anything?"

"True, but how many grow and flourish?"

The demon broke into a sneering smile that cast his hideous features into an even deeper look of evil. "Wide is the gate and broad is the road that leads to destruction, and many go through it. That's how many seeds never amount to anything."

Lutis nodded. "We'll see."

Arnold considered her question for several seconds before shaking his head. He didn't want her praying for him, here, in front of everyone.

"It won't be like those crazy snake oil televangelists you see on TV and the internet, with all the screaming and shouting and jumping and hollering and knocking you to the ground." she whispered. "All that is an unnecessary show."

He shook his head again and threw the truck into gear. He needed to get out of here, and the sooner the better.

"Woah!" Hyacinth gripped the handrail tighter when the truck lurched forward.

He threw it back into park and clutched her hand. "I'm sorry. Are you okay?"

"I'm fine. It just startled me for a second, that's all."

"Can I call you if I ever want to, you know, learn how to pray or something?"

"Call me anytime, day or night, but don't make coming to Him too hard. Confess your sins. Submit to Him through your repentance. To repent means turning from your sinful ways. You don't have to pray a single word to turn away from your sins, you just do it. He knows your heart before you even speak." She patted his hand then hopped back down to the ground. "I mean it. Call me anytime."

He held his hand out the window as he inched past her. In the rearview mirror, he watched her watching him drive away.

He turned the rig around the corner and rumbled past the restaurant. The man and woman who had accompanied her stared at him like a strange curiosity. He nodded and gave them a friendly wave.

His heart squeezed in his chest at the thought that he may never see or talk to Hyacinth again. He stole another glance in the side mirror before she disappeared from his view. "Something about you touched me in an unexpected way."

"She's not the one who touched you," Lutis said. "She pointed you in the direction of the One who wants you more than any other."

Chapter 43

It was two o'clock in the morning and a black and white Cary Grant movie flickered on the television screen in her bedroom. He was one of the handsomest, classiest men to ever grace the movies, yet not even he had the power to rip her away from her thoughts tonight.

Alice tossed back the covers with a hacking cough and made her way to her feet with an unsteady sway. She held onto the wall for several seconds until she was able to take a step.

She unlocked the bedroom window and yanked it up. A healthy breeze pushed into the room, and she sucked in several deep cool breaths. The branches of the trees across the street danced in the wind, and the shadows that pooled onto the street and yards gave the neighborhood a ghoulish aura.

Across the street, Pauline's living room window had the subtle blue glow of a television screen through the slits of the curtains. Was her friend, too, in the throes of a grueling sleepless night?

Too exhausted to stand on her feet for another second, though the breeze felt nice, she dropped into the armchair below the window.

She picked up the ancient Dorothy Gilman book that she had read so many times that its edges were dog-eared and yellowed and the cover's corners had dulled to ratty and rounded. She wasn't an avid reader, but it was her favorite book. On the occasions that the inclination hit, she read the same book over and over because the characters were familiar. They were the only friends she needed. She didn't like investing the time to learn to like people in real life, and the same went for fictional characters.

It was too dark to read, and she was too tired to reach up and turn on the lamp, but the tattered book still comforted her. She leaned her head back on the chair and closed her eyes.

***

<u>1971</u>

Arnold sneaked to the doorway and peeked into the room where Alice lay propped on a mountain of pillows flipping through the same magazine that she read night after night. On her face was a thick layer of goopy Noxzema. The room reeked of the medicinal smell that he at one time hated, but now it had grown on him. The scent was her, and he loved it.

He hid the package behind his back, tiptoed into the room, pushed the magazine into her lap, and pressed a kiss to her lips.

She giggled and pushed him away. "Don't smear my cold cream otherwise I won't look pretty tomorrow."

"The most beautiful woman in the world doesn't need cream to look pretty."

She thought a blush hit her cheeks at his words, but it was hard to say for sure due to the tingle of the cream. "Maybe she doesn't, but I do." She picked up the magazine and flipped to the next page.

He sat on the edge of the bed, wacked the magazine out of her hand, then looked up at the ceiling and whistled a zany tune.

"Arnold Mueller Collins. You want me to whoop your britches?"

"More than you can imagine."

"Oh, stop it." She gave him an amused grin and picked up the magazine again.

He pulled the package from behind his back and laid it in her lap. He had bought it at the retail store and one of the ladies in the office had wrapped it in a brown paper bag and tied a yellow satin ribbon around it.

She set the magazine aside and stared at it as though it were an alien rock from Mars. She looked up at him then back down at the package. "What is it?"

He spoke with an exaggerated country twang. "Well, ma'am, that's one of those newfangled things folks like to call a gift."

She picked it up and fanned herself with it. "I love you for it, but you need to stop buying me things. We shouldn't splurge on stuff we don't need."

"I wish you'd stop worrying so much about our finances. We're doing fine."

"I know we are, especially now that I'm contributing to the finances. Sally says I'm doing a great job. Who knows?" She raised her eyebrows in a hoity-toity manner. "Maybe I'll be a manager one day and we'll really roll in the dough then."

He hated that she insisted on working that job and was convinced it was a factor in her losing the baby. He kept his sentiments to himself, though, because the last time he had given his opinion on the matter, she got mad and locked herself in the bedroom for several hours. It had taken countless apologies through the door to finally get her to open it.

She tugged on the tail of the simple bow and unraveled it. When the paper fell away, she squealed with delight at a paperback novel by Dorothy Gilman. "Oh, Arnold. Thank you. I can't wait to read it."

"If you don't like that one, we can take it back so you can pick out another. A woman in my office loves that author and promised that you would love everything she writes."

"I wish you hadn't spent the money, but I'm sure I will love it."

Her comments about their near perpetual lack of funds made him feel like a heel every time she mentioned it. It wasn't like they had no money. They just didn't have an excess of it. "I picked it up in the clearance bin at the drug store. I thought you might enjoy having something different to read other than that ratty magazine your mother gave you months ago."

"Maybe on Saturdays when you're off work I can go to the library and borrow some books?"

"Any time you want to go to the library, or anywhere else for that matter, you can drop me off at work and go wherever your heart desires."

Chapter 44

It was the early morning hours, but he was too wired to pull over and sleep.

He had driven across Tennessee and was now pulled over at a truck stop in Van Buren, Arkansas, a town no bigger than his own in Iowa.

Much like he had expected, nothing was open at this hour except the Wal-Mart, McDonald's, the Waffle House, and a couple of 24-hour gas stations.

He munched on a premade deli sandwich with stale crusts and limp, tasteless lettuce. As far as sandwiches went it wasn't the best, but it was better than nothing.

He needed a game plan. His original idea had been to drive aimlessly across the country until his next job was ready, but the more he drove the less it was something he wanted to do.

He crumpled the crinkly sandwich paper and thrust it into the plastic bag along with the Fritos bag, the Snickers wrapper, and the empty bottle of Mountain Dew.

He laid back in the bed with his head cradled in his hands. Fifties music played on the radio, but the volume was just low enough that hopefully he could catch a few hours of shuteye before sunrise.

Images of Alice floated through his mind as he drifted into sleep.

***

Their wedding day, surrounded by friends and family, hadn't been a grand affair worthy of notice in the society pages, but it was everything to him. His eyes bulged as he watched her and her father dance across the Veteran's Hall, where all the poor people went to throw a shindig.

Dancing behind Alice was a dark and wiry creature with long and spindly fingers. Its face was gnarled and scary.

Alice and her father laughed with joy as they cut across the dance floor while *Ain't No Sunshine* blared from speakers around the room. How did they not notice such a hideous creature?

He glanced around the room as wedding guests smiled and applauded the father-daughter dance, eagerly waiting for the announcement for everyone else to join in.

The creature circled around them like a vulture on a dead carcass, and its focus was mainly on Alice.

He rushed onto the dance floor to protect her, but the creature held up its hand in his direction. "This doesn't concern you."

"If it concerns my wife, it concerns me," Arnold screamed. He threw a punch at the ugly creature, but his fist hit nothing but air. It had disappeared before his eyes and materialized on the opposite side of the dancing couple.

It gave Arnold an eerie smile then reached out and placed his hands on either side of Alice's head.

"I said stay away from my wife!" Arnold rushed to slap the beast's hands away, but they went through his arms like they were made of a dark, evil fog.

In disbelief, he glared at her father then at the rest of the room. They all laughed and clapped like nothing was going on. "What's wrong with you people? Can't you see this ... this thing?"

No one paid him even a moment of attention, so he turned to the creature. A rage boiled inside of him. "Who are you and what do you want?"

The creature raised an eyebrow and smirked at him. "Why, I couldn't miss your wonderful soiree, now could I?"

Arnold clenched his teeth. "Who are you?"

"You may call me Fraush."

His jaw dropped open when around the perimeter of the room, behind the celebrating guests, more similar creatures than he could count materialized. His heart thundered in his chest, and it was suddenly difficult to breathe.

In the corner of the room was a solitary being in glowing white that was so tall his head nearly touched the ceiling. "What the—" Arnold sniffed his punch and took a sip. Had one of his coworkers spiked his drink as a wedding party joke?

Alice glanced over at him with a beaming smile. "Did you say something, sweetie?"

Arnold gestured at the creature who shuffled around the room, never more than a few inches away from her. "Am I the only one who can see all this?"

A concerned look crossed her face. She took a sweeping gaze across the room. All the while, she and her father never missed a beat to the music. "What's wrong? I don't see anything."

"Are you kidding me?" He pointed at the creature. "Right there beside you. You can't see that?"

Their guests stopped clapping and smiling and looked from one to the other.

Her dad looked at his half-drunk beverage. "Boy, I don't know what you're drinking, but you might want to stop."

Arnold tossed the drink back and gulped it down in two glugs then tossed the cup at the nearest trash bin. It bounced off the edge and rolled under the table that held the three-layered wedding cake. "You don't see all these ... apparitions?" His gaze flit from Alice to her father, then back to her.

They paused their dancing, to Arnold's relief.

Alice looked around the room. "What apparitions?"

The creature stepped to Alice's side and positioned himself in such a way that he could keep visual contact with Arnold.

"Boy, if you're going crazy on us, I wish you'd done it before we spent all this money on the wedding," Alice's dad said.

The creature tossed its head back and released shrieks of maniacal laughter.

The hairs on Arnold's arm stood straight up. He glanced around the room at the dark creatures. Some of them were stooped over like old men, some were as tall as the room, and others were knee high little runts. Most of them were hideously ugly, but a few were handsome in a creepy, otherworldly sort of way.

When he stepped up to the creature, its laughing ceased, but it kept a mocking grin. "I said, who are you and what do you want?" He punched a finger in its chest, but it went right through it.

Alice looked around the room at the guests' worried—even scared—looks. She placed her hand on Arnold's forearm and squeezed it. "What's wrong with you? Are you sick?" Her heart deflated inside of her. Maybe marrying Arnold hadn't been such a good thing after all.

"What do I want?" The creature spoke in a slithery tone that sounded like it belonged in the most wretched horror movie. He pointed at Alice. "I want her." The tip of his finger had a blood-red nail that was filed into points so sharp that it looked like it could slash the flesh of anything that came against him.

It turned with an amused grin and pressed its fingernail into Arnold's chest, and the pressure of the point felt like it could break into his skin with the slightest increased pressure. "And I want you."

Fear rippled through Arnold's insides like it was a living being. "What do you mean you want us?"

The creature leaned toward Arnold until they were nose to nose.

Arnold wanted to take a few steps back, but his feet wouldn't move. The being's breath smelled like rotted death. He gagged then swallowed several times to keep down the contents of his stomach.

"I want you both, and I always get what I want."

Chitters of laughter and grunts sounded around the room until it swelled into a fiendish chorus.

***

Arnold bolted up in bed with a scream.

Sweat rolled off his face and saturated his clothing.

He was more scared than he'd ever been. He scooched to the side of the bed and looked out the windshield. The landscape was an orange-pink, and birds sang and swooped back and forth in the tree line just outside the truck.

"What the ... was that?" A few profanities sliced through his mind.

He hated to say it for fear of sounding crazy, but had those been demons in his dreams? It had been a dream, and he knew it. It was so real, though. So vivid. Even now he smelled the lingering breath of the beast that had spoken to him. Or maybe it was nothing but his imagination. Maybe the sandwich from last night was having its final revenge on him.

Something in his spirit didn't feel right, but he didn't know what it was. He couldn't recall the last time he'd been scared, but now he was so scared that he was afraid to move.

He raised his eyes toward the sky and squeezed them shut. "Lord, I don't know what happened last night but even now it seems so real. If it's alright with You, I'd like to never have a dream like that again."

Chapter 45

lice hadn't done it in years, but she cancelled today's card game. Pauline had given her what for about it, but she was quick to tell her where she and her disappointment could go.

Irritated, Pauline informed her that she would have the card game at her house instead. "You can come if you want or not," she snapped before hanging up on her.

Alice shuffled to the window, looked across the street, and flipped off Pauline's house. When she imagined Pauline doing the same thing to her, her raspy laugh turned into a coughing spell that left her gasping for breath.

She clutched her chest and wondered if this was the day that she would breathe her last. "Not that dying would be any worse than living," she muttered as she fell into her seat in the living room.

She reached for the spot on the table where her cigarettes always sat, but they weren't there. She spat as many obscenities as she could before another spasm of coughs prevented her from continuing.

She was too tired to go to the kitchen next to the coffeepot, where she now remembered having them last.

After a few minutes, she grabbed the remote and turned on the television. With the girls here every day, quiet was never a thing in this house, but now it was too quiet, to the point that it freaked her out.

She snarled at the images of the soap opera that filled the screen. A rich woman dripping in jewels that made the Queen of England look like a poor peasant was in the midst of an overly dramatic emotional breakdown over the loss of her child who'd been kidnapped by mobsters and had been found dead. She turned off the television, hefted herself from the chair, and made her way to the bedroom.

On the edge of the bed, she sat and removed her clothes then wiggled into her nightgown. When was the last time she'd been in bed in the middle of the day?

She wasn't sick, nor was she well.

She wasn't sad, nor was she happy.

Outside, the sound of pitter patters splashed on the roof and windows. Thunder rolled in the distance.

***

<u>1972</u>

Pasta boiled on the stove and fragrant meat sauce simmered next to it. It was canned sauce because she wasn't talented enough like her mother to make it herself. "Maybe I'm talented enough, but I'm too lazy," she whispered as she pushed cheesy garlic bread into the oven.

Arnold would be home any minute, so she took glasses to the freezer and filled them with ice. She set them on the wire rack to keep them frozen, but as the freezer door closed the front door opened.

"Hey, sweetheart, I'm home."

Her heartbeat sped up at the sound of his voice. "Dinner's ready. Go clean up and come on in when you're ready."

At the counter, she piled spoons of buttercream icing onto the spongy red-velvet cake. Again, not her mother's recipe, but a box cake with homemade frosting. One of these days she would keep her vow to take the time to make food from scratch, just like her precious momma always had. She slathered the thick, sugary concoction over the cake. She took special care to make it as smooth as possible to make up for the box job. At the last second, she didn't like the way it looked so smooth, so she pressed a butter knife into the icing and pulled it straight up, giving the icing curled points.

From the back of the house, Arnold's muffled, offkey voice belted a Patsy Cline song. He was in the shower and experience told her that he would be at the table in five minutes or less, famished, and ready for his dinner.

She turned off the fire under the meat sauce, poured the pasta into a colander, and pulled the bread from the oven.

The house was an extravaganza of succulent scents.

"I'll be there in two shakes of a lamb's tail!" Arnold called out.

She opened the freezer to pull out the glasses and pour the tea, but a rumble of thunder followed by pelting rain grabbed her attention. She rushed to the kitchen window and looked out at a dark gray, water saturated evening. Where'd that come from? She wondered. The last time she'd looked out it had been warm and sunshiny.

A shiver of excitement worked its way down her spine. This was her favorite kind of weather, and she hoped it would stay around through dinner so she and Arnold could enjoy cake and coffee on the front porch.

She took a few minutes to enjoy the rain falling into sloshy puddles in the backyard until Arnold's footsteps brought her back to the task at hand: dinner.

She rushed to the refrigerator and grabbed the glasses from the freezer then whirled back around toward the table.

A searing pain slashed through her abdomen in a fiery fury.

Her mouth dropped open as she tried to catch her breath. Another stab of pain hit her abdomen. Sweat drenched her body and when another pain hit even worse than the last, she dropped both glasses and clutched her stomach.

Shards of glass and ice slipped in all directions, but the mess was the least of her concerns.

She bent over as another spasm worked its way through her body followed by a warm gush at her groin. "No, God. Not again. Let me keep my child."

"Alice!" Arnold rushed to her side, but she screamed in pain when he tried to help her straighten up.

She dropped to the floor and cried, no longer from the pain but from what she feared would be yet another loss of her unborn child.

Arnold dropped to the floor and cupped her tear-stained face in his hands. "What's going on, honey? Are you okay?" It was a stupid question, but he didn't know what else to say or do.

She tried to answer, but another ripping pain doubled her over.

Arnold shot up and ran to the phone.

She laid back against the wooden cabinet as the world around her moved in slow motion. She could only hear snippets of Arnold's phone conversation.

"Ambulance."

"Wife."

"Road."

"Hurry."

His words tumbled into silent oblivion as the world went dark around her.

Chapter 46

A series of beeps niggled their way into her consciousness.

She opened her eyes, but the glare felt like tiny arrows penetrating her eyeballs. She grabbed her stomach, which was now barely a noticeable throb, and groaned.

"Alice. Oh, thank God. You're okay."

The bed rattled as Arnold jumped up and took her hand into his.

She opened her eyes into slits until she could keep them open.

Memories of what happened flashed through her mind, and she wept. "The baby. It's gone?"

He pressed his lips to her forehead. "Ssh. It'll be okay," he whispered.

She already knew the answer but needed to hear the words. "The baby's gone?"

He nodded, and his eyes flooded with tears. "The doctor said you'll be okay, though."

Anger surged through her. *Okay? I'll never be okay for as long as I live.* She wanted to scream the words from the rooftops, but she didn't have the energy to do it. *I want to die. Lord, just let me close my eyes and die.*

When her weeping subsided, Arnold held a cup of iced water to her lips. "How about a little sip?"

She took a couple, enough to moisten her mouth, then moved her head away from the cup. "What happened?"

He sat the water on the rolling table and took her hand in his again. "I don't know. When I came into the kitchen you were clutching your stomach and screaming. You sat on the floor and passed out while I called for an ambulance.

"When they got there, your blood pressure had dropped to dangerous levels, but you're okay now. They had to perform a D&C to—" He dropped his head because he couldn't bear to finish the sentence.

She cradled her stomach even though nothing was there.

The room was silent for several minutes except for the sounds of a clanking metal cart traveling down the hallway.

A man somewhere coughed followed by a woman's laughter.

The sounds of joviality offended her. How dare anyone have anything to laugh at, today of all days.

When the shattering wails of a baby rose above the fray, Arnold went to the door and slammed it shut.

At the bedside, he leaned down and pressed another kiss to Alice's forehead, then her nose, then softly on her lips. "Thank God you're okay. I don't know what I would do if you had—"

She whipped her head to the side and stared out the window. Rage like she had never felt boiled below the surface. *I hate you, God. I swear, I'll never set foot in another church for as long as I live. I'll never utter Your name in another worthless prayer. You're dead to me, and I'm dead to You.* It had been a year since the last time this had happened, since she had last begged God to not let it happen. He had, though, and now, here she was. She would never trust Him again.

For an entire year she had sat in church and sat on God's promise that He would once again give her the desires of her heart.

He gave her the desires of her heart alright, then He brutally took it right back away from her. God isn't a good God. He's mean and vindictive.

"How long have you known you were pregnant?" Arnold's words pierced through her seething hatred.

"What does it matter?" she snapped. "It's done and over with now."

He squeezed her hand and rubbed his thumb over it, but she yanked it away.

"This happens to couples all the time, honey," Arnold whispered. "We can try again as soon as you're ready."

She released a deep sigh and looked across the room at a *Leave it to Beaver* episode that flickered noiselessly on the television screen. "I didn't know for sure. I missed my cycle, so I suspected," she said in a snide, snippy tone. "I had a doctor's appointment for later this week."

She had been so sure that she had baked a cake as an early celebration. She hadn't planned to tell him until the doctor confirmed it, but she had known. That's the last time I'll ever bake a cake to celebrate a child. I'll do everything possible to make sure I never get pregnant again.

***

1972

She was somewhere between sleep and reality when the familiar squeak of the door grabbed her attention. She didn't want to see anyone but if it was someone from church, she would unleash on them. Kicking God out of her life meant kicking His people out of her life, too, and she was more than happy to do it.

Those church people had been dropping in like kids at Halloween ever since she arrived home from the hospital. She had managed to be nice while getting them out of her house as quickly as possible, but her patience with them was thin.

When Arnold slipped into the bedroom with a cautious, somber greeting, she gave him a pert nod.

"You about ready to go?"

At least he had the decency to not come in with a cheery smile.

"Go where?" she snapped.

Arnold sat on the edge of the bed and ran his fingers through her hair. "You have a follow-up with the doctor today, remember?"

She shook her head and looked away from his face that radiated love and patience. She had treated him like garbage since the incident, yet he continued to treat her with compassion. "What does it matter? The baby's gone. What's to follow-up on?"

"The test results are back. We want to find out why you keep losing babies so maybe we can fix it. Remember? After living through this nightmare more than once, we need to find out what's happening."

"Stop asking me if I remember things. I'm a bad mother not a mental patient."

He stood, extended his hand to her, and nodded toward the door. "Let's go, okay?" He nearly promised her lunch at her favorite Mexican restaurant afterwards, but she had refused to leave the house for anything since arriving home from the hospital. He would wait and see her temperament after the appointment then decide on whether to broach the subject of lunch.

***

<u>1972</u>

"Why does she keep losing babies? This is the third time it's happened in a year."

The doctor sat behind her desk with a grim expression. "As you know, we drew plenty of blood from you both and did several tests. I had a suspicion of what could cause so many nonviable pregnancies, and our tests now confirm it."

Relief flooded through him. He took Alice's hand and gripped it. "That's good, right? If we know what's wrong, that means we know how to fix it."

Alice stared at the wall with a blank expression, so Arnold focused on the doctor instead. She may have given up on everything, but he refused to do it.

"I'm afraid it's not good news." The doctor's silvery hair was sleek, and her modulated voice spoke of years of confidence and experience. "It's what we call a Protein S deficiency."

He stared at the nameplate perched on the edge of the desk. Geneva Murphy, M.D. "A Protein S deficiency? What does that mean?"

She gave him a warm smile of understanding. "Protein S is a vitamin K dependent protein that is synthesized in the liver. It is a rare disorder that can increase the risk of blood clot formation. In pregnant women, blood clots form in the placenta which leads to lack of vital oxygen and nutrients to the baby, which causes repeated miscarriages. This explains why Mrs. Collins has yet to carry a child to term."

Arnold shook his head. She might as well be speaking Greek for all he could understand of what she was saying. "I'm sorry, Dr. Murphy. I'm not ... I don't understand. This is something we can fix, right?"

"I'm afraid not, Mr. Collins. The Protein S deficiency is either a genetic disease process or an inherited one. Unfortunately, since we are unable to track family history due to Mrs. Collins not knowing who her natural parents were, we can't determine if the disease process is inherited or genetic. Protein S diseases that are inherited could go away on its own at some point and could possibly be treated with medication. Unfortunately, even treatment with medication would still result in pregnancy complications and miscarriage. If I remember correctly, Mrs. Collins, you indicated that your adopted mother never learned information about your birth parents."

Alice stared at the doctor's diploma on the wall without answering. What good was answering her questions if God would never allow her to have the baby she had always wanted. She despised God and everything that He stood for.

Arnold stepped in when it became evident that Alice wouldn't. "Her adoptive parents never had information on her birth parents. An unknown person dropped her off at the local hospital days after her birth because the mother didn't have the means to take care of a baby. She was adopted weeks later and to this day has never heard a word from her natural family."

"I see." The doctor gazed at Alice with eyes of compassion at the emotional pain the woman was forced to endure. Her job was rewarding in so many ways, but this was the part she hated.

Arnold closed his eyes and took a deep breath. "Are you saying that we'll never have a baby of our own?"

Dr. Murphy looked at him then at Alice. "That's what I'm saying, yes. It's likely that you will never be able to carry a child to term."

Alice stood to her feet, glared at the doctor, and left the room.

Arnold stood to follow her, but his feet wouldn't budge. "Thank you, Doctor," he finally muttered. He was numb to his very core.

"I'm so sorry to deliver such devastating news." She stood and moved to the front of the desk. "This isn't what you hoped for, but don't lose heart. Natural pregnancy isn't an option at this point, unfortunately, but there's still adoption for you to consider. I have pamphlets to send home with you. Mrs. Collins may not want to look at them now but set them aside and share them with her as soon as she's ready to talk about it. My nurse and I are happy to make an appointment in the future to discuss your options. Don't hesitate to let me know what you need." She grabbed his arm and squeezed it. "This isn't what you expected, but you can still have the family you both want."

Chapter 47

Once again, Arnold found himself driving down the interstate somewhere in the boondocks of Missouri. In the shadows of the night were when his memories, both good and bad but mostly bad, burrowed their way back into his mind.

His and Alice's lives had been horrible for so long that it seemed it was all they had—all they deserved. He had been a horrible husband, and Alice wasn't much better as a wife. As the man of the house, though, he should never have given up on his marriage.

What kind of man would do such a thing? A real man who loved his family didn't bury his head in the sand. He fixed what was broken no matter how hard it was.

"I should have done better by Alice. She deserved better than what I gave her. Instead of falling apart when we found out we could never have a baby, we should have clung closer to each other."

He wondered how different their lives would be now if their babies had lived instead of died. Would the paths of his and Alice's life been happy instead of a smelly trash heap? Or was their pathetic marital state their lot in life that ruined not only their lives but also would have ruined the lives of their unborn children?

Before he could stop it, bitter stinging tears flooded his eyes.

He pulled his rig to a screeching stop, slammed it into park, and jumped to the ground.

The car that whizzed past blew their horn at him for several seconds, payback for the sudden pullover without warning.

It was steamy and humid, but he barely noticed.

He went to the grassy side of the rig, fell to his knees, and looked to the sky.

It was inky black and dotted with pricks of light and a sliver of moon that yielded little light. "Lord, I've messed up our lives so badly. Alice and I are both old and set in our ways, but surely we can die in a better state than we've lived for all these years."

Lutis walked around the human in one direction while Fraush and Mondaci walked around him in the opposite. "Call out to your Father in Heaven, and He will answer you," Lutis encouraged in a soothing tone. "He will show you great and mighty things which you do not know."

"Beautiful," Mondaci spat with mocking laughter. "How grand if the human could hear you, though."

"If he listens to the Holy Spirit's still small voice, he will hear and believe."

"He'll never hear that in which he doesn't believe."

He ignored his evil counterparts and kept his focus on his charge. "I waited patiently for the Lord. He turned to me and heard my cry. He lifted me out of the mud and set my feet on a rock."

Fraush bent down and screamed at the human. "Don't entertain such flights of fancy. You don't believe in God because you don't believe in myths."

"He put a song in my mouth, a hymn of praise to our God. Many will see and fear the Lord and put their trust in Him."

"How can you trust something that doesn't exist?" Fraush hurled one lie after another at the human, confident that all of it would stick.

"You don't need a God who has abandoned you at every turn. If He was there, you would know it, wouldn't you?"

"What shall separate us from the love of Christ?" Lutis' voice rose above the enemy taunts. "Shall trouble or hardship? Persecution or famine?"

"You're alone and always will be, you weak human." Fraush said. "Your wife doesn't even love you, and neither does an imaginary God."

"Paul and Silas were in prison, yet they still sang their praises to Almighty God."

"Lord, if You're there, show Yourself to me. I want to believe, but I don't." A cool breeze moved across the earth and rustled Arnold's hair.

"You'll never believe because there is no God!" Mondaci shouted.

"Come, let us sing for joy to the Lord. You must sing the praises of His name." Lutis didn't need to raise his voice to be heard above the evil rantings. "You're in a spiritual war, so sing war songs to the One who saved you."

Mondaci and Fraush erupted into maniacal laughter. "He's too far gone to sing."

"Sing unto the Lord a new song," Lutis said.

Something was happening to Arnold. Nothing tangible, nothing he could discern with his physical senses, but something was different.

Where it came from, he didn't know, but it bubbled in his spirit from nowhere. He longed to release it into the world, but people would think he was crazy.

Maybe he was crazy. With a final burst of emotion, he raised his hands as words he hadn't thought of in years made their way from his mind and through his lips. "Amazing grace how sweet the sound that saved a wretch like me."

The song that spilled out was crackly and not pretty, but the words resonated in his heart like never before. *That saved a wretch like me. That saved a wretch like me.* "Lord, save a wretch like me. I'm a wretch who needs saving. Save me."

His cries bounced off the trees and intermingled with the breeze. "I once was lost but now am found, was blind but now I see." His voice croaked out the lyrics, and with every word his emotional resolve crumbled. "Save me Lord!"

"You're a fool!" Fraush sneered. "You're out here in the middle of nowhere. It's just you. There's no one to save you."

"From the creation of the world the invisible things of Him are clearly seen, understood through the things that He made." Lutis' words soared into the heavens and echoed through the portals of time. "Even His eternal Godhead is seen, so that they are without excuse."

"You think a fool like him will understand a word of that," Mondaci screeched.

"He may be a simple human alone in the night, but God speaks to him through the nature He created, through the nature that surrounds him. He will hear and be saved. The Holy Spirit will speak truth to his heart."

Mondaci and Fraush unleashed roars of anger to drown out the spoken Truth even though they knew that Truth was always stronger than lies. All they had to do was work to keep humans under the delusion of their lies. Their delusions worked with most humans, even this one, but they both sensed the delusion slipping under the power of Truth.

Again, they howled and roared in the night.

Hyacinth's face and voice materialized in Arnold's mind. "To be saved, God must first draw a sinner to His call." Her words came back to him as clear as if she were standing in front of him. Is that what's happening now? This feeling that I can't explain? "God, are You drawing me to You? Maybe I'm not too far gone for You to save me?"

Hyacinth's words that still rang in his mind sounded as sweet as honey. God convicts sinners of their sins by the power of the Holy Spirit.

He pressed his hands to the grass and dug his fingers into the moist earth. Tears fell from his eyes and splashed onto the blades of grass. "Lord, I'm a sinner. I'm a horrible sinner who's unworthy of Your forgiveness. Aunt Deborah says that You're a forgiving God. She said that You'll forgive me if I ask. I will turn away from my sins and never look back if You'll forgive me. I'll do everything to help Alice turn to You."

The moment a person confesses their sins, makes a conscious effort to turn from their sins, and believes that Jesus has saved him, then he is saved. Hyacinth's words pelted his spirit in a way that he couldn't ignore, not even if he wanted to.

His mind went back in time to curse words he had said, to lies he had told, to wrongs he had committed. "Lord, I can't remember everything I ever did, but I ask You to forgive me anyway. I'll do better. I'll be better. I give my heart and my life to You now if You'll have me."

Though the night was dark around him, blurred by a steady stream of tears, a piercing light from Heaven covered him—a light that his physical eyes could not see.

The worship and rejoicing of hundreds of millions of angels funneled from the Throne Room and circled around the human who was unaware of the spiritual happenings around him. "Holy, Holy, Holy is the Lord God Almighty for a sinner once lost has now been saved. Holy, Holy, Holy, Lord God Almighty."

Mondaci and Fraush released roars that vibrated through the heavens. How could this one who had been theirs for so long have slipped through their fingers?

Lutis placed his hands on the human's head as the heavenly worship continued. "It is by grace that you have been saved, Amen." He raised his hands to heaven and joined in the heavenly worship. "Another soul is won for the King of Kings and Lord of Lords, hallelujah. Everyone who calls on the name of the Lord shall be saved."

Chapter 48

As the sun peeked over the horizon, Arnold awoke with a surge of energy and new purpose. For the first time in more years than he could count, he was eager to go home to his life and to Alice.

He glanced at his reflection in the rearview mirror, raked his fingers through his hair that needed a vigorous washing, and cranked up the air conditioner.

He gripped the wheel, bowed his head, and whispered a quick prayer. "Lord, I love you more than I've ever loved anyone in my life." The words made his eyes fill with tears, but this time happy ones, and he wondered if this would always be his life—crying over everything and nothing. "I don't understand what happened or how, but I believe that You're with me, now and forever. If You can save this old heart of mine, surely you can save Alice's heart of stone."

He wiped away tears as he pulled onto the interstate. How could he feel the same yet so different? He couldn't put his finger on what was different, but something was.

As he drove through Missouri at a leisurely pace and entered Iowa under the filtered rays of dusk, he marveled that the first day of his new life was behind him. At least he hoped this was his new life. "What if I accidentally cuss or do something I shouldn't. Does that mean I'm screwed?" The minute he uttered the words, guilt hit his mind. "Sorry, Lord. You probably don't like the word screwed, do You?"

When the sky was dark and the stars peeked out for the first time, he took the next exit and parked his rig at the massive gas station/truck stop.

He grabbed his tote and toiletry bag and ran inside for a scrub in the truck stop showers. He hated using them and rarely did, but his body needed a cleansing to match the one that his soul had recently gotten.

He hummed one of the only gospel songs that he could remember from back in the day, "Bringing in the Sheaves." It was his grandmother's favorite song, and probably her grandmother's favorite song too. "What in the heck is a sheave?" he wondered aloud through a veil of bubbles that traveled down his face. "Sorry, Lord, I guess I shouldn't say heck either? Though it's not really a cuss word, so what's the harm?" He wasn't sure, but something inside told him it wasn't something he should say. "You'll have to be patient with me, Lord. I might screw up a lot until I get the hang of what I'm supposed to do and not do."

After the shower, he dressed in fresh clothes that would still look dirty no matter how many times he washed them, but it was all he had. He shaved the ever-present stubble from his face and splashed some Old Spice cologne that he always carried yet rarely used.

He always slicked his hair back with pomade, but he tossed it back into his bag unused. He wanted a brand-new look. "A new hairstyle for a new life."

He felt like a new man on every level, inside and out, as he pulled out of the truck stop, but he took the next exit when he remembered that a Wal-Mart was just off the interstate.

Inside Wal-Mart, he grabbed new white undershirts and socks, a dozen new shirts, and three new pairs of pants. For a moment he considered new shoes, but that could wait for another day. For the first time in years, he was excited to go home to Alice.

He swung his bags in wide arcs as he walked back to the rig humming "Bringing in the Sheaves." As soon as he got back in the truck, he resolved to find a gospel station and learn some modern songs. He might not have a great voice, but it wouldn't stop him from singing.

He gave a bright smile and a nod to a woman who strolled past him with her attention on her smart phone. "Howdy, ma'am. Have yourself a blessed day."

"Hm?" She looked up at him, frowned, and returned her attention to the phone.

In the old days he would have turned around and flipped her the bird for ignoring him, but today it didn't matter because he had pure sunshine in his soul. He chuckled to realize that yesterday, a few hours in the past, already felt like the old days. "Incredible," he said as he jumped into the truck.

He surfed through radio channels until he found one that played gospel songs that sounded like country music. The announcer said it was "the area's best in Southern Gospel music." He hummed along to songs he'd never heard, yet they felt at home in his heart. He changed into a new outfit and took his place behind the wheel.

A group called the Hoppers—what a funny name for a band, he thought—sang a peppy song called "Shoutin' Time in Heaven." He didn't know why, but the song made his eyes leak again, and he cried for the third time today. "Lord, if I'm gonna cry every time I turn around, someone back home will have me admitted to the insane asylum."

He put the truck in gear then put it back into park. He pulled out his phone and with a sly smile began to dial.

Chapter 49

Hyacinth placed her hand over her eyes to shield the blinding sun. "Paige, honey. If I have to tell you again, we're going home. Big girls like you have to be careful around the smaller kids, okay?"

Sheri watched as kids of all ages played at the public splash pad.

Paige ran up and tugged on the hem of Sheri's coverup. "I'm hungry."

"You are not hungry. We had waffles and bacon barely two hours ago," Hyacinth said.

"I'm hungry."

Sheri picked her up and balanced her on her lap. "What sounds good for lunch?" She tickled her stomach and spoke in an animated funny voice. "How about a nice sardine and mushroom salad with green slime dressing?"

Paige tossed her head back and erupted into laughter.

Hyacinth picked up her phone to check the time. Though technically it could be lunchtime, 10:35 was too soon to think about it.

Paige kicked her legs with excitement. "No! Pizza!"

Sheri clapped her hands. "Yay for pizza."

"And ... Donald's!"

Sheri looked at Hyacinth and cringed. "McDonald's. How did I know that one was coming?"

"And ... smashed tatoes!"

Sheri tussled her hair and set her back down on the ground. "Well, I can say one thing for you, kiddo. You've got a bizarre taste palate."

"I'll tell you what, baby. If you'll go play for another thirty minutes, we'll all go have pizza, okay?"

Paige jumped up and down and clapped. "Pizza, pizza, pizza."

Hyacinth kissed the top of her head and coaxed her back toward the splash pad. "First you have to go play for a little longer."

"Uncle Jenn will be there?"

The little girl's wide eyes of innocence broke Hyacinth's heart. No matter how many times they explained his absence, it was hard for someone of her age to understand how death worked. Hyacinth's heart plummeted as the familiar strains of grief worked their way back up. "Not today, sweetheart. Remember? Uncle Jenner is in Heaven with Jesus."

Her lip trembled and crocodile tears rolled down her cheeks. "I don't want Uncle Jenn to play with Jesus today. I want him to play with me."

Hyacinth pulled her close and hugged her tight. "I know, sugar. I miss him, too." She raised her face and smothered it with loud kisses that soon had her laughing. "Now go play, and we'll eat soon."

She darted away and jumped through a series of dancing sprays of water.

Hyacinth puffed out her cheeks, looked at Sheri, and let out the breath slowly. Though she had made her peace with Jenner's untimely passing, talking about him, especially with Paige, was like a punch in the gut every time.

"You have a fabulous pool at home. Remind me why we're at a splash pad with all these screaming kids?" Sheri looked at her with a sarcastic expression.

Hyacinth settled back into the mesh poolside recliner with a chuckle. "Girlfriend, I rue the day I introduced her to the splash pad. She still likes the pool, but I think it's all the ankle biters running around here that she likes."

Their conversation lulled as they listened to a podcast on being a Christian mother, an interesting topic considering neither was a mother yet.

She grumbled aloud when her phone rang. She almost ignored it but picked it up to read the name. "Hm."

Sheri paused the podcast. "Who is it?"

"It's Arnold."

Sheri cocked her head and snarled her nose. "Who's Arnold?"

"The guy who came to see me. Arnold."

Sheri wilted back into her chair. "I told you that guy was bad news. It's bad enough that he had the audacity to come here to see you, but now he's calling you?"

"I told you, he's not a bad guy." She pointed to the splash pad. "Watch Paige while I'm on the phone." She slid her finger across the screen. "Hey, Mr. Arnold, what's up?"

She smiled at his reluctant voice. "I'm sorry for calling you like this, but I—"

"Nonsense. When I gave you the number and told you to call me if you needed to, I meant it."

"Something ... something kind of ... kind of cool happened after I left you."

"Oh yeah? What's that?"

"I kind of prayed to God, for real this time, not just because I needed something. I can't explain it, but it's like He's inside me now. I never understood that saying in the past, but I get it now."

Hyacinth slapped her hand over her mouth and tears of joy spilled into her eyes.

Sheri bolted up in her seat. "What's wrong?"

Hyacinth shook her head and swatted her away. "Arnold, that's the best news I could've ever heard."

Her squeals of excitement floated through the play area, and several people turned to stare at her, but she didn't care.

She settled back into her seat. "Tell me all about how it happened, and don't skip a single detail."

Chapter 50

She clicked off the television at the sound of a sharp rapping on the door.

With a grunt of exertion, she lifted herself and made her way to the foyer. "I love you, Ellen dear, but nobody likes people who show up for the party two hours early."

When she opened the door, it wasn't whom she expected. "Arnold?" Aunt Deborah clasped her hands then opened her arms and swept him into an energetic hug. "How wonderful to see you."

He entered and closed the door behind him. He had nearly burst with the excitement of coming to visit but now that he was here his nerves were on fire. "I should've called first, but I was on the road and didn't take the time to do it."

She motioned for him to follow her into the living room. "Oh, stop it. Family and friends never have to call first. I'm delighted to see you anytime you stop by, expected or not."

As she sat, he looked around the place that was spotless, as always, and a tinge of vanilla scented the air. At least he thought it was vanilla. He cracked his knuckles. "Can I get you something to drink?" He needed something to do with his hands.

"Oh, my. Where are my manners?" She pushed to the edge of the seat to stand, but he placed his hand on her shoulder. "You sit. I'll get it."

She nestled back into the chair with a contented sigh. "Thank you dear. I'll have—"

"Iced tea with a ring of citrus?"

She chuckled. "You know me well."

"Not as well as I should, but I promise to do better from now on."

"You're a working man. I understand that you can't spend every day entertaining an old woman like me."

"You're hardly old, Aunt Deborah." In the kitchen, he pulled down two tall beverage glasses and filled them with ice, then chilled tea, followed by a sprig of fresh mint and rings of orange and lime slices. He wiped away the melted chips of ice from the countertop and resealed the citrus and stashed it back in the refrigerator.

He handed one of the glasses to her then took a seat on the sofa. "I know you like those tiny glasses, but today I needed more than a couple of swallows."

"What brings you out on such a lovely day?" She swatted her forehead. "I haven't been out since the weekend nor looked out the window even once today. For all I know it's gnarly and rainy."

"Every day is a good day when the Lord's in it." One of the announcers on the radio had said it, and he liked it.

Her shocked look almost made him laugh out loud, but she recovered with a dainty shake of her head. "What a wonderful thing to say, and how true it is. The Lord is always good to us, even when we don't deserve it."

He didn't know what to say in return because all this religious talk was still a foreign concept to him, so he turned up his glass and took several perfectly sweet swigs.

Aunt Deborah gave him a looking over then cocked her head to the side. "You look different today."

"Do I?" A smile that he couldn't stop spread across his face. "How so?"

"For starters, your hair isn't sticky like it usually is. I like it dry and styled like that."

"It's called pomade. I decided to skip it and try something new."

"I like it. You look distinguished with your hair dry and parted at the side like that."

As soon as she said it, his smile widened, and she realized that was what was different. He rarely smiled but today he hadn't stopped. "Plus, look at that pretty smile of yours. I don't think I've seen you smile like that since you were a little young thing. If I didn't know any better, I'd say you were the cat that ate the canary."

He set the glass on the coaster and cleared his throat. "Something kind of happened." His heart thudded in his chest and suddenly he could barely breathe.

She almost asked if Alice was okay, but he wouldn't smile like this if something bad had happened—at least she hoped not. "I haven't had any good news in a while, so lay it on me." Her heart took a dip when she remembered that he wanted to talk Alice into moving to Florida one of these days when he retired. She hated to think that they might be moving away now that they were back in touch.

"I ... I said a little prayer the other night." He sucked in a deep breath as soon as he said it followed by a few slower ones. Why is this so awkward to tell?

Lutis walked behind him and placed a hand on each of his shoulders. "She's been waiting and praying for you for years, child. Her prayers carried you to this moment."

"It never hurts to whisper a few prayers every day," she said when he didn't continue. She was curious to see where this was leading but didn't want to rush him.

"I asked—" He patted his chest and before he could say the words, tears welled into his eyes. "Jesus lives in here now."

Aunt Deborah rocked in her seat as the words swirled through her mind. She closed her eyes and whispered a prayer of gratitude. She stood to her feet and wiggled her fingers at him.

He wiped his eyes and stood to face her.

"Oh, Arnold. This is everything I've ever prayed for."

She wrapped her arms around him, and he wept like a little boy. The hug lasted forever but this time he didn't mind.

When they pulled apart, her eyes were glassy. She pulled a tissue from the box on the table and wiped it across her nose. She moved to the sofa and patted the cushion next to her. "This is the most amazing thing that will ever happen in a person's life. Sit and tell me all about it."

They wept and hugged several times as he gave exhaustive details. The more he talked about it the easier it was, and she devoured every word he had to say.

He yanked a tissue from the box and blew his nose. "I'm just so darned happy," he said when he couldn't think of another word to say on the matter. "I never dreamed I could be this happy."

She gripped his hand and squeezed. "That is wonderful, sweetheart."

He was taken aback by her sudden look of reluctance. Embarrassment replaced the happiness, and he suddenly wished he hadn't told her. Maybe he should have kept it to himself. "What is it? You have a funny look. I shouldn't have talked so much."

Lutis walked around the couple and listened to every word they spoke. He focused on Arnold. "The enemy will tell you lies about your salvation, about your relationship with your Father, but you're always covered by His blood. Now that you've submitted yourself to Him, resist the devil and he will flee."

"Oh, honey, no. This is news that you should scream from the rooftops. I'd rather hear people talk about how they came to the Father more than anything else we could talk about."

Reluctance, or something similar, still lurked in her eyes.

"I have to warn you, though, that it may not always feel like this."

His spirit took a nosedive. "What do you mean?"

She patted his hand. "It's nothing bad, but this happiness you feel right now may not always be there."

He didn't think it possible, but his spirit dived even lower. "You mean, Christians aren't happy like this?"

"Sometimes, yes, but always, no. Having Christ in your heart doesn't mean you'll always be happy. Christians often feel sadness, and depression, and other negative feelings. Deciding to follow Christ doesn't protect you from the bad things in life. The Bible tells us that Satan is like a roaring lion seeking people to devour. Now that you're one of God's children, the enemy of your soul will fight you harder than ever. Satan is a powerful foe, and his goal is to steal, kill, and destroy as many of us as he can before the Lord calls us all home."

This wasn't what he expected to hear, and it disheartened him. What's the point of being saved if it feels no different than it did before?

"Now, now. Don't get me wrong. As a Christian, you'll always have joy, even when you're not happy, and that's okay because your joy is the most important thing."

"What's the difference? I thought they were the same."

"They're as different as night and day. Your joy is a result of your salvation and your relationship with Christ. The Bible says that the joy of the Lord is our strength. No matter what happens in life, a Christian's joy will never cease.

"Happiness is a result of external factors. A new job, or new love, a new home—these things cause happiness but not joy. Happiness is fleeting because it's contingent on what's going on in your life. Your joy, on the other hand, is always there because the Holy Spirit produces it in your life. Does that make sense?"

He nodded. "Believe it or not, it makes perfect sense, even for an old lunkhead like me. Basically, you're saying that we can have lasting joy even when we're spitting mad, but you can be happy and not have any joy?"

"Exactly, but at some point, we must address the anger in our lives if that's a problem for us. Ephesians says that we are to do away with things like wrath, anger, and slander and replace it with tenderheartedness toward one another."

He let his shoulders drop in an exaggerated manner. "I always thought all this Christian stuff was a cop out, but it sounds like a lot of work."

"It is a lot of work, and it's supposed to be. The Bible calls it sanctification, which is the process of being freed from sin. No human on earth is fully sanctified. We're all growing and working toward sanctification, but we'll never achieve it until we're in the physical presence of God."

Fear bristled inside of him. What if I mess up? "How do you know if you're doing it right?"

"Oh, that's easy, dear. You must know God's word and then be obedient to it. When that thought pops into your mind and the Holy Spirit tells you that you shouldn't say it, or do it, or think it, and you're obedient to that little nudge, that's evidence of the process of sanctification in your life."

He could stay and talk to Aunt Deborah about this forever, but it was time to go. He stood and held out his hand to help her to her feet. "I'll probably have a lot of questions and need a lot of help with this. I'm not as smart about this religious stuff as you are."

"I'm here for you night or day, and I really mean that." She gave him another long hug. "I hope I didn't disappoint you too much with all that happiness talk but I didn't want it to take you by surprise when it inevitably happens."

"I'm glad you did." He thrust his hands in his pocket and leaned in and whispered, "I'm even excited to see Alice, and we ain't been excited to see each other since the seventies." It sounded like an embellishment of the truth, but it wasn't far from it.

She tapped his chest with her finger. "See, the Lord's already working in your life. The closer you get to Him and the more you love Him, He'll soften your heart and give you more love for people than you ever thought possible, even the ones you don't like all that much."

He held her hand as they walked to the door. "Will you pray for Alice, that she will learn to love God, too?"

"Honey, I've been praying for you and Alice to come to know Him for more years than you or I could count. I'll keep praying, but you don't forget to pray, too. God is your Father, and He wants you to talk to Him as often as you can. Never give up on your prayers, even when you don't see Him answering them. You're proof that God answers prayers in His time, even if He takes years to do it."

Chapter 51

Arnold drove to the city park overlooking the lake and sat on the bench even though it was almost midnight.

After leaving Aunt Deborah's he didn't go home, partly from nerves and partly because he wanted the card hags to be gone. He lifted his eyes to heaven and grimaced. "Sorry, Lord. I guess I should stop calling them hags, huh? I'll probably be slow at this sanctification stuff, so I hope You will bear with me. I'm a screw up and might need lots of Your forgiveness."

Lutis walked around the bench as the human communed with his Father in Heaven. "I think this guy will be a strong one in our Kingdom one day soon."

Mondaci and Fraush stood several feet back, seething at the turn of events. "He may be yours now, but we'll work him over until he's sick and tired of your God. He'll be one of those seeds that withers up and dies."

Lutis heard every word, but he didn't interact with them. In the tree line behind the two, multitudes more stood in wait. He glanced up into the portals of Heaven at the untold millions of angels who looked down over the Earth.

When the hooting of an owl brought him from his musings, Arnold checked the time on his phone. 12:30. "The card ... ladies, not hags—" he looked to Heaven and smiled, "—should be gone by now."

***

<u>Present Day</u>

He tiptoed down the darkened hallway and cracked open Alice's door. The only light was moonlight that spilled through the crack between the curtains.

At the bedside, he watched Alice as she slept. The woman got on his ever-loving last nerve, but he had never loved her more than he did right now.

"Lord," he whispered. "If You can save me, You can save her too." He wanted to say more but didn't know what. "Oh, and keep her under Your protective hand." He opened his eyes then closed them again. "Oh, and I love You. Thank you for saving me."

Thank you for saving me. He didn't think he would ever get tired of saying those words. How had it been so hard to believe in God for all these years when He felt so close to him now? Arnold wished he knew how that worked, but he moved it to the back of his mind. Maybe it could be a topic of discussion with Aunt Deborah tomorrow. He leaned down and pressed a kiss to Alice's forehead.

She stirred and looked up at him. "Arnold? What in the living—"

He pressed a finger to her lips and smiled. "I just got home and had to see you before I went to bed," he whispered.

"Why? You always make a habit of watching me while I sleep?"

He sat on the edge of the bed and placed his hand on her leg. "I just … something happened to me while I was gone."

She pulled herself up in the bed then reached over and turned on the lamp.

They both squinted under the light.

She looked at his hair then his clean-shaven face with the slightest stubble then down at the clothes that looked brand new. Even the scent of Old Spice caught her attention. "You look different. Have you been sleeping around with whores?"

He chuckled and shook his head. "Something amazing happened, but it's something way better than women."

She narrowed her eyes at him. "If you're telling me that you like the men now, you can pack your bags and leave. It ain't politically correct, but I ain't having none of that nonsense."

"Jesus saved me. That's what's different. He lives in my heart now."

She didn't like how that sounded. They had put an end to the religious mumbo jumbo decades ago, and she preferred that it stay that way. "Saved you? From what?"

He shrugged because he didn't have all the answers. "From myself. From Hell. From everything, Alice. God is real and He saves people from their sins. He saved a crazy old coot like me beside the interstate somewhere in Missouri."

She shook her head, turned off the light, and scooted back under the covers. "I think you've had a little too much of the hooch. Why don't you go to bed and sleep it off?"

As she settled back into the indentation of her pillow, a slice of moonlight fell across her face. "Alice Marie Collins, I ain't been a good husband to you in so many years that I don't even remember what a good husband looks like, but I'm changing that. We've turned away from each other in our grief. For the longest time I wondered what happened to us, but now I know that it started with losing our babies all those years ago. Starting tonight, I'm running toward you, not away. From now on, I will love and cherish you until the day I die."

He paused to wipe his eyes when they filled, yet again, with tears. "I'm sorry for being such a lousy husband for all these years and I hope you can find it in your heart to forgive me."

Her heart melted at his words. This didn't sound like Arnold talking. It sounded like the Arnold she hadn't seen or heard from in years. He even looked good to her, and she hated that. She closed her eyes and hoped he would leave.

He leaned down and pressed a gentle kiss to her lips. "I love you. Sweet dreams, my love."

When the door clicked closed behind him, tears pressed into her eyes, and she wiped them away with the sheet. She didn't know if this was real or not, but she would hold onto his words for the rest of the night.

***

Arnold paused just outside the door for several seconds before moving to his own room. He clutched his Bible to his chest and knelt beside the bed. "Lord, thank you for giving me such a lovely bride. Bless and keep our family in Your care forever."

Chapter 52

He, along with Aunt Deborah's help earlier in the day, had placed the finishing touches on the pergola in the backyard.

The structure had seen better days, but with white Christmas lights strung across it, it would look a lot better once dusk was upon them.

For the past three months he had fought tooth and nail to prove the resurgence of his love for Alice despite their decades-long estrangement.

In the beginning she had scoffed at his every effort. If he bought her an unexpected gift, she didn't want it. If he invited her out to dinner, she preferred the entertainment of her friends. If he tried to kiss her, she pulled away.

He nearly gave up on trying several times, but thanks to Hyacinth's and Aunt Deborah's encouragement, he kept trying.

A month ago, he had, against all hope, invited her to a Mexican food restaurant on a Friday evening. To his surprise, she accepted because Pauline was sick, and they couldn't play cards with an uneven number of people.

He hated to rejoice in another person's ailment, but he couldn't help giving God thanks for His help. Whether God had anything to do with it or not, he didn't know, but whatever it was, he had no problems accepting the help.

Their first date night in decades was steaming fajitas and a blaring mariachi band, though he would never call it a date in front of Alice.

It was awkward, and she barely said a word to him all night long despite his efforts at keeping the conversation going, but they had made it through it.

He told Hyacinth that it was the last time he would do it, but she convinced him to keep trying. Their estrangement hadn't happened overnight, after all, she reminded him, so it made sense that their romance wouldn't rekindle overnight.

He doubted they would ever have a romance again, because Alice was too emotionally distant for anything resembling romance, but he would be happy if they at least treated each other with respect again.

By what seemed a miracle—and he hated to call something as mundane as a date with his wife as a miracle, but it's how it felt—Alice had grudgingly agreed after their Mexican food date to one dinner per week with Arnold at a restaurant on two conditions. It had to be an early meal, no later than four thirty in the afternoon, and their meal could last no longer than an hour and a half, which gave ample time to return and finish the night with cards.

Her conditions had angered him at first. She gave seven days a week to her friends and their card games. Why couldn't she give him one night out of seven that was only theirs?

Though he was bull headed in his anger most of the time, Aunt Deborah had reminded him that baby steps in rebuilding their relationship were better than no steps at all.

Thank God for Hyacinth's and Aunt Deborah's dedication in holding him to perseverance because his near daily frustrations in Alice made him want to throw up his hands in defeat on multiple occasions.

Last Tuesday, she shocked him by accepting his invitation to a night of dancing at the VA Hall with, in her words, the other local geezers.

She was quick to preface her acceptance with, "but only because they're serving fried catfish for dinner." Fine. He could accept being second foot to a fried catfish.

They had limped around the dance floor with the physical grace of an elephant, and every few steps were accompanied by someone in the room nearly hacking up a lung, but they were together and that had been all that mattered.

He snapped himself out of the memories and back to the present. The new card table he bought at the discount store was covered with a vibrant fall tablecloth in hues of greens, oranges, and golden yellows and set with Aunt Deborah's coveted vintage Lenox china plates and Waterford beverage glasses.

In the middle of the table was a bouquet of orange mums and yellow sunflowers in a silver vase, compliments of Hyacinth and the local florist.

A second table contained a smorgasbord of Aunt Deborah's best cooking, which would be great even on her worst day.

The sun sank below the horizon giving the air a sudden cool nip, and a thin blanket of fog had rolled in out of nowhere.

He leaned down and plugged in the Christmas lights. The strings cast the backyard in romantic filtered light.

Groupings of gold, silver, and creamy white pearlescent helium balloons dotted the periphery of the pergola. It was a step up from a cheesy high school prom, and Alice would probably scoff at the attempt, but Aunt Deborah was convinced that it would be a nice touch to the evening.

He pressed play on the CD player boombox that he hadn't used in decades, and Nat King Cole's voice drifted across the yard in sweeping warm and dreamy overtures.

He trembled as he made his way across the grass toward the house. He brushed his hands over his brand-new shirt and slacks in a nervous gesture.

Alice would hate all this, and he wondered not for the first time why he allowed Hyacinth and Aunt Deborah to talk him into such a grand gesture, but it was too late now.

The Friday card game wouldn't be a problem tonight because he had pleaded with Pauline to contrive a reason to cancel it. She had complied with stingy reluctance then complained that his obsession with Jesus and a sudden compulsion to act like a newlywed husband was messing with their fun and games.

He slid open the back door and slipped inside. The smell of cigarette smoke nearly choked him to death, and he prayed that Jesus would remove the disgusting addiction from his wife's life.

She sat at the table with a cigarette dangling from her fingers.

"Dinner's ready."

"I can't believe we're eating outside like cavepeople," she snapped. "Wild animals eat outside. Humans are supposed to eat inside."

Maybe I can taste my food better if my mouth isn't clogged with cigarette smoke. He accepted her criticism with a warm smile. Maybe she was right. Maybe it was a ridiculous charade for people of their age, but he didn't care. He hadn't romanced his bride in years, and even if she didn't appreciate it, he would do it anyway because he had lots of time to make up for.

"I can remember a few times back in the day when we enjoyed a picnic or two." He held his hand out to her. "May a gentleman escort a lady to dinner?"

She fixed a cautious stare on him, stubbed out the cigarette, and stood to her feet with a series of grunts. She mumbled a string of profanities. "Let's get this over with."

The words stung his heart, but he took her arm into his and escorted her to the door without a word. He was glad to see that she had made a semblance of an effort by trading the ratty housecoat she always wore for a style of smock that any grandmother in town would be happy to have in her closet, coupled with thick polyester pants and tennis shoes.

Outside, King Cole's lush rendition of "Unforgettable" rippled across the yard.

"I haven't heard any of his music in decades." Alice allowed Arnold to help her into one of the kitchen chairs that he had dragged out.

Birds sang their final songs before settling down for the night. Their neighbors would think they were crazy old loons, with all the food, music, and lights.

Without asking for help, Arnold dished out generous helpings of meatloaf, steamed green beans swimming in butter and garlic, mashed potatoes, and Arnold's favorite fluffy sweet cornbread.

As their plates emptied, Alice's eyes glassed over at a familiar strain of music from yesteryear. Even as a young bride in the seventies, she had adored Nat King Cole. Arnold had whisked her around their tiny living room more than once, to her delight, to the tune of his music. Her favorite to this day was "Around the World," though she hadn't heard it in years.

The song brought comfort to her soul, and she swiped her dinner napkin under her nose to hide her fragile emotions.

Arnold stood and held his hand out to her. "It's been a while, but I think we can remember how to do it."

She looked up at him. "Huh?"

He nodded at the music player then wiggled his fingers at her.

"This is the silliest thing I've ever seen. We're too old for shenanigans like this. We're both lumpier than a bag of potatoes." Even as she said the words, a longing rose in her heart, so she slapped her hand into his and got to her feet.

With slow steps, they waltzed to the rhythm of the music with all the grace that their stiff and unused joints would allow.

Alice was rigid in his arms for the first couple of songs, but she finally melted into him and rested her head on his shoulder as Old Spice cologne wafted around their dance space like a familiar friend from the past.

"I know I ain't been a good husband for years now, but this old man still loves his gal with his whole heart," Arnold whispered into her ear. "We can't fix years of neglect with a few date nights, but I promise to be a better husband from here on out if you'll give me a second chance."

"I ain't the sweet girl I used to be. I'm old and cranky and I ain't likely to change." She pulled away and gave him a playful smile. "And don't expect me to jump into all this Jesus stuff with you."

He didn't need her to commit to a relationship with Jesus right now, and he had no intention of pushing her where she didn't want to go. He would go to church and change his life in meaningful ways that Alice could see, and maybe that would sway her.

Aunt Deborah's advice bounced through his thoughts. "Preaching at people never wins them over. Living a holy life in front of them will speak more than any words ever could." That's what he intended to do. Go to church more, watch television less, study the Bible, and pray.

There was a lot of himself that he needed to work on too, like not mouthing off when he was angry, cutting the habit of cussing and flipping people off, and changing his overall attitude.

"Plant the seeds in her life when you can," Aunt Deborah had said, "and let the Holy Spirit do the rest."

"As long as we're together and you learn to love me again, I can put up with your crankiness because I might still be cranky sometimes too." He pulled her close and closed his eyes under their gentle sway.

I still love you, you crazy old man, Alice thought. It's been so long that I don't know how to show it anymore.

Things weren't perfect in their life by any stretch, and they never would be, but he had the smallest glimmer of hope that they would end their lives on a better note than the middle part had shown.

He glanced up at the star-strewn sky. "Thank you, Lord, for giving us a second chance. Help us to do it right from here on out."

***

If you enjoyed reading "A Time for Redemption," you might also enjoy "Unprotected," a fictional cautionary tale of when the American government seeks to strip citizens of their right to bear arms. Visit this link to check it out on Amazon:

https://www.amazon.com/Unprotected-Clean-Small-Town-Family-Drama-ebook/dp/B0BYBKZZSW

To watch the "Unprotected" book trailer on YouTube: https://youtu.be/ETprHvGZEfg?si=zycpb6mglFNz8HNm

Afterword

"A Time for Redemption," Book Two of the War Songs series, begins in the days following the events of Book One. The story shifts the main character status away from Jenner and Hyacinth and primarily onto Arnold and Alice. I recommend reading "War Songs" prior to reading "A Time for Redemption."

As with the previous book, I ask that you keep in mind that this is a fictional story from my imagination. I merged the spiritual and earthly realms in a way that allows readers to experience it from both perspectives while characters see only what happens on the earthly realm. Whether or not the spiritual realm interacts with humans in exactly the way I depicted it on the pages of this novel, I can't say, but it's the creative license I took to propel the story forward. It's not my objective to argue beliefs nor to impugn differing opinions on the matter. I endeavored only to offer readers a story they will hopefully find entertaining and thought provoking.

In the novel, I needed a medical explanation for why Alice couldn't have a baby in her younger years. After bouncing around a couple of scenarios, my medical team and I landed on an extremely rare disorder called Protein S Deficiency.

Protein C and Protein S are vitamin K-dependent proteins that are synthesized in the liver. It is so rare, in fact, that severe forms of Protein

C Deficiency affect about one in approximately 750,000 people, and men and women are equally affected by the disease.

If the deficiency isn't genetically inherited, it usually goes away on its own. Non-inherited deficiencies can be caused by several different medical situations, such as: liver disease, kidney disease, chemotherapy, a lack of vitamin K, and taking birth control pills, just to name a few.

If it is inherited, it can be treated with medication though pregnancy complications and miscarriage are still significantly higher risks. Genetic studies are required to determine why a patient has the deficiency.

Protein S Deficiency fit the story perfectly until further research revealed that Protein C Deficiency was discovered in 1976 and Protein S Deficiency was discovered in 1979. Since integral parts of the story take place in 1971 and 1972 and Protein S had not yet been discovered, after much conferring with the medical team, we decided to leave it as written even though the dates are off by a few years. We thought this slight embellishment would be fine due to the interesting and rare nature of the illness coupled with the opportunity to introduce readers to a medical disease process of which they might not otherwise have been aware.

As authors, we always strive to write books that are accurate on all levels. That said, I hope readers will forgive the slight date discrepancy that I allowed into the final novel for the sake of progressing the story.

Dedication

This novel is dedicated to the two people in the world that I love the most—Larry and Teresa Nelson to everyone else but to me Dad and Mom.

Even though I didn't appreciate it at the time, thank God I grew up in an era when 'whoopins' were given liberally when needed, which was often—because of Chad more often than not (that's my story and I'm sticking to it...LOL). You taught us how to treat others well (my hot temper is on me, not you), and more importantly, you taught us that Jesus loves us and were an example of how to love Him in return. That's the greatest legacy a parent could ever leave to a child, and you did it well. I love you.

***

I also dedicate this book to the memory of Glenda S. Waldrip (July 27, 1943 – August 13, 2022). In the medical field and in life, you were my mentor in more than one way. Our family didn't know what God was doing when he moved us to Norman, Oklahoma for the years that I was there, and I'm glad He did because our paths might not have crossed otherwise. You taught me how to be a professional in my first "real job" in the medical lab. My heart hurt the day I heard that God took you home, but you and Bob are now where you belong--in the arms of the Lord that you loved with all your hearts. I love you, dear friend, and I'll see you soon.

About the Author

Brett Nelson lives in Arkansas and is the author of six books, five of which have hit the Top 10 Amazon Best-Seller list in Christian Fiction. "A Christmas to Live For" won the 2021 Readers' Favorite gold medal in the Christian Fiction genre, and "War Songs" (Book #1) won the Global Book Awards silver medal in Christian Fiction in 2022.

When he isn't writing, he enjoys reading a wide range of fiction books, from Christian fiction to secular fiction, and he specially enjoys seeking out and reading the works of his fellow lesser-known Indy authors.

On weekends, you're likely to find him snuggled in with a great movie.

He is hard at work penning his next novels.